"**I**F I EVER LOVE A MAN GREATLY ENOUGH TO MARRY HIM, I WILL BELIEVE ANYTHING HE WOULD EVER TELL ME."

Cissie raised her head, her face radiant, and fixed her eyes on Julian's. "I would trust him to the death!"

And then suddenly, as without volition, Julian's arms were around her and he was pressing her to him, while his lips fell upon hers. And the kiss went on as though they were being fused into each other by its power, by a kind of utter sweetness that could know no end.

A moment's breath separated them and then they were together in a passionate union that made them one in flesh and spirit.

All at once, Julian broke away and roughly pushed Cissie aside. "What have I done? Oh, what have I done? Can you ever forgive me?"

THE TWO BISHOPS

a novel by

Agnes Sligh Turnbull

FAWCETT CREST • NEW YORK

To all good clergymen
in memory of one

THE TWO BISHOPS

This book contains the complete text of the original hardcover edition.

Published by Fawcett Crest Books, a unit of CBS Publications, the Consumer Publishing Division of CBS Inc., by arrangement with Houghton Mifflin Company

ISBN: 0-449-24464-4

Printed in the United States of America

First Fawcett Crest printing: November 1981

10 9 8 7 6 5 4 3 2 1

1

The warm effulgence of the late June day fell upon the Bishop's garden with a pleasing variance of light and shadow here and there. When a soft puff of wind stirred the leaves of the big maple tree in the center of the lawn small golden stars of light flecked the ground underneath. When the breeze died away the leaves settled into their former place and all beneath was shadow.

The man cultivating the roses in the bed that circled the small fountain mused upon this: a small thing and yet interesting, this light and shadow business. Perhaps he might be able to work this sometime into a speech. Not a bad description of life itself, was it? Sunshine and shadow? Well, he would chuck that idea into his mind and see what he could make of it. Two addresses were just coming up in the next weeks, nursing school graduation and the university commencement. Already he had the framework for each, but all the rich substantive material to clothe them was still to be acquired by hard head-work. It was to escape this cerebral tension that the man had doffed his clericals, put on an open necked shirt and old slacks, and come out to dig in the soil.

> When Adam delved,
> And Eve span
> Who was then
> The gentleman?

He was pleased with himself for remembering the old rhyme just now. This urge to dig in the earth was inherent then, as in Adam. Well, he for one would not deny it. He felt more relaxed even now.

All at once he stood still, listening. He was sure he had heard a call. It could not have come from the Old Rectory, the

Bishop's house that was just behind him. It sounded more as though it had come from somewhere about the great church of St. Michael and All Angels, which lay in all its grace and beauty just two wide lawns from where he stood.

He listened. It came again, louder, but strained as though given with a great effort. Then the owner of the voice appeared just outside the porte-cochère at the back, which was still kept so that past memories of the days when fine equipages brought great ladies and gentlemen there should not be forgotten. The voice belonged to Harris, the old verger of St. Michael's, who was signaling desperately for help.

The man at the rose-bed dropped his digging tool and started across the lawns in a sort of lope. The verger had not been well, and now this fright he apparently had might go hard with him. As soon as Harris could be heard he began:

"Oh, it's glad I am you're here. We've got a problem this time we've never had before. Man and boy I've never known the like an' I'm too shaky entirely to deal with it!"

The man facing him now caught his arms and held them tightly. "Control yourself, Harris, and for the love of heaven tell me what you are talking about. What *is* the problem?"

"There's someone, or an animal mebbe, in the *Attic,* an' it's cryin' an' callin' an' moanin' an' I never heered such a carry on."

"In the *Attic?*" the younger man said. "How could anyone get there? Was the trapdoor down tight?"

"Tight as my fist. I shut it myself when I took those old Prayer Books down this morning, an' I just was sayin' . . ."

"Come along now and help me. This whole thing is ridiculous. Who on earth would play such a trick? And, by the way, why didn't you call the Rector? It's his study."

"Oh, he's at the hospital. His little girl had an operation, you know, and he runs in and out to see her."

"Of course. I know the news is good. But about this business of the *Attic,* I'm sure what's down there is one of those rascally little boys who were around selling tickets for the Fireman's Ball or chances on a Toyota or something. I know they've been bothering the Rector. They somehow sneaked in, so I sent them over to the Bishop. *He'll* manage them."

"I'll bet you he buys all their tickets," said Harris. "He's that soft on the kids."

They had traversed the hall by now and entered the office, where they stood listening. All was quiet.

"It's mebbe killed itself," Harris whispered hopefully.

6

"Bangin' around the way it did, it could 'a hit its head an' be done for."

"Don't call the creature *it*," said his companion sternly. "I'm sure this is a very bad little boy and I intend to deal with him."

"You'd better not tell the Bishop. He'd likely say he's been tryin' to save his soul."

"Well, I won't touch his soul, but there may be some other sensitive spots I can grab. . . . There he goes again!"

The silence had, indeed, been broken by long moans and high, pathetic wails, accompanied by blows of some sort of stick against the stairs.

Harris gave a shiver. "It scares me somehow. It might be one of them exercizen spirits like in the movie!"

"Exorcizing, if you must use the word, but don't talk nonsense. I'm going to call now and I hope the kid feels scared. Here goes!"

"*Listen you, down there*," he shouted. "Stop that noise and start up the stairs. I'll open the door here and let you out. Watch your head as you come," he added sternly.

He turned toward Harris. "You see how the kid quieted as soon as he heard me. The little devil! When I get my hands on him, I'll shake the liver out of him. I'm going to kneel so I can grab him the instant he appears. Stand back, Harris. Here we go!"

He grasped the handles of the trapdoor, gave a strong pull, the door stood up on the side, and the man looked eagerly down—to meet the face of a young girl with rumpled blond hair, a smudge of dust on her nose, and wide eyes full of laughter. In that first split second of recognition the girl took one more step up, leaving her face now almost on a level with his.

"Boo," she said distinctly, and giggled.

The kneeling man drew back and got quickly to his feet.

"I fail to see any humor in this situation," he said crisply.

"But that's because you missed your cue," the girl answered. "When I said 'Boo,' you should have said 'Boo, yourself,' and then we would have been friends, in a way. Will you please give me a hand to help me up and out?"

He gave it and the girl sprang lightly to the study floor. He made a business then of closing the trapdoor and dismissing Harris for the day, hoping the color he felt in his cheeks did not show. The trouble was that in his rather large palm, the girl's hand had felt so unbelievably small and soft. And why in the world had he noticed anything about it?

"I should introduce myself," she was saying. "I'm Cicely Lansing, but I've always been called Cissie—with a *C*," she added. "And you?"

The man glanced down at his gardening clothes. "My name is Julian Armstrong. And I should like to ask you if you are in the habit of entering strange places without being invited."

A look of bland innocence spread over the girl's face. "Oh, never," she said decidedly, "except"—she paused a second—"except when I see a trapdoor. Then I'm lost. I just have to see what's below. The urge comes from reading too many mysteries, wouldn't you think?"

The man passed over the levity. "Please be serious. How does it come you are here at all?"

"May I sit down?" she asked. "I'm really pretty tired from all my banging and shouting."

"Of course. Excuse me. I think the large desk chair is comfortable." He remained standing to indicate the conversation was to be brief. He had just decided her eyes were a very dark blue. Like violets. As this thought crossed his mind he heard his voice coming more sternly than ever.

"Please go on."

"Well, you see I live with my grandmother, Mrs. Andrew Lansing, who has just lately moved here from New York. She hasn't been well and so has not been to church. And she asked me to come to see the Rector and tell him please to bring the Word of the Lord to her. That's the way she put it." The girl caught her breath.

"And when I got here the secretary was just leaving, this being Saturday, but she showed me in here and said the Rector expected to be back within the hour, if I didn't mind waiting. So I waited until I was finally so bored I decided to try the trapdoor to see if heretics and special sinners were kept down there. Quite an idea! But when I found I was shut in, I was scared so I yelled and banged. But now tell me, please, how the trapdoor ever came to be in this unlikely place."

"It's a simple story. Many years ago there was a Rector here named Dr. Lovejoy, a very fine person, but with one phobia: he couldn't bear noise. You can tell now how the sounds from the Avenue come in. It was much worse then. Trotting horses instead of cars. The Rector was unhappy. So the vestrymen got together and arranged for a little room to be partitioned off in the basement to be reached by some stairs and a trapdoor in the study. It was done and the good

Doctor was then content, going down every morning to study and write his sermons in perfect quiet."

"So that's the way it's used."

"Not for a long time. When the Bishop first came—only he was not a Bishop then—he was like you, he wanted to see what was below the trapdoor. And when he found the old record books on the shelves and pieces of pewter and plate wrapped in cotton wool and stacks of old choir music and all sorts of odds and ends, he said, 'Why, bless my soul, *an attic* in the basement!' and it's been called the *Attic* ever since."

The girl leaned forward. "You spoke of the Bishop. Do you know him? Bishop Ware?"

"Oh, yes. I live with him, as a matter of fact."

"You live with him! Oh, I've heard so much about him. It must seem like living with one foot in heaven to be with him!"

"I'll tell him that. It will probably make him smile."

"He's quite different from you if he smiles. Do you know," she said, pointing an accusing finger at him, "you have never once smiled at me since I came up from the *Attic*. Come on! I dare you to smile!" Her lips curved bewitchingly.

But the man's remained set. "I can't smile to order. It must rise of its own accord from a deep sense of humor or pleasure."

"And you felt neither. I think that is true. I must go now," she said, "but if it isn't impolite I would like to ask you one more question. How do you happen to rate the honor of living with the Bishop?"

The man's features relaxed, but if it was a half smile, it was the girl who did not return it.

"It is a very unusual thing for two Bishops to live in the same house, but when I came, a bachelor, Bishop Ware was so kind as to invite me to make my home with him. We are fond of each other, but you are right, it is a privilege to live with him."

"But—but you spoke of *two Bishops*. Can you possibly be one—yourself?"

"Yes, I am the new Bishop. Bishop Ware has been retired for several years but still active in many ways."

The girl had risen to her feet as he spoke. She continued staring at him as though frightened, a mist clouding her eyes.

"I'm so utterly ashamed and distressed at all my rudeness and silliness." She spoke the words with difficulty. "But you see I never dreamed . . . I never once guessed you were the Bishop. Your clothes . . ."

9

"Yes, I was doing some gardening in the Bishop's rose-bed when Harris, the verger here, called and signed to me to come at once."

"That was about *me*," she murmured. And the mist became tears.

She moved quickly toward the door while he remained as though galvanized to the spot.

"Please try to forgive me, if you can." She had reached the door now. "Only I hope you'll give Gran's message to the Rector when you see him. And thank you!"

As Julian sprang at last to overtake her the door had opened and closed and a sound like running footsteps came back from the turn of the corridor. She was gone.

The man, Bishop Julian Armstrong, paced back and forth and, to use one of the older Bishop's expressions, "thought *small* of himself." An inner monologue formed in his mind. "She asked *me* to forgive *her*, when I'm the one to be forgiven. What on earth possessed me to act like an oaf? As though I had never had any social experience or any normal courtesy of manner." He had been startled, of course, and provoked, but even so these were not reason enough to make him act with the rigidity of a robot, were they? Certainly not. It was all very strange.

And then as though a shutter had dropped in his mind, allowing him to look beneath into his very self, he suddenly knew exactly why he had acted as he had done, and he was shaken by the truth. He stood still, his brows drawn, his face sober. At last he slowly made his way out again as he had come. He could hear strains of music as the organist went over his next day's arrangements. It sounded soft and soothing. Fenwick, the Rector, was not back yet. He was probably in the arms of his family. Oh, well, he was a good fellow and had made the usual choice.

Julian slowly crossed the two lawns and reached the rose-bed where he had lately been working. He had almost finished when called away, so now he picked up the long gardening tool and leaned slightly upon it, looking across to the church, now the Cathedral, since it was the seat of the Bishop, thinking of its beauty, which had always moved him. There was the gray stone pile with its spire rising, delicate in its strength, up to heaven itself like an architect's dream. On either side of the doors were carvings of little angels in the stone as though to invalidate the church's name, "St. Michael and All Angels."

But it was the inner beauty of the church that most stirred Julian's heart: The great chandeliers, which sent down showers of light as soft as angels' wings; the tall stained glass windows with color fitted to color until all emerged in the glory of a dream when the sun shone through. Then, turning toward the altar, slowly, as though the soul should be prepared for its ultimate beauty, one could see rising the pure white marble reredos, carved in Italy and sent to the church when it was being built.

At last Julian put his gardening tool in the garage, and walked toward the back door, thinking as he did so of Bishop Ware's remark that the church had been designed on lines of absolute and chaste beauty but when the architect turned toward the Rectory he was tired of being chaste and became lascivious. How else could you explain the small unexpected dormers, the saucy looking little pergola effect above the front door, *and* the carvings!

For through the first floor there were, in odd corners, bits of sculpture: a diminutive girl winking at you from under a May-apple leaf, a tiny kitten coyly holding up one paw, a dancing bear, definitely cross-eyed! These and the others caused Bishop Ware to say that the expression of each was either malevolent or seductive, he couldn't tell which. "But," he always ended, "I'm sure the architect put the sculptor up to it. How else can you explain it?"

How else, indeed, Julian thought as he entered the door under the slant-eyed smirk of two little leprechauns carved in the lintel.

As soon as he was inside, Mrs. Morgan, the housekeeper, met him. No matter which door he chose, she was there, by some weird transference of thought, to greet him.

"Well, sir, here you are. Go right up and change and I'll have your drinks ready for you on the porch. Bishop Ware wanted sherry on ice, but I feel iced tea is better for you both on this hot day. Hurry now. He's been looking for you."

"Fine, Mrs. Morgan," he assured her, thinking all the while that if she had suggested nice cups of hemlock he would probably have said the same.

As he went on up the stairs and prepared for the evening he considered Mrs. Morgan. She was at once the bossiest and the kindest person he had ever encountered. She took charge of them and loved them both, he knew, but with Scottish inhibition would never reveal it by word or look. In her own capable, managing way, however, she made a home for

11

them. He remembered the week last winter when she had been away at her niece's because of illness. Nothing then had been right, though Cook had done her best. The wheel had stopped turning; the clock wouldn't strike the hour. He and the Bishop had both felt bereft. All the pleasant little habits to which Mrs. Morgan had accustomed them were now gone. When she returned suddenly one morning, in thick hood and plaid shawl, they had both hurried to inquire for her health and to welcome her back. In a minute she had raised her hand. "Tut! Tut!" she had said. "That's enough. I'm quite all right. I was just a bit doncy, that was all. Now get to your work and I'll get to mine. Look at those newspapers lying all about. I doubt you haven't picked up a one since I've been away. Well, I never!"

When she had gone to the kitchen, the Bishop had winked at Julian. "We've been bad boys. I doubt we'll get no jam for our muffins at lunch." They had laughed together and gone their separate ways contentedly knowing that home was now secure again.

When he was showered, shaved, and dressed in the whitest of linen and elegantly pressed clericals, Julian made his way down to where Bishop Ware waited in his favorite spot. The widest end of the long veranda had been screened and now made a pleasant living room. Here the Bishop sat in his big wicker chair with the peacock back and side pockets for his books and papers. He was past his mid-seventies now, with white hair and a face wrinkled by all the sorrows and vicissitudes of his flock, to whom he had been a Shepherd indeed over the years. A well-developed body left him able for his long daily walks, though these he often noted wryly to himself were growing in little shorter each birthday.

As Julian stepped into view the older man smiled delightedly. There was a strong bond of affection between the two. This had begun long ago at the graduation of Julian Armstrong from the Theological Seminary. Bishop Ware, newly come to his office, ahd been there and had spoken to the young man after the exercises. Then it had happened, as occasionally it does, that a spark of affinity struck them both. The Bishop looked at the handsome young face, its eyes ablaze with religious commitment, and felt his heart knit to that of the other.

Julian, aside from his natural awe, was somehow conscious of the strength, wisdom, and compassion in the face of the great clergyman. He found himself daring to hope that the

12

warm handclasp might not be merely the end of a casual meeting but the beginning of a friendship. And so it had come to be.

It was not hard for the Bishop to keep up with Julian's career. Even holy men enjoy the exchange of religious gossip. Bishop Ware learned that Julian had gone rather quickly from a small parish to a bigger one, and now after some years was called to a large one indeed, where he was making a name for himself in public speaking. He was a good sermonizer but also a clever after-dinner speaker and, most of all, the giver of eloquent addresses to various groups and societies.

On one occasion when to fill an important engagement he passed through the Bishop's own city, he stopped to spend a night with him in the Old Rectory. Then, as father and son, or as Brothers of the Cloth, they had talked until morning, so infinitely more satisfying than their occasional letters. From then on the friendship was fixed forever.

When the time of Bishop Ware's retirement loomed, he already had made his plans. He asked for an assistant, a coadjutor who would automatically succeed him. Before the election took place the Bishop deftly pulled a few strings. He arranged for Julian to preach on Sunday at St. Michael and All Angels; he spoke to key laymen of the diocese, expressing his views diplomatically, and even wrote notes to various neighboring Bishops whose opinions he knew, like his own, had weight.

On the day before the election Bishop Ware spent most of it in prayer. (He couldn't manage the fasting under Mrs. Morgan's watchful eye.) On the day itself he hoped he would not show how nervous he was. But at the end, the Reverend Julian Armstrong was the new Bishop Coadjutor.

"Well, my 'son in the Lord,' come in. I'm glad to see you." Bishop Ware went on now as Julian entered the porch room, "I've been thinking just now of an analogy that won't work. Mrs. Morgan has brought iced tea and little plates of some hors d'oeuvres that she calls 'fiddle faddles.' All very good. Help yourself and sit down and be comfortable while I air my problem."

"Good, I'd like to hear it."

"Well, as I guess you know, this is my favorite hour of the day, when the western light pours in, not diffused, but concentrated as though for a great consummation of glory before the sun slips out of sight. Now, I say, why should not a life go out the same way, why should all its accomplishments

13

and aspirations not be concentrated in a great radiance instead of just squeaking out in weakness? Where's the flaw in the argument?"

"Well, my dear Bishop, I believe you are confusing soul and body a bit there. It's the body that, as you say, squeaks out, but who can tell what glory of light envelops the soul as it goes on its way? No watcher can see that."

For a moment the Bishop looked a bit stricken, then smiled as usual. "You're right, as you always are. How could I have made such a foolish mistake? Sometimes I'm afraid my mind gets a bit foggy. I'll tell you what I'll do. I'll push this whole idea aside until later on, when I'll straighten it out and perhaps write a little piece about it for *The Churchman.* The editor has been asking me for one. And now let's hear what you did when you stopped digging the roses."

"A perfect lead," Julian thought. "Now I can speak casually of the incident." "Oh," he began, "I had an amusing little thing happen. I saw Harris at the side of the church signing to me and calling me to come over fast, so I went thinking the old soul might be sick and Fenwick was out. When I got there Harris was in a tizzy, for he said there was someone or something down in the *Attic,* making queer sounds. He rather inclined to the idea it was an animal or one of them exercizen spirits like in the movie!"

The Bishop gave his deep-throated chuckle. "Good for Harris. He has imagination. Go on, I can't wait. What did you do?"

"We went on to the study where all just then was quiet. I had decided the creature below was one of those rascally small boys who have made such a nuisance of themselves getting in somehow to the secretary and to Fenwick to sell tickets for the Fireman's Brigade and chances on the Toyota automobile in the market. I had decided if I got my hands on him I'd shake the wits out of him for playing such a prank as going down there. So when the noise began again I opened the trapdoor and knelt down to be able to grab him easily and shouted to him to come up . . ."

"And was it the boy?" the Bishop broke in excitedly.

"It was a girl," Julian said in clipped tones.

"A girl? Good heavens! What did she say?"

"Just nonsense."

"What she said when caught in that position would give a clue to her whole character. I want to know. Tell me."

"Well, if you insist, she said 'Boo.'"

14

The Bishop laughed now until the tears came. "Wonderful! Wonderful! I wish I'd been there. Did she go on and tell you why she had opened the trapdoor and gone down in the first place?"

"Just silliness. Said she never could resist a trapdoor and in this case she wanted to know whether heretics and special sinners were kept down there. You couldn't talk sense to her."

"I haven't had such a laugh for many a long day. Did you get her name?"

"Oh, yes. She's Cicely Lansing called Cissie for short, with a C. She's visiting her grandmother, Mrs. Andrew Lansing. Do you know her? You always seem to know everyone's grandmother."

"I've certainly heard that name, but it belongs I'm sure with my very early years. I may though recall the connection later. Was this girl pretty?"

"I didn't notice," said Julian shortly, at which the Bishop gave him a level glance.

"Ah, yes. Well, I think I can guess her looks from the nature of this episode. Her hair must be *black*."

"No," said Julian decidedly. "It was light brown, sort of blond."

"Just so," the Bishop agreed, "but the eyes *have* to be black, a piercing black!"

"Not at all. They were blue, not that thin watery kind of blue so many eyes have, but a dark, dark blue."

"Like violets," said the Bishop.

Julian started in his chair and replied almost angrily, "What made you say that?"

At this the Bishop shot another straight glance again, then smiled. "Don't bite me, Julian. I said that because I have occasionally seen eyes like that. Very beautiful they are, too."

Mrs. Morgan appeared in the doorway. "Dinner is served, Bishop," she said, looking at both of them.

"Thank you, Mrs. Morgan," Bishop Ware said, rising, "And I want to say your little 'fiddle faddles,' as you called them, were perfectly delicious. I'd like to have them every day for a while at least."

"I'm glad you liked them, sir, but they're very rich so I couldn't let you have them that often. I'll make them as often as I think best. I wanted to speak of the dog, Bishop Ware. Of Marcano."

15

"Is he all right?" the Bishop asked anxiously. "I've been missing him."

"Oh, he's in fine fettle now but you should have seen him a couple of hours ago. He heard the children shouting at the Russells' pool along the Avenue and he took off to them. They know him so they threw him in the water. He struggled and wiggled, but I was watching from our back lawn and had no fears for him and since he's a spaniel I knew he could swim if he had to . . ."

"Poor Marcano," the Bishop said softly.

"But when they let him alone he got to the edge and scrambled out. Then he shook himself and you'd never guess. He went right over to the big dirt bed the gardener had made to plant bulbs in and he rolled an' rolled in it an' then came peltin' home, very pleased with himself—but what a mess."

"Poor Marcano," the Bishop repeated.

"It was poor *me,* if I may say so. I brushed him for one solid hour, an' he took it fairly well. I guess he knew he'd never get to you in the state he was in. At the end, though, he did come up beautiful. Then I washed every paw of him with soap an' water an' dried them with a bit of a towel an' now he's as clean a gentleman as you'd care to meet."

As she turned, an unseen force propelled the dining-room door open into the hall where the men were now standing and threw itself upon the Bishop's feet, with small barks of joy. The dog reached up then to lick the large hand that began to stroke the brown-and-white head and scratch the sensitive spots back of the ears and below the throat, while small tremors of pleasure went through him.

"Good lad!" the Bishop kept saying. "Good lad! You ran off to swim like all the bad little boys, did you? Well, all is forgiven. Would you like to carry my cane in to dinner?"

He presented the middle of the cane to the dog, who grasped it delicately between his teeth and slowly started off toward the dining room. Once there he stood beside the Bishop's chair until the cane was accepted with thanks.

The dining room, like most in the Old Rectory, was worthy of a Bishop. It was a spacious room with dark walnut paneling and tall windows with leaded panes that gave upon the garden. At one end was the great fireplace with its wide stone hearth. Above it was the portrait of a young woman. A little light was turned on at each meal, bringing new beauty to the young woman's smile and pink gown. Mrs. Morgan never forgot this light.

Upon the opposite wall above the long Sheraton buffet was a panel picturing the noble heads of a half dozen hunting dogs, their identification given by name beneath each head, as Marcano, Sereno, Calypso, Nicano, and so on. Guests always studied the picture with interest. Had the Bishop ever known the dogs? They were too real to be imagined. He gave his answer simply. The picture had been in his father's house, but, unfortunately, he had never heard its history, just accepted it as part of the familiar furnishings. Since it had been his own, a number of artists had studied it but were unable to decide upon the medium. Of course, no photograph, and no etching. Possibly an engraving, but no one was sure. As to himself the Bishop always added, "I just love the dogs and let it go at that."

The table, as usual, sparkled with crystal and gleamed with silver, a bowl of pink roses from the garden gracing the center. The tall candles were lighted when the men sat down, Julian having helped the Bishop into his chair at the end of the table where he faced the portrait of the young woman who had been his wife. After grace, the meal proceeded rather quietly, for the two Bishops were accustomed to discussing clerical problems in private before or after dinner. Now Mrs. Morgan served them meticulously in silence, pausing occasionally as she passed Marcano sitting expectant on the hearth beside his pewter plate. When she put some tidbits upon it, she spoke in a stern whisper, "Be a good dog now, an' you'll be the mair thought on."

It was as the two men were finishing dessert that Bishop Ware suddenly slapped the palm of his hand upon the table making the nearest candle flicker. "I've got it!" he said jubilantly.

"Got what, my lord?" asked Julian.

"Why, the name, Andrew Lansing. You asked if I had known the girl's grandmother. I knew if I recalled anything it would be from my very early days, and sure enough it was when I was serving my first parish up in Connecticut. There was a river flowing past the town and the great diversion for young people was boating in the evening, singing as they rowed or drifted on the water. I was young then so I often joined them."

The Bishop paused a moment, lost in his memories.

"There was one girl—I think her name was Sally—who always seemed to be the center of the fun. She had a lovely voice, I remember, and she always started the songs. Curious

17

about memory. You start with only a name and all at once a whole scene comes back."

"But that's wonderful," Julian answered, trying to make his tone fit the words.

"We were going on our pleasant way with the boating and the singing once in late summer when a young man came from New York to spend his vacation in the little town. He was very handsome and very nice. The other fellows envied him his smart clothes, and we all admired the ease with which he met every situation. Before long we saw that he and Sally were in love. One of the other fellows was quite broken up, for he had hoped to win Sally himself. I was leaving that fall for my next parish so knew little more of the old boating crowd. I did hear, though, that Sally and this Andrew Lansing had been married at Christmas."

"So, that's the story," Julian said with polite enthusiasm.

"Not quite all, for to my surprise one of the old songs came back to me. You would think it completely silly but I want to tell you, that sung by good voices in the moonlit dusk over the water, it had an absolutely haunting sound. I warn you I'm going to go now to try to get a few chords. I think I remember some of the words and even the crazy refrain!"

Julian followed him into the drawing room as did Marcano, and Bishop Ware fumbled with the keys of the piano as he hummed to himself. All at once he found the chords he was searching for and raised his clear tenor voice in the song.

> *"Oh, who will raise my green umbrella*
> *Green umbrella!*
> *Oh, who will raise my green umbrella*
> *When I am far-r away?*
> *Allebezan, Patsy Moran,*
> *Kalamazoo, Shoo, Shoo!*

> *"Oh, who will smoke my meerschaum pipe*
> *Meerschaum pipe!*
> *Oh, who will smoke my meerschaum pipe*
> *When I am far-r-r away?*
> *Allebezan, Pasty Moran,*
> *Kalamazoo, Shoo, Shoo!"*

"Well," said Julian with a laugh, "if I didn't know your incredibly serious capabilities, I would be shocked to hear you waste your good voice on a song like this."

The older Bishop turned quickly. "I'll tell you something, Julian. When I've been almost wrecked by some problem, so hard I felt I couldn't solve it, I've saved myself many times by relaxing into some bit of humor or nonsense like this song until I could think straight again. I prescribe this remedy, Julian. Don't belittle it."

"I won't," the younger man said still smiling. "And I certainly hope you are not being plagued just now by any *wrecking* problem."

Bishop Ware turned back to the piano and softly struck a chord. "Could be," he said quietly. "It just could be."

2

Mornings began early in the Old Rectory, when Mrs. Morgan rang a bell in the lower hall at six o'clock. The bell had been made with the idea of alerting a drowsy elephant and Bishop Ware had been fond of it ever since he had found it long ago while on a trip to Egypt.

"I don't like to be wakened harshly," he had said as he placed the bell on the hall table, "and this tone just suits me. It's decisive enough, but there is in it, a sweet resonance that sort of 'gentles' the sound."

The two Bishops prepared differently for their breakfast at eight, set at this hour so that there would be the long time they wished for their devotions. Bishop Ware had his first cup of coffee in leisurely fashion in his dressing gown, along with Mrs. Morgan's detailed report upon the weather, and, unlike yesterday's fair June warmth, this day boded clouds and chilly showers. He read then from the Psalms and *The Imitation* until nearly seven, when he returned the books to the table and settled more deeply into the upholstered chair that seemed to support every curve of his body. Then the old question assailed him.

"Have I the right," he thought, "to be so *comfortable* while I pray for all sorts and conditions of men, the destitute, the sick, the sorrowing, the starving, the homeless?"

Sometimes he feared his prayers must have a hollow sound in the ears of God. And yet the fact remained, that while he could still kneel in the normal posture of prayer, he could not rise from it without the greatest difficulty. It was only after he had been compelled to call for help one morning, that he had decided upon the comfort and safety of the armchair.

"I rather think," he had remarked one day to the younger Bishop, "that if God hears my prayer, he will also know the state of my knees."

On this particular morning, Bishop Ware added, to his regular requests, new and agonizing petitions for a man known, and a woman unknown.

In contrast to the older man, Bishop Julian Armstrong rose quickly at the first sound of the bell, took a cold shower, some setting-up exercises, and then dressed with meticulous care in his finely tailored gray suit. For himself, he rather blessed the rain, for it would insure him a quieter day to work upon his next speech, an important one to the university graduating class. He would also have time to catch up some loose threads in the pattern of diocesan life, make a half dozen telephone calls, plan the next days' work, and check his own Bishop's account book. Thank heaven he had had a course in bookkeeping along the way, for financial problems reared their ugly heads in a diocese as in everywere else.

When he was dressed, Julian opened his Bible, as he often did, at random, realizing it was a childish gesture and yet half believing, backed by experience, that he would find a special message on the pages thus before him. He used the little device now and felt quick tears sting his eyes. For he was reading some verses that had always touched him about the young boy, Samuel, who ministered to the Lord before Eli, the old priest.

Julian pictured the scene as he had always done. It was night in the great Temple. Old Eli was asleep with the young Samuel also asleep nearby. Darkness soon brooded over them as the Lamp of God went out where the Ark of God stood. A great silence, a holy quiet, filled the place. Suddenly, the boy started up. He had heard a voice. He went quickly to old Eli.

"Here am I, for thou calledst me."

The old man roused slightly. "I called not. Lie down again."

But once more the boy heard the voice and went to the old priest. "Here am I, for thou *didst* call me."

20

But Eli only answered, "Lie down, my son. I did not call."

When the voice came the third time and Samuel went to the priest, Eli perceived that it was the Lord who had called the child. "Lie down again," he said, "but if you hear the voice, I will tell thee what thou shalt say."

So Samuel went back to his bed and waited in the darkness. Once more the call came, and this time he answered. "Speak, Lord, for thy servant heareth."

Julian still sat, thinking over the little scene. Out of the darkness and the silence, a voice. And so must it ever be, the Divine Call and the human answer. He remembered how it had been with himself as a youth. Strangely enough he, too, had heard the voice in the darkness and silence of a sleepless night. And the call had seemed so clear that he had made his first great commitment before the dawn came.

But oh, Samuel's words of response, "Speak, Lord, for thy servant heareth," brought for him a question. Was he always able, even now as a Bishop, to *hear* the voice? Did the busy secularities of everyday living drown it out? Or dim its message? Was his mind so spiritually attuned that it could receive impulses from the Great Source of all Power? He wondered, he feared, he hoped. This morning, this very day, he meant to concentrate upon his address to the students, and he wanted desperately to hear creative ideas flowing into his mind.

He closed the Bible, laid it on the table, and walked over to the Prie Dieu, which stood against the wall opposite his bed. He had found and bought it after he had just become a Priest of the Episcopal Church, and had felt, over the years as he used it, that its beauty of line and delicacy of color lent a certain dignity to his devotions as he made his petitions to the Throne of Grace. He knelt, bowed his head upon his hands, and prayed.

Breakfast in the Old Rectory was a hearty one, for Mrs. Morgan said that, after the long night, both body and mind needed nourishment. The two men read their morning papers and discussed the news of the world as they ate. When they had finished their last cups of coffee, Bishop Ware rose slowly.

"Are you going to be at home for a while?" he asked.

"Yes, until about ten I should think. A wet day always seems to me a good day to work. If I could just muzzle the Archbishop when I get down to the office. He's such a good man, but he drives me distracted with his interruptions. Then just when I'm ready to explode, he comes in with a very important matter that should be decided immediately, and I have to thank God for him. For one thing today, I thought I would put the finishing touches on my talk to the university students. It strikes me they must be just the age to be facing their first serious religious doubts. I would like to say something about that. What do you think?"

"Very good. Only be honest. They'll know it if you're not."

"But of course I will be. Haven't I told you how I wrestled with my own doubts in college and came through them?"

"Yes, well, it's my judgment that it's only when a man stops *thinking* that all his doubts leave him."

"I don't believe I could use that in my speech. If I say anything on this subject, I want it to be encouraging."

"It will be, Julian, don't worry. By the way, the reason I asked if you would be home for a while was that I would like you to come to my office in about a half hour. There is something I want to tell you."

"You look ominous. Is it as bad as that?"

"I'm afraid so. I'll see you then. Thank you."

Bishop Ware's office was a gracious place, developing that quality over the years he had used it. It had a mellow look with its wall of books, one or two of which and some magazines usually lying on the low table with the large lamp suggested many comfortable midnight readings. The chairs were mostly easy, except for the one behind the desk. Here Bishop Ware was seated with Marcano beside him when Bishop Armstrong came into the room.

"Pick a comfortable seat," the older man said, "and I'll begin at once. I think you know Will Babcock, don't you?"

"Certainly, a fine fellow he is! What about him?"

"I'll tell you the story just as Fenwick told it to me. He was not at the hospital yesterday as you supposed. He was here. He came to me because I've known Babcock for twenty years. Another vestryman, John Carson, is connected with a big real estate firm here and they would like to buy a certain piece of land out near the end of Long Island. Carson went there to find some facts out for himself. As he stood sizing up the locality, he saw a cab stop before a good-looking brick house set in a wide lawn. A man got out of the cab and went quickly up the walk to where two children were playing. Carson heard them shout, "Daddy! Daddy!" He took something from his pocket and gave some to each child. They

22

looked to be about five and three perhaps, Carson said. Then the man went on to the front steps where a very pretty youngish woman waited, smiling. He put his arm around her and drew her into the house. The man was Will Babcock!"

"I don't believe it!" Julian was vehement. "Carson just saw someone who *looked* like Will. You know yourself how often resemblances are deceiving. It is ridiculous to think it was Will Babcock! It simply was another man and a case of mistaken identity!"

Bishop Ware sat silent for a long minute. "That's what I thought when I first heard the story. But John Carson had more proof. The next day being Saturday, he went back and took his wife along. They had both been friends of the Babcocks. They parked the car at a little distance and walked through a small grove opposite the brick house, which stood quite apart from its neighbors. They waited then, behind some trees, which concealed them but between certain branches allowed them to see clearly what went on in the brick house. This next part seems, for a strange reason, the hardest part to tell you." The Bishop paused again.

"They first saw Will coming out the front door with a wicker chaise longue that he set upon the lawn. Then the woman came out with the children. They played with a dog and their toys and the woman and the man seemed to be joking playfully about who was to use the chaise. Suddenly Will picked her up. Carson said she was slight—and put her comfortably on the cushions, then took a chair beside her and sat down. Carson said they seemed to have a great deal to say to each other, and once, when the woman leaned to whisper something, smiling, Will threw back his head and laughed and laughed. I think this should be noted, for in all the twenty years I've known him, I've never seen him give way to great mirth. The Carsons left after that. So, that's the story."

"It's outrageous! It's indecent! It's unbelievable! What about excommunication? Has that been done away with altogether? This would seem to me a perfect case for it. What are you going to suggest?"

"I don't know. I have a strange feeling of sympathy for the man."

"Sympathy! I can't quite understand that. Here is a man breaking the laws of God and the church and society itself. Do you mean you condone his actions?"

"Of course I don't. You know that. But before I pass any judgment I want to know what lies behind these facts we

23

already know. I promised Fenwick I would speak to Will, but before I do, I intend to pay a sort of social call on Mrs. Babcock. I may know more then."

"She seems to me a very fine, dignified, *ladylike* person. Does Fenwick say whether she still comes to church?"

"Oh yes. And once in a while, Will himself, usually when the boys are home. Then they make a family pew."

Julian suddenly stood up. "I *hate* the deception of all this. To me it seems worse than the crime—the error—itself. I have no feeling of mercy for that man! How can I get on with my work today?"

"I'm sorry to upset you, Julian, but I believe it is good for you to consider all the facts as they come in, because you will have to take the leading part in resolving this whole sorry business in some way."

For three days there was not a word spoken in the Old Rectory about the problem. On the fourth day, Bishop Ware dressed with especial care, explained to Marcano why he could not go along, and then, taking his best cane, he walked past St. Michael's and over several streets beyond, to the large distinguished-looking house of the Babcocks'. A neat little maid answered his ring and showed him into the "drawing room," as she called it. Here he looked about him. The furnishings were rich and absolutely correct, he thought, but they gave the impression that no one ever sat in the velvet chair or struck a chord on the grand piano in a corner. A dead room, he was thinking as his hostess entered. She was tall, dressed in a rose-colored gown that was becoming with her graying hair. Her face was unwrinkled as a child's. She was really good looking.

"My dear Bishop," she began, extending her hand, "I am so honored and pleased to have you here. Do sit down. The fact is, there is a certain coincidence about your coming, for I had been actually planning to go to see you at your office."

"I am the one who is honored," the Bishop said gallantly. "Did you feel there was something I could do for you?"

"It seems a bit strange to tell you, but since we are together—it's about Will."

The Bishop gulped mentally and took hold of himself.

"Do tell me, Mrs. Babcock. I would be so happy if I could help you."

"Well, it's really about an article I read in a magazine about heart disease. It said a person could feel fine and look well and yet not know there was anything the matter if he

24

hadn't been checked by a doctor, and then some extra strain could bring on a sudden heart attack and just—take him off! Have you ever heard anything like this?"

"Yes, I believe I have."

"Well, the way I look at it, for long years, Will has had to make trips for his company which would take him away from home for several days. But in the last few years, he's been away so much more and this would make the extra *strain* the article talked about. Don't you see?"

"He looks well?" the Bishop inquired.

"Why, he looks wonderful. Better than for years, I would say. But there is this threat hanging over him."

"Does he get enough exercise?"

"I've wondered about that. I don't think he has gone on walks much for years. Not since the dog's been gone."

"Oh, you had a dog?" The Bishop's voice was eager.

"We certainly had, until I couldn't take it any longer."

"What happened?" His voice was full of sympathy.

"Well, in the first place, Will brought a puppy home that wasn't even housebroken. If I didn't have a time! But I 'broke' him in short order. Every time he made a mistake in the house, I slapped him hard and he soon learned. It was funny though, he never forgave me. He wouldn't come near me. I didn't care, for he was Will's dog. He just made a baby of the creature. I had my own troubles with him. He grew so fast and had the biggest paws I ever saw. He would slop over the dish every time he drank and I would be always cleaning up after him. Will always walked him, and one day Will said they would go for a walk even in the rain. When they got back you never saw such a sight. The dog bounded into the kitchen and his paws were pure mud. He raced all around on the clean, waxed floor until it looked like a cattle pen. It was the last straw. I told Will I couldn't stand it any longer. The dog had to go."

"And what happened?" The Bishop's throat sounded a little dry.

"Oh, of course Will pleaded, but I stood firm. I did feel a little sorry for Will the day he took the dog away, but when I thought of all the trouble I had to put up with, I didn't blame myself."

"I suppose Will stopped his walks then?" the Bishop asked.

"Oh, yes. He had several long trips, close together at that time, so I think he got over it. But Bishop, I should not have spent so long talking about the *dog*. What I really meant to explain to you was how much of the time I am alone, and what I could plan to do about it. Even on vacations the boys are always dashing off to visit their friends. And what of me?"

The Bishop spoke quietly. "I can see your problem, Mrs. Babcock. But you have a beautiful home here. Have you thought of entertaining even when Will is away? You could have your women friends to luncheons and teas, for example."

His hostess stared at him as though amazed. "Entertaining," she said. "Dear Bishop, I am sure you are psychic! You have just led me to confess an experience I was questioning whether to tell you or not."

"Please do," said the Bishop.

"I always *loved* to entertain until one time some years ago. I had planned a really beautiful dinner party for eight. How I worked on every detail of that! I engaged a butler for the evening so that all would go perfectly. He and I decided that since it was spring, leg of lamb would be nice, with everything that went with it, curried rice, little green peas, chutney, and so on. I invited three couples who I felt were among our most distinguished friends."

She hesitated a moment, then went on. "When they came to the dining room I could feel they were impressed with the table, hand-painted place cards, and a mound of spring flowers in the center. The first course was perfect, with nice, low-voiced, well-bred conversation, and then the butler brought in the roast. It did look ravishing! And here I should mention, Bishop, that the guests were all members of St. Michael's and had, dozens of times, repeated the words of the General Confession, 'All we like sheep, have gone astray.' Will stood up to carve. He looked down at the leg of lamb and then around at everyone at the table and said, 'Do all we like sheep?' For a second they didn't get it, and then there were simply roars of laughter. And they kept on laughing all through that wonderful meal. I had the feeling they didn't even know what they were eating. My face was scarlet. Are you sure you are all right, Bishop?"

"Perfectly," he said. "I have had these little seizures before upon occasion." For at one point in his hostess's story he had suddenly brought forth a snowy handkerchief and clapped it over his mouth, behind which he struggled with something between a sneeze and a cough.

"I will talk to Mr. Fenwick," he went on, "to see if he cannot find you something in connection with church work

26

that might be congenial to you and keep you busy. Now, I really must go. It has been most interesting talking with you."

"Oh, thank you, Bishop. It has been so good for me to unburden myself, especially, perhaps, about that dinner party, for I've never forgiven Will, *never!*" She added with vehemence.

Bishop Ware walked slowly and soberly back to the Old Rectory. Once, unfortunately just as he was passing another pedestrian, he broke into a short, uncontrolled laugh, then, with brows knit, went on as before. Once at home he called Will Babcock at his office. When his voice came, it was cheerful.

"Why Bishop, this is a pleasure! Are you starting a new Boy's Club? Or what can I do for you?"

"Can you come to see me one day soon for a little visit?"

There was a slight pause. "Of course. Would tomorrow be too soon?"

"Perfect. Could you come about four?"

"I'll arrange it. Thank you, Bishop."

The next day, Mrs. Morgan showed Babcock up to the office, where the Bishop met him with a warm handclasp.

"Would it make this interview any easier for you, my good old friend, if I were to tell you I think I know the reason for it?" Will asked.

"Yes, it would. Also I want to tell you that my feeling for you is the same this minute as it was when we first knew each other."

Will drew a deep breath.

"That certainly makes it all easier for me. Thank you. Do I have to sit while I'm questioned?"

"No, walk a bit if you wish. Why?"

"My thoughts always congeal when I sit."

"Pace around then. I've a few good pictures you can glance at as you pass. Now let's begin, since we understand each other. Could you tell me something of your later boyhood and early manhood at the time of your marriage?"

"That's easy. I like to remember it. There were four brothers of us, and we certainly enjoyed our home. We were a noisy bunch, as you can imagine. One would be banging on the piano while another was pounding away at a small boat he was making—oh, I don't know what all. Then we were always playing tricks, with my father often joining in. He was a great prankster. I suppose you might sum it up by saying we were a happy, affectionate, rather noisy lot. I'll end this part by telling about our last big spree. My oldest brother had fallen in love with a nice girl and was to be married in a week. We liked her very much, but were a bit sunk at the thought of losing him. We were all in my room when Bob, our youngest, threw his pillow and hit the coming bridegroom right in the face. That was enough. Within ten minutes, we had taken all the pillows in the house except for those in our parent's room. There was a big upper hall and there we waged battle. You may not know that if you shake the feathers all to one end and twist the empty end of the slip, you'll really have a weapon. We made the most of it, for we'd learned this trick when we were kids. When the fight was over, we'd busted one pillow, so we gathered up the feathers and quieted down. The next morning our parents confessed they had looked at the fray from their bedroom door and thought it was very funny. But I'll tell you something, Bishop, from that wedding day on, we were all grown up. We were men. Do you get the picture?"

"I do. Now what about your own wedding?"

"This is hard to explain. When I met Elizabeth I was simply stunned by her beauty. Not only her face, though she was pretty, but by the dignity, the gentle withdrawal, I guess you could call it. She seemed to me remote in some lovely, virginal way. I simply bowed my heart before her. After our wedding, I began to feel disturbed. I found that, in our relations as husband and wife, what was sheer joy to me, was for her, a distasteful chore to be endured as infrequently as possible." He moistened his lips.

"When our first son came, things were better for a while. But when the second child came, I had a shock. She told me she would never take any chance on having more children. I needn't say any more about that."

After a few moments, he went on, "But my little boys! I certainly had pleasure with them. The only trouble was that Elizabeth was so strict with them, even severe at times. And, Bishop"—he stopped pacing and looked almost piteously into the face of the older man—"they were such *good* little chaps! As good as any normal boys could be.

"But Elizabeth demanded perfection. The house was *her* idol. When something was accidentally spilled on the table-cloth or a glass was broken, it was a serious matter for punishment. I interfered as often as I dared, but as the boys grew older, I knew they would be happier if I could find a good homelike school for them, and I did. When they left I was sunk. I missed them so. But I think Elizabeth was relieved. She could devote all her time to decorating the house. I believe," he added thoughtfully, "that the last vestige of feeling I had for her left me when the boys were gone."

The Bishop raised a finger. "That's enough, Will. I think I understand. Now, could you tell me a little about your—your present—"

"Wife," he said. "The first real wife I've had in all these years. I met her at my brother Tom's house about six years ago when I stopped to see them while on a trip. Rose is a friend of Tom's wife. My first sight of her was when she was kneeling beside a big springer spaniel, removing a thorn from his paw. The dog was wise and understood, but it hurt and he trembled with little moans of pain while she had to wipe her own eyes to see clearly. I went over and knelt by the dog to hold him more steady, and with a lot of skill, she got the thorn out, washed the cut, and bound the paw with a little gauze bandage. He lay down contentedly before the fire and she and I stood, facing each other with a long look. We fell in love at that moment. You probably can't believe that."

"Oh, yes," said the Bishop calmly, "for it happened to me just that way, many, many years ago."

Will breathed a long sigh of relief. "Wonderful!" he said. "Then I needn't elaborate on that. We talked our very hearts out all that weekend, and as soon as I got back, I told Elizabeth I wanted a divorce. She was calm, but adamant. Never, she said, would she suffer such humiliation. What she wanted was for me to spend more time with her so the marriage would look correct. Then I bared my soul. I told her I loved another woman. To my horror, she smiled and said she understood. Men had these infatuations, which passed, as mine would do. As to divorce, she never wanted the word to be mentioned again. And this was *final*.

"Her face was set in lines I had seen before. I knew there was no hope. The worst was telling Rose. She thought for a few minutes and then said we must go on with our plans. She said her heart had at last found a home and would never leave it. So I bought a nice house in a quiet section out on the tip of Long Island and when it was furnished, we moved in. That evening we read together the marriage service and declared to each other we were man and wife. Without benefit of clergy but, I was sure, with the blessing of God, to whom all hearts are open.

"In a year a great desire of mine was granted. A little girl,

29

as pretty as her mother. Later on, a sturdy little boy, named for me. As to my two older boys, nearly through college, they spent a few days with their mother and then hurried out to our home and at once became a part of it, as they still are. Rose mothers them and they adore her. And sometimes, for example, one of them will be belting out a new hit song, the other, perhaps shouting to me to come and see a truck, the little children squealing with delight, and the dog barking—it is so gloriously noisy, it makes me think of my boyhood."

"I think I understand that, Will. Could you tell me something more about Rose, and your own feelings," the Bishop said.

"I'll try, but this is hard to do. Rose is thirty-six years old and for ten of those she has been a nurse. She's been taking this year off as a sort a sabbatical. She never talked much to me about her work except to say she loved it, but my brother Tom has a doctor friend who has told him how wonderful she is. I believe I'll repeat one of his stories.

"There was a patient who had to have a delicate operation in a few days. Meanwhile he could not relax. He *couldn't sleep*. They had given him all the opiates they dared, and yet he was restless, feverish, with his mind working overtime. The doctor was in despair until he thought of Rose and, luckily, got her. She entered the room, about nine in the evening, smiling delightedly as though coming for a social call. She acknowledged the introduction, for the doctor was there for a final check.

"Hello, Steve," Rose said, beaming upon the man on the bed. (Of course she had read the chart outside.) The doctor told Tom she had gotten rid of him in a few minutes as airily as you please, saying it was so nice of him to stop in, but they really wouldn't need him anymore for she and Steve were just going to have a pleasant time together. He said he made her tell him next day everything she said or did. The relief nurse had prepared the patient for the night, but Rose now bathed his face, smoothed back his hair, put ice pads on his eyelids, and told him a good way she had found to change her position in bed. Lie on your right side, stretch your right leg down, and draw your left leg up. You should try it sometime, she told him. He did at once and said it felt good. Just as he seemed to settle, he raised his head. 'Don't I get some more of those damned pills?' and Rose said, 'Not a damned pill,' and laughed. Wonder of wonders, so did he. She knew there was then a break in the tension. 'If you don't mind keeping quiet for a little while, I think I'll sing to you.' (Not a word about *sleep*, you'll notice.) So then she began, in her sweet, gentle voice, on the old nursery rhyme, with its slow, dreamy tune.

"The Frog went a wooing, he did ride,
With his sword and pistols by his side,

Ah Hmmm.

"He rode till he came to Miss Mousie's den
And said, Hi, Lady Mouse, are you within?

Ah Hmmm.

"He took Lady Mouse upon his knee
And he said, Lady Mouse, will you marry me?

Ah Hmmm.

"O, not without Uncle Rat's consent
That his niece should marry the President.

Ah Hmmm.

"Uncle Rat has gone to town,
To buy his niece a wedding gown.

Ah Hmmm.

"Those last lines were the ones I liked best when our mother used to sing it to us whenever we got sick. So Tom knew the way it went and so did I. There is more of the song, but this will give you an idea. Rose sang it over and over, then over again without a break, checking her watch and the patient all the while. At ten she could feel him relax. At exactly eleven-thirty, she saw that he was asleep. She turned the light out and set herself for a careful watch through the night. At a quarter to *seven* he was still asleep. She looked at him with satisfaction. They day nurse was due at seven, so Rose went softly out of the door and stood with her back against it. Not only the nurse, but the doctor was there. He said he had been so anxious to hear how the night had gone that he couldn't wait. Rose put her fingers to her lips and then very quietly told them the patient had been sound asleep for nearly eight hours and if it broke all the rules of the hospital she would not allow *anyone* to enter that room until she called. The patient must not be wakened even if he slept all day. The doctor said he was a very staid man, but when he saw her standing there with her back to the door, ready to fight for that man's sleep, his eyes got wet and he leaned down and kissed her and said he would arrange everything.

"So, Bishop, that is part of the story of Rose. I'm afraid it's been rather long."

"Not at all. I've been very deeply interested. How long did the man sleep?"

"Till one o'clock. Then he woke refreshed, but said he wanted to apologize for going to sleep while she was singing."

"Wonderful!" laughed the Bishop. "Wonderful! Now, a little more about your own feelings, if you can, and hers too," he added.

"This is hard," Will said. "I never knew before there was such a love as I have, and Rose has the same. The wonder is that she fell in love with *me*. I have so few attributes—"

"I can think of some," the Bishop said. "Just go on."

"I'll add one more little illustration. When the big boys were very young and I put them into a school where I thought they would be happier, I had many nightmares, dreaming something had happened to them. Now, once in a while I dream that Rose is gone and I can't find her. It is so real that I wake in sheer terror. Then I reach out and touch her softly and am at peace. I love her like that.

"I'm afraid I haven't answered your questions very well. I know you wanted just the essence, and I've gone off on tangents and talked too much about the wrong things perhaps—"

The Bishop rose. "You have told me exactly what I needed to know," he said, and came around to where Will was standing stiffly as though waiting for a sentence. He put his hands on the younger man's shoulders.

"Perhaps you will be good enough not to repeat this, for I am speaking now just as one who himself has known a great love. As man to man, I rejoice in your happiness, and as your long time friend, I send my love—to Rose."

Will still stood stiffly for a few more moments, then with hands that trembled, he grasped the arms of the Bishop, dropped his head on the broad shoulder before him, and wept without restraint. Bishop Ware waited quietly until Will raised his head and moved back.

"I'm ashamed of that breakdown," he said. "I don't think anything like that ever happened to me before. I hope you will forgive me. You see, I was uptight when I got here. I didn't sleep last night, for I was sure I would hear words of censure from you, and that would be hard for me. Then the whole sorry situation that I can't marry Rose and give her and our children an honorable name, cuts into my soul sometimes, especially when I'm away from them. When I am with them, I'm so happy I forget it. But it all came over me last night. So you see, everything sort of hit me together."

He walked to the window and stood there, looking out. Suddenly he turned and went on speaking.

"And then, when you didn't say a word of reprimand, but just the beautiful kindness of that man-to-man speech, my self-control just left me. I'm sorry."

That night Bishop Ware dined alone. Julian was away in a distant end of the Diocese on church business and would not be home until late. Bishop Ware was rather glad of that. He wanted to be quiet and think about the strange life story he had just heard and his own reaction to it. But above all, there was a nebulous recollection of a verse, which he must have read long ago, probably in the Scriptures, but had not committed accurately, or remembered the source. However, there still came the haunting suggestion that there was somehow a relation between it and the emotions he had felt that afternoon.

When he had finished his dinner, he decided to go up to the office and look for the verse. Once there he seated himself in what he called his "reading" chair with Marcano in his favorite position, lying beside him with his head on his master's feet. The Bishop turned up the light, reached for his Bible, and began his search. "Not in the Old Testament, certainly," he murmured, nor yet in the Gospels he felt. It sounded more like St. Paul. He started then, slowly and carefully to scan the Pauline letters. But at the end he leaned his head against the back of the chair. His eyes were tired and he was disappointed. There were three other letters, shorter ones that he would now go on reading, those of James, Peter, and John. But they, also, did not produce the thing he sought. It left now only one brief missive, a page and a quarter long, written by St. Jude, and placed before Revelations, which he had not even bothered to examine. But he would try St. Jude. Since the letter was so short, he read it aloud, savoring the words. The theme of the writer was the *Ungodly*, whom he described as,

> *Raging waves of the sea, foaming*
> *out their own shame.*
> *Wandering stars for whom is reserved*
> *the blackness of darkness forever.*

"What imagery!" spoke the Bishop. "What writing!"

The author went on to indicate various types of the *Ungodly*, and always with strong denunciation.

But suddenly at the last, he spoke directly to his Beloved, the Good People who would be working against the *Ungodly*. As though his inherently gentle spirit had risen to the surface, he gave them a command:

> *And of some have compassion,*
> *making a difference*

The Bishop read this over and over. He had found it indeed, and it was more than he had vaguely remembered. While written hundreds of years ago, it was now perfectly related to the case of Will Babcock. When the little tribunal of vestry and clergy met to pass upon Will's irregular conduct, surely the substance of his story and this verse of St. Jude would incline their hearts to mercy.

Bishop Ware stood up and walked about the room for relaxation. He held Marcano's proffered paw, stroking his smooth silky head and explaining he was not going to bed just then, and then he sat down to think. While the discovery he had just made would certainly alleviate one hurt in Will's heart, there was something much more important and of greater immediacy that must be considered. This was the baffling and sinister problem of the *divorce!*

Just before twelve, Julian came back and tapped softly on the study door, since the light showed through beneath.

"I'm all right," Bishop Ware called. "Just working late. See you at breakfast. Good night!"

The footsteps died away and the Bishop grew more tense as he called upon all his inner resources to aid him, and, a praying man, called also upon the Divine Light. Once in a while he spoke aloud.

"There must be a way!" he repeated.

He pursued several options, having Will try again; having

34

Fenwick, the Rector, try; even to try, himself. But all of this led to the same end. There was only, alas, one solution and cure. This lay in the person of Elizabeth herself, but how? What? For he could see, all too plainly, her fiercely set face as she ended the account of what she called her ruined dinner party. "And I'll never forgive Will! *Never!*"

The Bishop was tired. He never gave up on a problem, but, sometimes he allowed himself to rest a little along the way. He sank more deeply now into the comfort of the chair and closed his eyes. Once or twice he had had the experience that when his mind was open and free of all dominance, a new idea came as tenant there. He could at least hope this might happen again. The clock had already struck one and when the chime of two came, the Bishop still sat quietly waiting.

But when the next hour sounded, something happened to the Bishop. He started up, wide-eyed, his whole face alight. He stood and smote one palm against the other.

"That's it!" he cried exultantly to the four walls. "That's it! Why didn't I think of it before? And if only I can do my part, this will work! Thank God! I'm sure it will work!"

3

On the evening of Julian's address at the university, dinner was served early since he wanted time to look over his notes before leaving. He would take his own car because he did not know just when he would be getting home.

"I'm really glad you are coming, but I'm sure it will make me a little nervous, knowing you are in the audience," he said.

"Nonsense!" Bishop Ware laughed. "I'm glad you broke down and told me of this engagement. You've been very secretive about a number of others."

Julian only smiled as he rose, leaving the Bishop to finish his dessert. "*Priez pour moi,*" he said.

"*Mais oui, sans doute,*" replied Bishop Ware gravely.

He sat on, with his coffee, after Julian had left, thinking about this phase of the younger Bishop's work, which had expanded, he realized, over the last two or three years. He had heard him speak, of course, but so far only to church-related smallish groups. He had been quick to catch Julian's gift of holding an audience and also of clothing a prosaic subject with some grace, but he suddenly realized now that he had not paid enough attention to the many calls that had been received from large organizations in various parts of the city. Their dialogue after these occasions had been like this:

Bishop W., "Well, how did the speech go?"

Bishop A., "Oh, I guess all right."

Once he had ventured a question, "Do you think these talks you give to all kinds of groups do not make too much demand upon your time and strength, which perhaps"—here he paused—"should be spent upon your own special work?"

"No, I don't," Julian had answered slowly. "I have strength enough, thank God, and I can *make* the time by cutting out nonessentials. But as Broad Churchmen—as we are," he said smiling, "we must try to be sympathetic with the social and intellectual development of the time. The Church must play a role in the nation's total life. I think, in my small way, I am doing that more than if I confined myself entirely to the diocese."

Bishop Ware had never questioned him again, and had gone on, he now shamefacedly admitted to himself, paying little attention to the nature of the various speeches.

But this one was different. Julian had spoken to him about attending it and had also said in some connection that the auditorium seated one thousand. This worried Bishop Ware now as he waited for the time to leave. Would Julian be able to meet this great demand upon his ability? His petitions rose earnestly as he finally drove across the city to the university building.

All that morning he had concentrated upon the solution of the problem that had come to him like a light on the sleepless night. He had been writing a sort of dialogue that might be the discussion between him and Elizabeth Babcock. The more he wrote the more uncertain he became of its validity and the more frightened he felt over his own part in it. He had left his desk with some features of the great climax in doubt. He was glad now to have this chance of a complete change of thought.

He parked in the place reserved and made his way to the great front door, where he found himself among many others arriving for the service. They seemed to be pouring in. A young usher recognized him and spoke deferentially. "Bishop Ware? We have a seat reserved for you on the right front. The center is all reserved for the students and faculty. Bishop Armstrong asked us to save this one for you. If you will come with me . . ."

The Bishop felt slightly lost as he walked up the aisle between the filled rows of people. In this great congregation he had no part.

He was no more than seated when a man behind him came up. "Bishop Ware, it's wonderful to see you again. I never come to the university affairs as a rule but I couldn't miss a chance of hearing Bishop Armstrong. He's a real spellbinder, isn't he? Well, glad to see you after so long a time."

The Bishop felt himself shrinking. A spellbinder? Julian? He remembered how they had playfully tried to see who should get the extra muffin at breakfast!

In a short time he could tell that the auditorium was nearly filled. Then came a burst of music and the familiar strains of "Pomp and Circumstance" fell on the air.

The graduates in their caps and gowns and the faculty in their brightly colored hoods marched in and took their seats. There were a few welcoming words by the Chaplain, an anthem, and then the President of the University rose to introduce the speaker. Though his words were brief, Bishop Ware noted they were not stereotyped, but spoken with feeling. Then at last Julian stood, tall and straight and handsome, behind the lectern, sweeping the audience with a friendly glance as though gathering them all to himself. Then he began to speak.

Bishop Ware had decided as he was driving over that he would listen carefully for the form and outline of the talk. Since he was the older man and had made a good many speeches he might be able to give Julian a word of advice.

But before five minutes had gone, the Bishop had forgotten all about form. He was listening to the compelling voice explaining his theme: "The Making of a Man." One by one, he described the phases through which any youth was likely to pass before reaching a useful and happy maturity. Once in a while the certain turn of a phrase sent a ripple of laughter over the audience, but in a few moments they were caught up again in the fervor of his earnestness. Once Bishop Ware started suddenly in his seat when he heard Julian say, "And now at this point I wish to speak of the matter of religious doubts which usually beset every youth along the way. Let us take one example, the doubt of immortality. I should guess that everyone in this auditorium has at some time or other had a glancing doubt about this. But there are many things to steady our faith outside of the Gospels themselves. For example, one of the finest thinkers in America once wrote: "The greatest proof of immortality is the fact that mankind has stubbornly refused to give up the idea.' Isn't that wonderful?"

Bishop Ware nodded. "He got around the *doubts* part pretty well," he muttered softly to himself, and then was engrossed again in the flow of the argument.

At last Julian paused and looked over the assembly as he had done in the beginning.

"I would like to close," he said, "with some words written by one who pursued his ideal of manhood even though he often fell so terribly far from it. He was musician, poet, warrior, and king. He knew all the good and the bad of life and this was his summary:

> *"Blessed is the man that walketh not in the counsel of the ungodly, nor standeth in the way of sinners, nor sitteth in the seat of the scornful.*

> *"But his delight is in the law of the Lord; and in His law doth he meditate day and night.*

> *"And he shall be like a tree planted by the rivers of water, that bringeth forth his fruit in his season; his leaf also shall not wither; and whatsoever he doeth shall prosper.*

> *"For the Lord knoweth the way of the righteous; but the way of the ungodly shall perish."*

When Julian had finished the President came forward to shake his hand. His words of praise were not heard however, for already the applause had taken over, as if by a storm, and as the front rows stood up so also did the whole audience.

Bishop Ware unobtrusively reached the narrow side aisle and started down. No one, it seemed, noticed him. The eyes of all were turned upon Julian and the crowd now standing near him, as he had come down from the platform. More than that there were *lines* of men and women waiting to speak to him.

The Bishop had no trouble in leaving quietly and reaching his car practically unnoticed. The ushers all seemed to be well inside joining in the plaudits of the multitude. Bishop Ware felt unable to start the car. He must sit quietly and think. He was weak from amazement and from another feeling that seemed to sear his soul. This was jealousy. For he himself had made many speeches, had, indeed, been gratified when asked to do so and they had always been—he hated the word—*adequate*. But never with the fine felicity of expression that Julian had! Never that mesmeric quality that drew and held an audience, as Julian had done; never with that power of thought transference between speaker and listeners that made men and women wait in *lines* to speak to the one who had moved them, as had just then happened with Julian.

And even worse, that miserable little part of the mind, called the subconscious, might have gotten in a lick at him, making him see the reason for his being uninterested in Julian's speaking because of hidden jealousies, waiting to spring.

At last Bishop Ware got home. He went to his study and sat down, leaving the door wide open. He tried to feel a faintly normal quality in his thinking. Did not every man, deposed from his high office, even for a valid reason, have a twinge of envy as his successor surpassed him in some phase of ability?

But he was too honest a man. He could not excuse himself. He sat in his desperate humility until he finally heard Julian open the outside door and come straight to the study. He snapped on the light.

"What are you," he began, "sitting here in the dark for? And why on earth did you go slipping down that side aisle? The President wanted to meet you and so did some of the faculty. And there you were sneaking out as though you had stolen the silver candlesticks or something! Was the speech too long? I thought it was rather, myself."

Bishop Ware was on his feet then. "Oh, Julian," he said, "your speech was wonderful beyond words of mine to praise it. I was amazed and overcome by it. But I have to make a

39

painful confession. I was *jealous* of you every minute. I hope you can forgive me. Of course, I've asked the Lord for strength to overcome it, but. . ."

Julian stared at him unbelievingly for a moment then threw back his head and laughed. "*Jealous of me!*" he said. "Oh, my dear Bishop, that's the finest compliment I've ever received, or ever will, probably." He laughed again.

But as quickly as he had changed in his address from humor to deep seriousness, he said now. "Please listen to me. When I'm speaking to a crowd who, in the main, are strangers to me, I can give way more or less to my emotions. But when I am alone with someone I care deeply for—you, for instance—I'm reticent, I'm inhibited, I can't say what I feel. Now, I'll try. In the few years I have lived with you, you have given me more practical help, spiritual example, wise counsel, encouragement—yes, I'll say it—*love,* than I could thank you for all the days of my life."

When Bishop Ware sat at his desk on a bright July morning some days later, his heart was light within him over Julian's touching and incredible confession. He almost forgave himself, the most difficult of all things to do. At last he could now enter into all Julian's problems and work with more confidence, born of the love between them, as spiritual father and son. The thin little curtain of withdrawal that he had always felt in Julian, had now been pushed aside. "All my heart, this morn rejoices," he sang softly, paraphrasing one of his favorite hymns. But then he bent to the completion of the paper upon which he had been at work.

Although the sudden light of a new perception that had shone on him that sleepless night in connection with the Babcocks still seemed to him both credible and possible, he realized he was nervous about his own part in the plan. He went over the paper before him where he had carefully set down what he thought could be the conversation between himself and Elizabeth when he went to see her, as he felt he should do very soon. But the tension mounted as he thought of it. He felt like a gambler, staking all his savings on a turn of the roulette wheel. For if he spoke a wrong word, the whole beautiful plan could be wrecked.

He read the conversation aloud, as he had set it down, like a play. It did seem to carry force and surely would touch her vanity. At least, he felt he could do no better. If he could wait for a possible lead from her it would help, but try he must today if she could see him.

She could, he found, at four o'clock. Good! If he could just do this well and get it over, he would relax, with, he hoped, an added joy.

He knew he was early when he finally started, so he stopped in the garden, where Marcano, with accusing eyes, was watching him from his tether under the maple tree.

"Now, Marcano," the Bishop said sternly, "I don't want you to be greedy! You know you had a good walk with me early this morning!"

At the tone Marcano put his head down upon his paws, as if in deep contrition.

"All right, laddie," the Bishop then went on brightly, "if you are greedy only of my company, I'll excuse you. It's all right, I say!"

At this the dog leaped to the end of his chain, wagging his tail violently, and sat down close to his idol, presenting his paw and leaning over to have his head stroked.

When the Bishop at last went on he decided to go past St. Michael's slowly, to calm his beating heart. When he reached the Babcock house, however, he knew the tension was still upon him. This time Elizabeth herself opened the door.

"Bishop Ware! How very kind of you to come! You always do me so much good! Perhaps the library would be best," she went on, showing him into a large room filled with bookcases, the contents of which looked unread, and many chairs with soft rose-colored slipcovers. "I wonder," the Bishop was thinking, "if anyone ever uses this room." "This is very beautiful," he said, aloud, looking about him.

"I'm so glad you like it. I do myself. I worked so hard to make it beautiful. But I must say I've had a problem keeping it tidy, especially on Will's occasional visits!"

"Oh?" said the Bishop.

"Yes. He will take a book out of the shelf and never think of putting it back where he got it. And the papers! Last time he was here was a Sunday, and I think he brought in three newspapers to read. They were scattered all over the floor and some of the chairs. When I spoke to him about the confusion he always made he just gave one of his silly little answers or questions . . ."

"Might I hear it?"

" 'Oh,' he said, 'Do you think the lawn would mind it if I sat on it for a little while?' What would you make of that?"

41

"It is a bit odd," said the Bishop, "but, Elizabeth," using her name for the first time and noting her pleasure, "I have come on a very important errand. I have given so much thought to your situation and Will's that I want you to consider carefully what I am about to say."

Her face hád hardened after the flush of pleasure at his using her name. "I think you have heard that Will wants to get a divorce and that I refused him completely. I will not be the object of humiliation. You know, Bishop, Will has been very successful in business and his company publishes a little trade journal. It has a line of any special happening to any of the company. I can just see the words: 'Will Babcock divorces his wife.' Never." she ended. "*Never!*"

"But my dear Elizabeth, please think of this. If the line you speak of should read: 'Will Babcock's wife divorces her husband.' Would that make any difference to you? Would that take away all the humiliation? Would it?"

Elizabeth was startled, but was evidently thinking while a certain light grew in her eyes.

"Why—why—yes, I suppose it would. I—I never thought of it that way."

"But you see now what a really queenlike attitude you could take if you divorce Will. One thing I would want to ask first. Is there any real affection left between you?"

"Not in me," she said, "and I don't think there is in him either."

"Well then," the Bishop went on, "my strong advice to you, Elizabeth, is to consult a good lawyer at once—I know a fine one who would handle your work with delicacy and promptness, starting right away to forestall all gossip. And one more thing."

"Oh, Bishop, how clear and easy you make it all seem!"

"And this I'm about to say seems very clear to me. When you told me you loved to entertain and described the details of the lovely party you felt Will had spoiled, I thought if you were free from all—all interruptions, you could make a real career of entertaining. I can see you becoming one of the fine hostesses of the city. Doesn't that sound attractive to you?"

"Oh, simply marvelous! How do I get the lawyer?"

"I can see the one I know best. I can tell him briefly that you are divorcing your husband and want him to handle it. He will then call you when he wants you to come to the office. You will be relieved of all details, I can assure you. If I were you though, when he begins working on your papers, I would

42

invite a very few of your most intimate friends in to luncheon perhaps and tell them you have a secret. They will all know soon but you wanted to tell them first. Then say you are divorcing Will but don't wish to talk much about it. That will be enough to spread the news far and wide."

When the Bishop left, Elizabeth took his hand in both of hers and for a moment bowed her head upon it.

"Life hasn't been right for me for a long time," she said brokenly. "But I think it is going to be better. And," she added as an afterthought, "it might even be for Will, too."

"It just might," agreed the Bishop.

He walked back with a firm, brisk step. It was not quite elation that he felt but a great gladness of heart. He had been the instrument of changing three lives from a distressed entanglement into a clear open path of living. He gave deep thanks. He wondered again if the sudden thought that had come to him in that troubled night might have been, indeed, the Divine Light he had prayed for. It was so simple and yet the one and only solution. At any rate he would always believe that out of the darkness of his spirit, light had come.

He went through the garden smelling the rich midsummer fragrances from the beds with delight. He loosed Marcano's chain and let him splash a paw in the fountain before they went around the house, Marcano to the back door to be dried and the Bishop to the front. Julian was home and stood in the front hall, sorting the afternoon mail.

"Hello," he called. "Look what we've got! Two elegant identical envelopes! I can smell what's in them. They will say, 'The blank church of blank town will hold its 75th Anniversary at a blank time and we hope you can come and make a few remarks on the blank occasion.'"

The Bishop had been holding his to his face. "Mine doesn't smell like church business," he announced. "It smells like violets!"

"Violets, you say. Why, by Cricky, mine does, too, when I really smell it. Who would be sending scented notes to us? Have you been treading a primrose path behind my back, Bishop?"

Bishop Ware chuckled, "Well, if I have, we've evidently been in it together. Come on. I've opened mine. I'll read it."

You are cordially invited to dine with me at half after seven o'clock on Monday evening, August fifth.

Sally Lansing.

At the foot was scrawled, "If this doesn't suit, set any night. Any time will suit me. Only come."

"Well, well, well," Bishop Ware said, as he finished reading. "Why, that's my old friend, Sally. Down in the corner she says if this doesn't suit, we can try another date. That sounds like her!"

"What do you mean?" Julian asked. "Do you know this lady?"

"I did long ago. Don't you remember I told you of our boating parties on the river up in Connecticut when I had my first parish and how a young man, named Andrew Lansing, came to the town and he and Sally fell in love and I left for another parish and lost track of her until your *Attic* girl brought it all back?"

"That needs a little explanation, please."

"It's simple. The girl gave her name as Cissie Lansing, staying with her grandmother, Mrs. Andrew Lansing; ergo, our hostess is that lady. And I hope the girl is still there. I want to meet her. She has spirit."

"I'm afraid I must decline," he said. "It is you she wants to see anyway."

"Julian, you can't do that. She says to set any evening we wish. So that means we'll have to go . . . Of coure, I want to, and I'm sure you'll have a very pleasant time. I fancy Sally will be as charming as an older woman as she was when she was young. Besides the girl, this Cissie, may still be there."

"That's what I'm afraid of, and I don't care to meet her again. She irritated me the last time I saw her."

"Julian, that was different. From what you told me she was evidently teasing you and you didn't respond to it. This would be quite a different thing. I think out of courtesy to the old lady and also to me—for I would be embarrassed to go without you—you should accept for the date she mentions. Check it right away and then we can both send our acceptances. If the girl should be there, she couldn't ruffle your feathers now."

Bishop Armstrong did not answer but gathered up his scanty mail—the bulk of his went to his office—and departed to his room.

Bishop Ware sat on in a pleasant reverie.

With the coming of August, the western light streaming into the porch sitting room had become stronger, there was a rich fragrance of phlox and nicotiana from the garden, the crickets had begun to sing in the hedges, and the divorce papers of Elizabeth Babcock were well begun in the office of Judson and Elliott, Attorneys at Law. As Bishop Ware had been sure, the suit had been uncontested. Indeed, an almost incoherent call had come from Will, thanking him for the magic he had used in bringing about the happy issue and telling him that, to his surprise, it was Rose who was most affected by the news of their coming freedom. She cried all the time out of happiness and relief, she said. Bishop Ware liked to think of this before he went to sleep at night. It justified what he had done.

Fenwick, the Rector of St. Michael's, came over to tell him the report was circulating that Elizabeth Babcock was divorcing Will. Might not this alter the whole story? The Bishop assured him it would. And that all that really was needed was for everyone to keep quiet until the divorce was a *fait accompli* and Will and Rose were legally married.

"When it comes to that," added the Bishop, "I would be in favor of letting the whole matter drop."

"So would I," said Fenwick.

Before he left at the door he turned back, "When the dust has all settled," he said, "do you suppose you could tell me all the story behind this? Secret of the Confessional, you know."

Bishop Ware smiled. He liked Fenwick. He was a good man and Mrs. Fenwick an ideal Rector's wife. "I'd like to do that," he said. "Secrets carried too long alone get heavy. Glad you suggested sharing them."

The evening of the dinner party was a pleasant one. After the high cicadas sang through a very hot day, there had come the little grace note of a shower at four. After that everything seemed refreshed. Mrs. Lansing lived across the city, and Julian remained silent most of the way. As they neared the address, finding it a residential section of large, chiefly stone, houses, Bishop Ware spoke to his companion, "I do hope, Julian, you will show your most social side tonight, even if you weren't keen about coming. I keep remembering funny little things in connection with my old acquaintance with Mrs. Lansing. I recall that back in those innocent days there was a great interest in riddles. Can you imagine it? Mrs. Lansing may have forgotten all about that now, though she always had the largest repertoire of them then, as I think of it. She just might mention the old pastime. Could you join in if you had to?"

Julian laughed. "As it just happens I could. The Archdeacon told me one yesterday. His attitude is so funny toward me. He still seems to stand in awe, and I had the feeling he had spent the night before in prayer to find out if it would be proper to ask me this."

Bishop Ware was amused. "Tell me what it is."

"No, sir. I'll keep it in case the matter comes up here. If it doesn't, I'll tell you when we get home. Here we are anyway!"

He parked the car in the drive, and they walked together to the front door, where a pleasant-looking manservant greeted them and showed them into a long, cool room where Mrs. Lansing waited to welcome them. She and Bishop Ware stood for a few moments looking intently into each other's face. Then the Bishop burst out, "This is incredible! After fifty years you *couldn't* look as young as you do!"

She smiled, "And you, Bishop, have followed the provoking example of all the men, you've grown more handsome as you got older. Where is the skinny youth we once knew? He is now a very well built man with broad shoulders and wide chest and a face full of the lines of living, as I call them. But the smile is just the same! Do you remember what we called you?"

"I suppose it would be—Larry."

"It was. May I use it now?"

"Of course, if I may call you Sally."

"You remembered. Oh, this will make us both feel young again. I'm so very glad to see you.

"And Bishop Armstrong," she went on, turning to the other guest, "It was so kind of you to come when you couldn't have the same interest as Bishop Ware . . ."

"You are the one who was kind to invite me."

"I've heard of you many times and, of course, my grand-daughter told me about the *Attic* espisode. I fear she was a bit naughty, but it was funny, wasn't it?"

"I'm afraid I was rude. Perhaps I'll have the chance to apologize again this evening."

"She's right here. Cissie darling?"

"Yes, Grammie," she replied, appearing at Mrs. Lansing's side. "I was just talking to Bishop Ware. He says the most beautiful things! Oh, Bishop Armstrong, how are you? It's very pleasant to see you again. Have you ever learned to smile?"

"Cissie! What a question. She's teasing, Bishop. Don't mind her. We must all sit down now and be comfortable, while we have something cool to drink."

46

When they had found chairs, the butler quietly came in.

"Will you have sherry, Bishop?"

"Thank you."

"On the rocks? It's been a hot day."

"Yes, please."

"And Bishop Armstrong?"

"I'll have the same, thank you."

"And so shall I. Cissie here will have some wild concoction—I guess you know what it is, Harris?"

"Grammie dear, don't make them think it is some witch's potion! It's just vodka with a dash of water and lemon juice. It looks so beautifully clear and pure and harmless if you don't take much. Of course, I know that sherry is the parson's drink. I should have made it unanimous."

"You added," said Bishop Armstrong, "a more sophisticated note to our more usual sober imbibing, and that is good."

Cissie smiled and Julian returned it. That smile, given and returned, made a special air of good fellowship pervade the room.

"Do you remember, Bishop Ware—oh, I can't bring myself to say 'Larry'—it doesn't seem respectful now."

"As you wish, Mrs. Lansing," he answered with a twinkle.

"Oh, you are just the same. But it can't be hard for you to say 'Sally.' I was about to ask you if you remember our little sherry parties on the low bank before time to get into the boats? We felt so sort of wickedly pleased with ourselves, and we girls transported the little glasses in our slipper bags. Then I don't think you could possibly remember, Larry, what we did as we sipped it?"

"But I could! You see, Sally, I've thought so often about this evening that all sorts of old details came into my mind about that lovely summer. So I do remember what we did as we continued in our debauchery. We told riddles! What a riotous evening! You know I asked my vestry if they thought my conduct was in any way unbecoming. They were all much older than I and they reported that since I worked so hard during the day—at sermons and calls—I deserved some diversion in the evening. So my conscience was clear—no matter how loud we grew over the riddles."

"They were fun," Sally said, "but I can't remember one of them now. Perhaps people never ask them anymore."

"Oh, they do," Bishop Ware said. "Julian was asked one only yesterday."

"Tell us," begged Sally.

"Do please," Cissie said, smiling across to him.

She was wearing a thin dress covered with flowers. The wide bateau cut showed the firm whiteness of her throat and neck. Her face was flushed and glowing now with interest and expectancy. The hair, tumbled and half falling at the time of the first meeting between herself and Bishop Armstrong, lay now in soft waves that were caught up in curls at the back of her head. Before her look Bishop Ware was thinking, "She's irresistible."

"Well, come on, Julian. You surely can't refuse such requests," he urged.

"I'm embarrassed. I'm shy," the younger man returned. "And it's not fair unless you all do the same. But here goes for mine. The Archdeacon told it to me yesterday after he had considered whether it was respectful or not, for it might sound indelicate.

"What is the last thing a man takes off before he get into bed?"

"His slippers," cried Sally. "That's easy."

"His wrist watch," shouted Cissie.

"Close, but not good enough," Julian answered.

"Tell us, for heaven's sake, and put us out of our misery," said Bishop Ware.

"Very well. The last thing a man takes off before getting into bed is his feet—off the floor."

There was a burst of laughter.

"By Jove, that's right," agreed Bishop Ware.

"It's priceless," said Sally.

Cissie was the last to speak for she was still overcome with mirth.

"That's so funny," she brought out at last. "Just when we were wondering how far we dared undress the poor man, out he comes with the most proper answer in the world. I'm going to have fun with this one."

"We can't top it, Bishop Armstrong, but Cissie knows the only one I really remember and when she says it, it sounds rather musical. Will you run through it, darling?"

"Of course. Here it is:

> *"What can't go up the chimney up*
> *But it can go down the chimney down*
> *It can't go down the chimney up*
> *But it can go up the chimney down."*

"I pass," said Bishop Ware promptly. "I have a slight case of vertigo."

"Sissy, you're afraid to try," Sally told him. "I know it so I'm out. What about you, Bishop Armstrong?"

"I like that," he said, "and I believe with a little time to study it I could guess it."

"Of course, you may have all the time you need for we will soon be going out to dinner. We have a large patio at the back with an awning over it. Cissie and I eat there all summer long. Today when all was set the rain came on, so Cook and I brought everything into the dining room. But when the shower stopped and the sun came out we took everything back. I do love to eat outdoors. Will you escort me, Larry? We'll go through the hall. And, Bishop Armstrong, will you escort Cissie? The only drawback," they could hear her saying as Julian proffered his arm to Cissie, "is that with the awning we can't see the stars . . ."

"Or the moon," finished Cissie. "There is none tonight, but we have a large outside lamp at the back of the lot that shows a fine light over the garden. We are very proud of the flower beds. Grammie and I did a lot of the planting ourselves."

"This is lovely!" Julian exclaimed. "What a scene of beauty!"

"You should hear him, Grammie," Cissie called, "expostulating over the garden and everything."

He dropped her arm quickly and moved near the front of the patio.

"You must say it all to her. She will be so pleased," the girl went on.

Mrs. Lansing was arranging the guests at the table. "I want both my distinguished gentlemen to have a good view of the garden so I shall sit at this side with Bishop Ware, Larry, on my right, and Bishop Armstrong at my left and Cissie opposite me, with her back to the garden since she sees it every day. Right, darling?"

"Right, Grammie."

It was a wonderfully gay dinner. Bishop Ware watched Julian in happy surprise, for he was not only being passably polite, he was being cleverly amusing. A good raconteur, he told of interesting little happenings in the line of his work. He was also quick to pick up the conversational thread when it dropped for a moment. Through it all there was much easy laughter, and just enough badinage to add a little spark.

They lingered over dessert as though loath to leave the garden, but at last Mrs. Lansing stated her plan. "I think it would be nice, Cissie, if you would take Bishop Armstrong to the library and let him see the old portraits while Bishop Ware and I will go back to the drawing room and tell each other all about our lives from the young days up 'til now. Are you all agreed?"

"I am," said Bishop Ware, promptly.

"And," agreed Cissie, "I love showing off the portraits and telling the stories that go with them."

"Of course," Julian's voice was rather quiet.

Once in the library Cissie, moving nearer to him, raised a glowing face.

"Bishop Armstrong, I couldn't begin to tell you how happy you have made me this evening—I mean because you gave my grandmother such a beautiful time. You see I had told her about that silly little incident of the *Attic* and how stern you had been, and she was afraid that was your natural attitude and you would be that way at the dinner. She was frightened. And then when you were so wonderful! So gay and full of fun and altogether charming. I wish I could thank you as much as you deserve!"

With a quick movement she had come close and put the lightest possible kiss on his cheek.

"Don't do that!" he said sharply, stepping back as though she had struck him.

Cissie stood still, her face amazed. "Why?" she asked slowly. "Why did you speak like that?"

Julian's red face had grown pale now. "I'm sorry for that," he said. "You see I was so surprised, and then it, I mean . . . because it, I mean it *bothered* me."

A faint smile crossed Cissie's lips. "I hope you know the difference between what I just did, and a real kiss?" she asked with a rising inflection.

"I prefer not to discuss that," he said. "Can't you just accept my apology and try to forget the whole episode?"

"Can you?"

"I think so. May we look at the portraits now?"

"Of course. The one just behind you is interesting. He was an old Puritan, but he committed a misdemeanor and had to sit in the stocks, according to his diary, which is still in the family."

"What did he do?" asked Julian.

"He kissed his wife on Sunday and was seen doing it. Wouldn't you think he could have waited until Monday? I mean to judge by his looks?"

"But the diary?" Julian questioned. "You mean it's a bona fide writing? From away back?"

"It is. It's in my great uncle's possession and he keeps it under lock and key. All the Historical Societies want to buy it like mad."

"Have you seen it?"

"Oh, yes. And it's fascinating. No wonder it's so sought after. The thing . . ."

"Yes," he prompted.

"Well, you see he has willed the precious thing to me, as the last of the Lansing name. I keep wondering if the possession of it will make me much more *eligible*, as it were."

When he did not reply, she gave a quick toss of her head. "There you go," she said, "missing your cue again. You really aren't very clever catching them."

"What do you mean?"

"Oh, you could have said, 'Nothing could make you more eligible than you are. No one could question your desirability with or without the diary.' You see?"

Julian looked angry. "I know what's the matter with me. You *irritate* me!"

"I know," she agreed with what could only be called a giggle, "but it's such fun! I promise though to be good. I won't tease you anymore. We'll finish the portraits and then go back to the others in a more pleasant frame of mind, as we were at dinner. Can't we?"

"I hope so," he said rather shortly.

"This portrait," Cissie went on, "is my great-great-grand-father. He was in the Revolutionary War as a quartermaster. He took care of his men by going about with a big wagon or a sled that harsh winter and collecting food and supplies as he knew the need. Always blankets from the home where he felt they could be spared. The story about him that I like best is the one where he went to check in a great upper room where thirty sick and wounded men lay on pallets on the floor. These pallets were made of some straw with a blanket thrown over it. Great-great-grandfather found there was so little straw that the poor men's bones must be touching the floor, so he took his help and drove to a barn he knew and loaded the wagon with straw and hay, came back, and filled up each pallet. Wasn't he kind?

"This portrait next to him is his wife. She's a plain little body, but her eyes are nice and every time I look at that little smile I think she's saying, 'I had a hard life but it was a good one.' Now we come to the last and the very best.

"These two are my grandfather and grandmother. Wasn't Grammie lovely when she was young?"

"She's still lovely," Julian said.

"Oh, I'll tell her that after you have gone. Of course, I think so, too. You may have heard about their romance. My grandfather was a young New York banker and he went up to Connecticut for his vacation and when he met Grammie they both fell in love at the first look. Do you believe in 'love at first sight,' Bishop?"

"I have never considered the matter."

"Oh, I have thought of it often. It seems to me that to be sure in one beautiful, blinding, shining moment and feel it will last forever would be so wonderful. I've always hoped that's the way it would come to me—if it ever 'comes,' " she added softly.

They were near the door and Cissie looked up at him.

"Is everything all right? I'd really like it to be."

"It is. Let's shake on it," he said, extending his hand.

She put hers at once within it and, as in the first time this had happened, Julian felt the softness of the palm inside his large one.

When they entered the drawing room, Mrs. Lansing greeted them eagerly.

"Oh, here you are. Now I am going to announce a treat for you both. Won't you sit down, Bishop Armstrong? And, Cissie darling, will you play for us now?"

"Of course," the girl said, going at once to the grand piano at the end of the room.

"This is amazing," Bishop Ware spoke, "and wonderful. I've heard a good many young ladies asked to play for guests, and each one demurred, apologized, and hesitated. You, Cissie, have at once agreed. I thank you for that."

"But I love to play when it gives me pleasure," she answered. "Shall it be Chopin, Grammie?"

"I think so, with a few little Preludes to set our mood, at first."

Cissie sat down and waited a few seconds; then began. Even before she had reached the larger and more intricate selections, there could be felt a quickened listening—a breathless, surprised attentiveness on the part of the guests. She played on with the ease and fervor of a great artist, while her fingers went with incredible swiftness over the keys. When the climax of the waltz and of the Polonaise were at last reached the room was stormed with music, and then Cissie raised her arms and allowed them to drop beside her. And there was silence.

Bishop Ware broke it after the first few minutes. "My dear," he began, "you have given us something magnificent! You have played like a professional such as we pay to hear in great auditoriums. We are so moved by the beauty of it but—I'm sure I speak for Julian, too—we are astounded. Can you explain it?"

"Tell them, Cissie," Mrs. Lansing said. "I'm sure they would like to hear."

Cissie moved on the bench to face them. "Perhaps you can guess that music began for me when I was quite small. The piano fascinated me. I had the best teachers all through my teens and after that—thanks to Grammie, bless her heart—I had a wonderful year in Europe with outstanding teachers. And when I got home I had a recital for music critics and the Press and it went fairly well."

"Now, Cissie, tell this straight," Mrs. Lansing interrupted.

"All right then. To my surprise, they were awfully kind. It was easy after that to get engagements. So I had many recitals and played soloist with big orchestras across the country. This is the way it would go: Pittsburgh, Cleveland, Chicago, San Francisco, Southern route, home by way of Texas. That was the general pattern I followed for three years. I was getting toward the end of my twenties. I was at a crossroad. Did I want to go on doing this?"

She stopped, looking over their heads as though still pondering it.

"I decided I did not want to continue. How could I ever marry and make a home, if I did that? Some artists do, but I'm not made that way. One thing I felt that I did want that I couldn't tell everyone. They would think I was sort of self-righteous, but you will both understand. I wanted a career where I could actually be of service. And I decided upon that of a nurse."

"A *nurse?*" the two Bishops said in one breath.

"Yes. You shouldn't be surprised. It certainly is a career of service and I knew I could keep up with my music on my off times, practicing and perhaps giving small concerts where it would give much pleasure. My mother was surprised, too, and very annoyed with me. She thinks I'm crazy. But Grammie dear took another view. She said it was not a good life for a

53

girl still twenty-nine to go all alone to and fro upon the earth like Satan. (You can see the company she put me in.) So I finally decided to go over to St. Michael's Hospital."

"St. Michael's," the two Bishops said at once.

"Yes, it seemed best. It's near to Grammie where I will be living. Of course, I couldn't take regular nurse's training, but I found I could become a very good nurse's aide. And I should add that I have loved the work I'm already doing. I feel I've made the right choice."

She faced the piano again. "Does either of you have a favorite selection you would like to hear? I think we've talked enough about me!"

It was Bishop Ware who spoke. "I have one that I would dearly love to hear you play. A man told me once it was the piece every high school girl played at her first recital. But anyway, it's Beethoven . . ."

"I think I know what you mean. I'll be happy to play it. Do you know how the music originated?"

"I'm afraid I don't."

"Good. Then I can tell you. The great composer was walking home late one night when everything was bathed in moonlight. As he passed one house he could see a girl playing the piano just inside the window. He couldn't hear the melody, only sweet sounds that seemed a part of the beautiful night. He hurried home and wrote 'The Moonlight Sonata.' So here it is."

When the last tender note had ended, Cissie sat with her hands at rest during the moment of silence. Then Bishop Ware stood up.

"Thank you, my dear, for that beautiful experience. I think we should make it the closing gift for this wonderful evening. Don't you, Julian?"

Bishop Armstrong rose, too, as he agreed.

There were warm expressions of pleasure and in the good-byes were sincere hopes of further meetings. Bishop Ware held Mrs. Lansing's hand in both his own as he told her what the evening had meant to him, and he kissed Cissie, saying it was an old man's privilege.

"And," he added, "I'll have the piano at the Old Rectory tuned at once so that I can persuade you to come and play for us there."

Bishop Armstrong bowed gracefully as he spoke his thanks to both ladies, and then the two men were out again in the car, driving across the city. Bishop Ware was eager to talk.

"Such an evening," he began. "Such utter delight even without the music. But that incredible performance! I'm afraid when I wake up tomorrow I'll think I dreamed it. The idea of that beautiful young thing, with the career of a great artist, used to the plaudits of thousands and famous from one end of the country to another, having reached this pinnacle before she was thirty, then tossing it all aside to go into training for a nurse's aide. To render service rather than give entertainment. How do you reconcile this, Julian?"

Any reply was slow in coming so Bishop Ware rushed on, full of his own emotion. "During that lovely sonata, I was testing myself. I wondered when I was elected Bishop whether I could have given up the prestige and the satisfactions pertaining to the office and gone to a poor little church in the slums where there was great need of a Shepherd of Souls. Could I? Could you? It would be very much like what this girl has done. Wouldn't it?"

"Her act was not all sacrificial," Julian said slowly. "She had other reasons."

"Even if she had, there still . . ."

But Julian remained silent. All the way to the Old Rectory he did not speak. When they got there, the good nights were brief and Julian went at once to his room. Bishop Ware was too excited to sleep, so he went to his study, relaxed in his reading chair, and thought it all over.

A pleasant warmth stole over him as he realized that the bygone little friendship with Sally was now revived and he was sure would be continued. She would provide something he had often wished for, a woman his own age with whom he could enjoy many of the small pleasures of life. Sally was perfect in this regard. She was intelligent, charming, and gay. This evening had proved how often their minds met congenially. They were amused by the same things. He had missed so many concerts, so many good evenings at the theater because he had said to himself as a small boy might have done, "It's *no fun* going alone!" Perhaps from now on, he dared to hope, there might be a change.

But the girl! The wonderful Cissie! As his mind turned to her it was not only the magnificent strength and beauty of her music of which he thought; it was also of the changing expressions on her face. There was, as she played, a sweet gravity, showing her inner concentration; there was a bright alertness as conversation quickened.

Here Bishop Ware was interrupted in his musings by a tap

on his study door and the appearance of Julian in his dressing gown.

"I saw your light on, and I thought I'd tell you I've just now got the crazy thing!"

"Got what?"

"Why that fool riddle that Cis—the girl—asked. I had never heard it but thought if I had a few minutes' free time I could work it out. Well, when I got back here, I couldn't get it out of my mind and yet I couldn't solve it, when suddenly an hour later the answer just popped into my brain."

"Things do that sometimes."

"Well, this did. You know how the lines of it went? It can't go up the chimney up but it can go down the chimney down, and all that nonsense."

"Yes, it made me dizzy. Cissie said it so fast. Well, what's the answer?"

"*An umbrella!* So confoundedly simple when you know it. Like most things. Well, with these few remarks I close. Good night."

When he got to the door, the Bishop called after him.

"Julian, are you going to call Cissie and tell her you've guessed her riddle?"

"I am not," he responded, with rather undue emphasis.

The Bishop went on with his own description of the changing expressions on Cissie's face, which he had broken off when Julian entered the study. Now he longed to put into words this particular manifestation of her beauty that he, himself, had seen only twice, once when she spoke of her grandmother in the midst of her surprising story and once at the dinner table. This was a light, which he could only call a *radiance*, which fell upon her features. He had noticed that it was Cissie, rather than their hostess, who once in a while tossed out a subject that might be interesting to discuss.

This particular moment he was now remembering was when Cissie had laughingly said, "Apropos of what we've just been talking about, why not ask, What *is* Truth? What do you think, Bishop Armstrong?"

And he could see again now that strange radiance on the girl's face as she looked at Julian. He saw, too, that Julian had immediately dropped his eyes!

But why did this happen? Was it because of shyness? But he had been talking easily with Mrs. Lansing only minutes before. Was it deference? Hardly with a young woman. He recalled how he himself had stepped into the moment's silent

56

breach by saying to Cissie that they must decide first whether they were speaking of Absolute or Relative Truth. Mrs. Lansing led the discussion eagerly, and had probably not noticed what he had seen, since she was at the time speaking to the butler about dessert. Furthermore, it had been only a short time until Julian joined in the conversation going on, with his usual alertness and humor, telling the story of their old cook who said she'd never tell a lie, *never*—except when she just *had* to . . . and they had all laughed, and the talk went on.

Bishop Ware now mentally shook himself, as he rose from his chair. "I'm an old fuss-budget," he muttered. "I'm going to get myself right off to sleep, for I think my brain is addled. No more foolish fancies tonight."

But in spite of his good resolves, when the Bishop reached his room, finished his evening prayers, and was comfortably in bed, he still lay awake for some time, wondering.

4

August had gone its voluptuous way and September was well begun before the promised dinner at the Old Rectory took place. The delays, however, had been from natural causes. Julian's calendar kept filling up so fast that he, himself, was startled. Bishop Ware was uneasy.

"How can you do it, Julian?" he asked, as he had done before. "How can you manage to go all around the Diocese, keeping in touch with every church and Rector in it?"

Julian gave a small laugh. "You should guess it if you have never realized it in full. It's because I have Miss Lamb for a secretary."

The Bishop said, "Um-mm."

"She has the most marvelous good judgment. I swear she could run that office without me—completely. That's why I don't have to be so generally tied to my desk. I can confess to you that I find the movement about the Diocese, drawing as close as I can to Rectors and church members, much more congenial than desk work most of the day."

"Aren't you afraid you may miss some appeal you should consider?"

"Miss Lamb takes care of that. She lays the letters I should deal with myself in a little pile on the right side of the desk. The rest she throws away or leaves with a question mark or a suggestion on each. So, when I come I can deal with them speedily. You can see how this lightens my office work."

"Hm-mm," began Biship Ware. "How old is this paragon of yours?"

"I've no idea. I never asked her ... I suppose middle forties. But if you have any ideas in that romantic brain of yours, she is just part of my office furniture, and that's all. Now about this dinner business. I'm not keen on it at all, as you know, but from my calendar I seem to have no free Saturday night until September twenty-second. Why must it be on Saturday?"

"Because Mrs. Lansing says it's the best night for Cissie to get off. I told you she asked for the ward with the poorest and sickest patients and she works there."

"I'll put down September twenty-second then, and hope the weather will favor us."

It did, as a matter of fact. A quiet autumnal fragrance, chiefly of chrysanthemums, filled the air. It was not that scent of the funeral pyres of scarlet leaves, but just a hint of October's bright blue weather, yet to come.

The ladies were received by both their hosts and escorted to the drawing room after Mrs. Lansing had noticed the carving of the tiny girl winking at all comers under the Mayapple leaf. Bishop Ware explained that the woodcarver who had made this and the other droll little figures did it for his own delight in his spare time.

"I'll have you see some others later," he said.

The conversation over sherry and again at the table, upon which Mrs. Morgan had lavished all the treasures of the house, was a little less animated than that of the first dinner they had all had together. This, Bishop Ware felt, was due to Cissie's attitude. She was as lovely as ever, but she was more quiet.

It was not until the beautiful dinner, which Mrs. Morgan and Cook had spent themselves preparing, was ended and the last echo of the strong and tender music had died away in the long drawing room that Cissie turned to the others and asked if they would listen to something that was happening in connection with her work. They all agreed eagerly.

"I haven't ever told this to Grammie, but tonight I feel I *must* tell it to those who will be understanding. It came about this way. I've been working in what the nurses among themselves call the *cheap* wards, where the very poor and some of the very sick find themselves. Since I've been there I've made friends with a wonderful doctor whom I think you know, Bishop Ware. Doctor Lindsay?"

"Of course, I know him. A man in a thousand."

"He is. He gives one afternoon a week as a free gift to the patients who need him most. I guess it was through me he got interested in a young black woman."

She stopped. "It's hard to describe her. She's in her late thirties by her record, but she is so frail it makes her look younger. She has a light brown complexion and pretty black hair that can be brushed over her shoulders. She's very gentle, and makes no complaint about her condition or her surroundings, but she cries most of the day and much of the night for her husband, whom she calls 'Big Tom.' She wants him."

"Why doesn't he come?"

Cissie's own eyes seemed to mirror the girl's distress.

"The doctor had grown very upset about it. He said last week he had to find that man, for he didn't intend to have his conscience hearing that young thing's cries forever. I don't know how he did it, but he found where Big Tom is. He's in jail."

"In jail!" her listeners spoke the words together.

"That's where he's been, on the hill just back of the city. I don't believe anybody ever thinks much about it, though. But Dr. Lindsay thought about it. He went straight to the Warden, told his story and what he wanted done. This was to bring Big Tom out under heavy guard and take him to the hospital, let him stay perhaps for twenty minutes, and then take him back to his cell."

"Sounds reasonable," said Bishop Ware.

"The Warden just laughed. He said the doctor probably knew something about running a hospital but he knew nothing about running a prison. Said Big Tom was a great brute of a creature and highly dangerous. That he had nearly killed a man who was cleaning his cell the week before just by choking him with one hand. The doctor asked what the cleaning man had done to Big Tom, and the Warden said nothing and then added it was likely some of the fancy talk that goes around amongst the men. Anyway, he said Big Tom was dangerous and only safe behind the strongest steel doors. But the doctor didn't give up. He asked if the Warden would obey an order from the Governor for this plan he had described. The Warden said he didn't care much for the Governor but he was sure he wouldn't be fool enough to send an order like that. But the doctor said, 'If he did, would you obey it?' And the Warden said of course he would have to, but he didn't think they need to worry about that."

"I suppose that ended the matter," Julian said. He had been watching Cissie, as she told her story, with an air of wonder.

"Oh never," she said. "You don't know Dr. Lindsay. He telephoned the Governor and got him. It seems they've known each other for a long time. He went over the plan and said he wanted the Governor to send an order to the Warden to release Big Tom under heavy guard for the time allotted. Would he do it?

"The doctor said the Governor went slowly over each detail and then said he couldn't see why it might not be done, and that he would write at the top of the order: *Brief Compassionate Leave,* and would send it by special messenger. It came this morning!"

Cissie stopped, her face shining. "I can hardly believe it. I should have had more faith."

"When will they take Big Tom to the hospital?" asked Mrs. Lansing.

"Tomorrow morning, about ten. We've changed the girl's room today. Dr. Lindsay said she must be alone, for if there should be trouble or—or shooting, it couldn't take place in a ward full of patients . . ."

Julian almost jumped from his chair. "Trouble, *shooting,* what do you mean?" he cried.

Cissie was calm. "Well, we don't expect any, but you can see that if Big Tom suddenly tried to make a break for it, the officers would shoot. Don't look so anxious. Everything will be all right. I'm sure of it."

Bishop Ware saw that Julian looked pale. The story had been a deeply moving one, but it surprised him that Julian had been so affected by it. Cissie was speaking again.

"The last act of the drama remains to be played out, but I'll try to see that you know how it went. I do have one strange

60

request to make of you, Bishop Ware. It sounds rather crazy I fear, but I'm so terribly in earnest. You see in all my talks with the girl I'm convinced that there is *real* love between her and Big Tom. When he sees her now he will know she hasn't long to live. I am sure that when he leaves he will be stricken. I want him to have one kind word. The police will be sharp with him. Would you, Bishop Ware, be willing to remain in the corridor as the officers start to take him back to jail. He would recognize you as a clergyman and an *older* man and your voice would be kind. Would you consider this strange request?"

"Of course, I would. If you will tell me just where to stand and at what time, I'll be there."

"Oh, I do thank you! I'll write directions on a slip of paper before we leave."

"And apropos of leaving," said Mrs. Lansing. "I'm sure we should be going soon. But before that I think it would be good for us to have some soft, relaxing music to quiet our spirits, for mine have been greatly moved by your story. Do you like this idea, Larry?"

"It's inspired," Bishop Ware said, "if Cissie is willing to play for us again."

"It might do you good, too, darling," Mrs. Lansing said and smiled.

"I'm sure it would. I talked too much. But it's done me good to talk it all out with you." She walked over to the piano and sat down.

Suddenly there came the sound of a little stream, rippling softly, chuckling over its pebbly bed. It moved on through quiet leafy glades, unhurried, happily continuing until, at last, its path lay between wide green fields where white flocks were straying. The sheep were nibbling idly, for here and there a sunset bell was ringing and it would soon be time for the shepherd to lead them home for the night. Away beyond the green fields the blue mountain ridges melted into the sky.

The evening song of a robin sounded above the ripple of the little brook, now heard again but moving on very softly, on and on, more and more quietly until, at last, it died away.

Cissie rose, smiling. "Did that help a little? It really did calm me. And now, Bishop, I'll write a sentence or two to help you remember how to reach the third floor of the hospital."

He led her to the little escritoire in the corner, where there was paper and pen. Cissie wrote slowly, speaking as she did so.

61

"Elevator Bank C going up. Push button for Floor Three. Get off. Turn right to end of hall and wait."

"When they bring Big Tom out, step forward and say 'It's all right, Officer. I just want to say a word to Tom.' "

She handed the paper to Bishop Ware, saying, "I can't begin to thank you, but I love you."

Mrs. Lansing rose, giving her own thanks, and in a few minutes the good-byes were over and the guests had gone.

When the two Bishops were alone Julian said irritably, "I don't see any good reason why you should allow yourself to be entangled in this affair. You heard Cissie say there was a possibility of danger. Why should you take this risk for the sake of a sentimental girl's idea that you say a word of cheer to a dangerous character? I'm dead set against this, Bishop."

"Well, now, Julian, I'm sorry to go against your judgment, but I don't think I could refuse, just because of the very remote possibility of danger. If she had pointedly asked you, would you have said no?"

"Well, I would have tried, at least, to point out the degree of pure sentiment back of this request. In fact, it looks to me as though the whole plan is shot full of *sentiment* instead of cold facts. Take that order from the Governor. That struck me as very strange. Didn't you feel that way?"

"No, I didn't. When he put Compassionate Leave on the order I knew he had assessed the facts and felt he was doing right. But he also had a personal reason for doing something Dr. Lindsay wanted done."

"What was that?"

"Lindsay saved his life once years ago when the governorship was a long way ahead. A man doesn't forget a thing like that. By the way, I couldn't help overhearing your good-bye to Cissie. I thought it was very touching."

"I don't know why you use that word. I only said . . . I mean after her confession I . . . I mean it would have been strange for me not to . . . You see I was only . . ."

"Oh, indeed I see, Julian. I just meant to commend you on your thoughtfulness. Now let's stop all argument and go to bed. You can call me up tomorrow about noon to see if I've survived."

But the next morning as Bishop Ware set forth on his peculiar errand of kindness even he began to have doubts of its validity. It was, indeed, the idea of a sentimental young woman. Might it even do harm to the big plan itself?

62

But, in any case, he must carefully follow his instructions.

With no confusion or mishap he finally reached the spot Cissie had indicated and walked along the hall past closed doors until he saw the open one at the end. The Bishop took his stand nearby and waited. Cissie had told him as she left the officers would bring Big Tom up in the service elevator. The Bishop checked his watch. At ten minutes to ten he heard the sound below of heavy doors closing, then the rasp of the ascent until the opening clang and a man's voice:

"Steady now. Watch your step! We go down this hall to that open door."

In only a few moments the three passed before the Bishop's eyes: the two strong policemen with the huge black man between them. When they reached the open door Big Tom was allowed to go through, and the officers stood close together in the doorway. Bishop Ware was taller than the policemen so he could see between their heads what went on in the little room. He saw the black man hold up his hands and look at the officers, who looked at each other. The one in charge spoke low, but his voice was sharp.

"We'll take another chance on you, Tom, but one move from you and we shoot." He unlocked the bracelets.

"I ain't makin' no moves," the black man said.

He went slowly toward the bed and sat down on the chair placed for him. He slipped one great arm under the head of the little wisp of a woman lying there, her eyes closed, as tears ran down her cheeks.

"Baby!" he said gently.

She looked up and the watchers could see a light spread over her face.

"Oh, Tom! Is you here at last? I thought you never gonna come." She seemed to choke a little on her tears and her joy.

"Me not come, Baby? Why, I come far as I could when I heard 'bout you. I was in a little mess of trouble or I'd a-been here when you got sick. How you feelin', Baby?"

She snuggled into the curve of his arm. "Oh, Tom, I'm so scared!"

"What of, Baby?"

"It's Pastor. He keeps prayin' an' talkin' 'bout me dyin'. I'm awful scared of dyin', Tom!"

The Bishop, watching, saw what he thought might be the expression of a killer on the man's face, but his voice when it came was gentle, with even a touch of humor in it.

"Now, you oughta know Pastor better'n that, Baby. He all

the time shootin' off his big mouth. That's just his business, makin' up stuff to scare hell outa folks, so they come to church. Now, 'bout this dyin' . . . it don't mean nothin' . . . just nothin'.'"

"Oh, Tom, you sure?"

"Sure I'm sure. I been readin' up on it. Want me to tell you the way it is, Baby?"

"Please, Tom. Maybe the fear'll go."

"Well now, first of all dyin's as easy as rollin' off a log. You take a little nap an' you wake up right where you goin'. An' it'll be somethin', Baby! I tell you it'll be somethin'! Mind the time I took you to the big night club where they was a lady playin' on a harp?"

"Oh, *yes!*"

"Well, where you goin', Baby, they's goin' to be dozens—I'll betcha hundreds—of gold harps all playin' at once."

"Real gold, Big Tom?"

"Real gold, Baby. An' the singin' will be fillin' the air so beautiful. You know how you always likin' music?"

"I loves it, Tom."

"Well, you never heard nothin' like this gonna be."

"But the river, Tom. Pastor's always talkin' 'bout the river Jordan. He says I has to go through it to wash my sins. It's deep an' maybe I'll . . . sink . . !"

Big Tom threw back his head and laughed. Those watching could see the anguish on his face, but the laugh sounded real.

"There you go, Baby, worryin' again 'bout Pastor. You know how he always talkin', makin' a mountain out of a ant hill or somethin'. I know 'bout that Jordan, Baby. 'T ain't no river nohow. Jest a little teensy bitty ole run like the one down at you Grandpappy's. I could spit across it. Nothin' to it!"

"You sure, Tom?"

"Sure, Baby! An' listen." The man's face suddenly lighted. "We forgot somethin'. We forgot your Mammy be there to meet you! You mind when we'd been away somewhere and come back she'd spread her arms out and she'd say 'Chile, where you been? I been waitin' for you. Oh, Chile, you done come home.' An' that's what she gonna say when you gets there, Baby."

She tried to speak and evidently found it difficult. But finally the words came slowly.

"The fear's gone."

She smiled and nestled her head closer into the curve of

Big Tom's arm. Cissie came out from behind the screen and stood closer, her eyes on the patient. There was then an audible sigh, then a small tremor. And then the slight form on the bed was still.

Cissie went over and softly straightened the head, releasing Tom's arm. Those watching could see her whisper something to him. He nodded and stood up, looking at the small smiling face below him. After a few moments he turned toward the policemen. His eyes were dry. But those of the officers were not.

Big Tom came up to the men in the doorway and held up his hands. The shining wristlets were double-locked upon him and his arms were firmly held by the officers. The three faced back and moved in the direction of the elevator.

The Bishop knew it was time for him. He stepped forward, meeting the sharp, questioning eyes of the nearest policeman. "It's all right, Officer," he said. "I just want to say a word to Tom."

After a few steps the men paused and Bishop Ware came close.

"Tom," he said, "your wife is now safely in the care of the Good Shepherd, and I want you to know that He is also watching over you."

The man raised his dry, anguished eyes. "Thank you," he said.

The Bishop stepped back to his former place to control himself. He had feared his tension would cause his voice to sound casual and lacking in feeling. But he need not have worried, for it had broken on the few words.

Cissie came out from the room, closing the door behind her.

"I have only a moment, but I had to see you. Did you manage?"

"I said something, and he answered me."

"Oh, I'm so grateful. Dr. Lindsay thought it might end this way, that her fragile heart might not stand the strain of such joy. But she had the joy first. Dr. Lindsay will be in around noon to see how it all went."

Bishop Ware took out his wallet and extracted a bill.

"Could you please order some flowers for her? Something beautiful. If Big Tom ever hears it might comfort him to know."

"The doctor will see him, I'm sure. The Warden gives him the run of the prison now. I must go, but my love to you, dear Bishop." She reached up and gave him a kiss on the cheek.

As he walked forward to the elevator he passed two order-lies and a nurse going back the way he had come.

After Cissie had given him the little kiss and started away, she had come back to speak very low.

"You'll be sure to tell Bishop Armstrong how it all was. He was so terribly afraid there would be trouble."

As he had given his assent he noticed a little flush come and go on Cissie's cheek.

On the way back to the Old Rectory Bishop Ware found the driving difficult. In spite of his efforts at self-control a tear would now and then come, dimming his vision for a moment. He was relieved to reach the house in safety and find himself sitting quietly in his study. But strangely all he could think about was the prison where Big Tom probably was now. He thought of the story of how Big Tom had all but choked a man to death, because, as the Warden had said, he was evidently doing some of the fancy talking which was going round amongst the men. "Fancy talk." That would be about *women*. And if this loose and ribald talk had been given by the cleaning man as though including the listener and his "Baby," Big Tom would reach out and try to kill him.

"And I wouldn't blame him!" the Bishop almost shouted.

Then his head dropped on his breast. "What have I said? What have I said?" he repeated. "A Bishop of the Church condoning murder?"

He sat for a long time thinking of all the smoldering fires, banked between those prison walls.

Julian called at noon. His voice sounded guarded.

"Are you all right?" he asked.

"Except that I am emotionally stunned. The little woman died while Big Tom was with her."

"So? He made no trouble then?"

"None. Only pulled our heart strings. I think even the policemen were touched."

"I would doubt that. As for me, I've had a perfectly terrible morning. I'll explain when I see you."

"I'm distressed to hear this. Any hint?"

"Not now. I can only say it's an unholy mess."

That day Bishop Ware changed his usual pattern. He lay down after lunch because he felt an alarming lack of physical strength and a great vacuity of spirit. He did not question the matter, but merely slipped into his dressing gown, found his bed soothing to a degree, and fell asleep. It was four o'clock before he wakened, only then because Marcano had gently licked the hand outside the cover. Mrs. Morgan had been hovering about the hall alarmed at this break in the calm monotony of the days.

The Bishop rose refreshed, then dressed and explained to Marcano that they were going for a long walk. He always liked to converse with the dog. In a very low voice he could murmur much that was on his mind. But while there was a listening ear, there was no argumentative reply, no irritating contradiction.

At the end of the walk, nearing six o'clock, the Bishop felt a great relief of mind. He knew he would be ready now to share a new burden, which he felt sure Julian's coming disclosure would bring.

Dinner was a quick affair. Bishop Ware knew he could not describe the tender poignancy of the morning's scene in the hospital, which still so moved him, and even if he tried, he doubted that the younger Bishop would share his own emotion. So they discussed the weather and news of the day, until they were free to go up together to the study.

Once there Bishop Ware said, "Now, Julian, please tell me the problem and don't keep me longer in suspense."

"I'm going to tell you. I have to have some help. But, first of all, I'll say that I have been humbled. I had a sort of self-satisfied feeling that the reason the affairs of the Diocese had gone on so smoothly for several years was because of my—shall we say?—administration. I don't believe that anymore."

"Why not?"

"Because yesterday morning I had a caller, a Mr. Howard Vail, the Senior Warden of Long Falls church. You've heard me speak of that town. It's in the western corner of the Diocese. About eight thousand, maybe ten thousand, population, you may remember. I've been there a few times, liked the old church, liked the Rector—slender, young-looking, forty-five perhaps. Mr. Vail said he had always had the respect and affection of the parish until this last year."

"And what then?"

"The old organist had to resign and they secured a young woman, fresh from the conservatory. Very pretty, he said, and a wonderful choir leader. Better music than for years. Everyone was delighted until nasty little rumors began to float about. Miss Dunbar, the organist, practiced often in the church. A parishioner, coming in one day on an errand, saw the Rector sitting close beside her on the organ bench, one arm protectively on the bench behind her."

"Ouch," said the Bishop.

"Even so," said Julian. "This was seen more than once. Then Miss Dunbar began to play after service until everyone had left the church. It was noted then that the Rector and organist emerged together, he carrying her music book and papers and walking with her to her apartment, where he was seen standing rather a long time to talk before he turned away."

"I'm afraid your plot is thickening, Julian. But you haven't said a word about the Rector's wife. Doesn't he have one?"

"That's a big part of the story. This Mr. Vail is the nicest kind of person. He says it's ironic that he should be the one to bring what we might call clear evidence against the Rector. Vail and his wife were invited to an anniversary party about thirty miles from here. They went and the festivities lasted on after dinner quite into the night. They didn't leave for home until after one o'clock. Then he skipped the highway and chose a quiet back road he knew. It was nearly two when they passed a small gasoline station in a very secluded spot. There was the Rector's car, and the Rector and Miss Dunbar beside it looking at the moon, holding hands."

"Good Lord," said Bishop Ware.

"And," Julian went on, "Mr. Vail wanted to be very clear about his own reaction. He said he knew perfectly well what goes on in our own very liberal society, but he said he felt that a man, ordained to be a priest of the Church, the Rector of a congregation, cannot be found at two o'clock in the morning on a dark lonely road, holding hands with a pretty woman not his wife, and just go on his way, bearing no stigma."

"Of course he's right," said Bishop Ware. "What do they propose to do? And, once again, what about his wife?"

"That can be quickly told. She was a high school teacher and he a student in her class, not so many years younger. They fell in love. He wanted college but had no money. She suggested a bargain. She would work and put him through the four years, after which they would marry. So they did. At that point he wanted the seminary, so she saw him through that. Now, as Mr. Vail says, she is still so in love with him she will hear no word against him. He has done no wrong, can do no wrong. All the trouble comes from that serpent of a

68

woman, Miss Dunbar. You know, she adds, how women always run after preachers."

"How true!" said the Bishop. "Now we get somewhere. They have confronted the Rector and his wife with the rumors, and this last fact?"

"Yes, but they have the answers al—most too ready."

"So, what next?"

"I'm coming to that. They are calling a meeting of the vestry for next Wednesday night, and his errand was to ask me to come, after he had given me the background. He has always had such a high respect for you, he wishes you could be present, too. Would you go?"

"Oh, no. That would be a little too irregular. But you may be sure that I will give you my very best advice if you feel like talking the matter over with me. Just now I think you should sleep on it, as the saying goes. We have both had a difficult day."

Julian rose and turned toward the door, then stopped. "My great trouble will be," said he, "that I've already in my mind decided in favor of the Rector. I've liked him both times we have met. He has a pleasant manner and his eyes look right at you."

"I hope they still will."

"So do I. I meant to ask you—I mean how Cissie got through the morning. It must have been pretty hard for her."

"I'm sure it was, but she was very controlled. She did what she had to do simply and quietly. She's a wonderful girl, Julian."

"Oh, yes . . . I think so, too. I mean she's an *interesting* person. Well, good night, Bishop."

In the days before the meeting, to which Julian looked forward with profound distaste, Bishop Ware was doing some thinking of his own. "About my new career," as he mentally called it. During the years since his retirement he had many times been haunted by a sense of futility. From an extremely busy and active life he had been retired by church law to what he felt was actually a rather useless one. It was true he always had a number of confirmations in the spring, a few weddings and baptisms because of long-time family friendships, occasional invitations to preach, but these were all sporadic incidents. What he longed for was a continuity of work. Something to engage his mind for each day and to make it reasonable to project his plans and hopes into the future.

He had once felt he had discovered this new career which he craved. He would *write!* His Diocesan experiences had not been spectacular, but they had been valid and, he thought, interesting. Overjoyed with his idea, he bought a large notebook and wrote on the top of the first page:

Memories of a Bishop

This gave him courage and a delightful sense of reality. He had difficulty beginning, three pages wasted, but he wrote on doggedly, his assurance growing a little less as he worked.

At the end of three weeks, he read over what he had written and closed the notebook. "If this doesn't seem interesting to me," he thought, "what chance has it with a stranger? No, *il ne marche pas,*" he said aloud, "I just can't write."

He laid the notebook in the bottom drawer of his desk, and took Marcano for a walk. His disappointment was keen.

Now there had come to him like a flash of light another idea for a new career. It had come as he watched Big Tom in a great act of love describe to his little dying wife the beauties of Heaven so she could imagine them. The Bishop wanted to visit Big Tom again if he could. And then there might be others whom he could help. Was there such a thing as a prison chaplain? He did not know.

There would be much to learn. Meanwhile, he could think about it. And from then on, he added to his prayers the petition of the Psalmist: "Let the sighing of the Prisoners come unto Thee. And in Thy great power preserve Thou those who are appointed to die."

On Wednesday evening, the night of the meeting, dinner would be served early, but Julian arrived still earlier to talk to Bishop Ware.

"I'm nervous about this thing," he began. "It's chiefly because I do not feel competent to pass upon the morals or ethics involved. For I feel a sort of weight of ignorance."

"Not quite, Julian. You are a very mature man, used to dealing with all kind of people, unconsciously making judgments every day. I think you will be a very discerning arbiter in this matter. Don't worry. Just listen!"

He sent him away with a warm handshake, and a promise to stay up till he came back. His trip was only an hour and a half long.

The Bishop's quiet evening was broken once. It was Cissie,

in deep apology for not telling him her piece of news sooner. She said she had been so worn out each night that she hadn't had the strength to call. Now her voice seemed to have recovered its lilt.

"Wait till you hear about this, Bishop! It's the most beautiful thing! Your money was so generous that an enormous box of flowers came. I made a great bouquet to go with 'Baby' and then since there were so many I made a small box for Big Tom himself, and Dr. Lindsay took it when he went that evening to the prison. He said Big Tom was just stony. He wouldn't speak. Even when he heard about the flowers for 'Baby' he didn't touch his own box until the doctor took the lid off and opened it up. Then Big Tom stared, unbelieving, at the beauty before him, reached for the box, and holding it to his breast sank down on his bed and cried. Dr. Lindsay said he had never *seen* such tears, floods of them, and great sobs followed. He was satisfied then and left quickly, knowing the tension was broken. So, you see it was really you who caused it to happen, dear Bishop, with the flowers."

She had gone on quickly before he could disclaim the credit.

"And would you be willing to listen to something about me, that has made me so happy?"

"I could listen to endless 'somethings' about you."

"Well, this is it. After the sad morning of Baby's death I was a little shaken and our good Supervisor said she was putting me in a different section, this time with the Premies. They are the tiny little babies, Bishop, who have to be kept in incubators, until they begin to gain or die, whichever. When I got there, there were only five, and four of them doing well. One little creature was not expected to live over the following night. The Supervisor there said they had tried intravenous feeding, but while she was too weak to cry she made little sounds of distress, little squeaks the doctor called them. She had gained nothing, rather lost, and he felt hope was so slight they should do nothing to disturb her. 'You can try the bottle again but I warn you she won't take it,' he said to me."

"But she did," interpolated the Bishop, "I know what's coming, knowing you."

"I simply *willed* her to live. I talked to her softly all the time. I touched the tiny hands with my fingers so she would feel there was someone with her. I made her comfortable and never left her that night. At two o'clock I slowly—gently, tried the little bottle of formula. It was very slow getting the

71

nipple into her mouth, but I kept trying. At last it was in. She lay quiet a few moments while I held my breath. Then slowly, incredibly, she gave one little suck on the nipple, the first since she had been born. I withdrew it gently, for one effort was enough for her feebleness. But I almost choked with my excitement!

"I stayed close, of course, the rest of the night, often stroking the tiny hands and sometimes the head, and whispering my messages to her. In the morning I rather let myself go. Here she was, still living and breathing normally—and something besides. I told her softly what a wonderful night she had had, what a nice breakfast was coming, how very much I loved her—then presented the small bottle again. It was easier this time and—wonder of wonders—she gave several little sucks, enough, though, I knew, to give her a good many drops of the formula. Just as I withdrew it, in came the doctor."

"What did he say?"

"He wouldn't believe it and then went a bit crazy."

"Tell me what he said."

"He's a very good doctor but sometimes he's a complete idiot."

"I wouldn't be surprised. Tell me a bit of his idiocy, then."

"Oh, I couldn't repeat it except for one bit." She giggled. "I did think this was funny. He asked if I took off my wings before I got into bed. That gives you an idea."

"Yes. A very good one. I'm so grateful to you for telling me your story of the little Premie, I think you called her. Is she doing all right now?"

"Oh, yes. I'll finish in a sentence. She's taking the formula regularly and they are going to weigh her soon to see what she has gained. She does best when I am with her. I love the little creature so. I'm so proud I could sing all the time."

"You saved a life, my dear! You chose the right profession."

"Oh, I'm sure of it. But apropos of professions," she went on, "I've been invited to give a concert in the new Lincoln Memorial Hall October fifteenth. I'll see that you and Bishop Armstrong get tickets. Oh, I'm so disturbed about him."

"Julian? Why so?"

"I like him very much, but he does not like me. On the few times we've been alone he is so lofty and unapproachable that it gives me an insane desire to tease him, and then we get angry and it's worse than ever. Does a Bishop never date girls?"

"You see, my dear, usually when a man is elected Bishop he is already married. Certainly Julian is an extreme exception. But I don't think there is any church law that would keep him now from having a date if he wanted to do so."

"I have dates on my off nights. Often it's only for dinner out at a country restaurant where we can visit for an hour or so and I can get back early. They all understand that. I've wondered sometimes—this sounds unmaidenly of me (to use an obsolete word)—but I've wondered if perhaps with your good offices if you might be able to help break this deadlock between Julian and me."

"My dear child, I could never have a commission more to my liking. But please don't count on results. Much as I love Julian, I think he is a very stubborn"—he paused—"critter," he ended, laughing.

Cissie laughed, too. "Thank you, dear Bishop. I think we understand each other. You have been so good to hear my long stories. I'm talking from Grammie's. I couldn't have held a phone up so long anywhere else. Are you alone?"

"I am. And you've taken the loneliness out of my evening. And I thank you."

They said the good nights quickly, and Bishop Ware was left with a new train of thought. He was ready, however, to hear Julian's report when he returned. It was that the meeting had been rather quiet, a going over the rumors and evidence they had with one new piece added. Miss Dunbar lived on the first floor of an apartment house. There was a front window looking on the street. Her piano was visible. Lately she had begun playing very soft and sweet music after dark, dressed in white, with a small light on the table behind her. Several times the Rector hurried past the house on his way to the drugstore in the business section and then walked slowly back, pausing a little for the music and, as many watchers pointed out, to glance occasionally at the figure in white inside.

"Probably a number of passers-by might have done that," Bishop Ware remarked.

"That's what I mentioned. The thing that is worrying them most of all is that the congregation has divided into two factions, one for the Rector against Miss Dunbar, the other for the organist against the Rector. Each side has become increasingly vocal and bitter. It's a regular schism."

"The worst thing that could happen," said Bishop Ware.

"Yes. And the men tonight seemed sort of helpless, inept at

coming to any idea of action. They finally begged me to present some sort of plan they could follow. So I gave one. I suggested that for two weeks we all pursue our normal ways and keep *quiet,* only setting a second meeting at the end of this period to which the three principals should be invited. My feeling is that if the Rector and his wife and Miss Dunbar are all there to hear the rumors, gossip, and the facts presented to them for questioning, their answers may somewhere show a slip, an error, a little contradiction that will make a clear decision possible."

"Good for you, Julian. That was a very discerning idea. Rather Solomonesque, I should say . . ."

"Odd that you should mention him for I've just been reading about him in my devotions. He fascinates me. However, I don't think I'm ready yet to threaten to divide a baby in two to find the true mother."

"A baby!" Bishop Ware repeated. "I've a wonderful story to tell you! Cissie called me tonight!"

"Oh?" His voice showed no enthusiasm.

"She recently saved a tiny baby's life."

"How did she do that?"

"I can't give the details—too professional. But I would merely say by the use of a strong will and a tender heart."

"She's still content with the new profession?"

"She says she feels like singing now all the time. On the other side of the coin, though, she told me she is giving a concert in the new Lincoln Memorial Hall on October fifteenth. Said she will send us tickets. So, of course, we'll be going."

"No quite *of course,*" he answered. "You will go, I'm sure, but I have no idea what I may have to do on that date. I think I will make no promises."

"It's a good while ahead so you could adjust your plans. I will hope to escort Mrs. Lansing and you could sit with us and then be of service to Cissie afterwards in helping her get away and back home. I don't imagine she will want any fuss and feathers after she's through."

"She must know plenty of younger men willing to squire her. That is not in my line, Bishop."

"Well, put the date down anyway. That won't commit you to anything."

"I'll put a large question mark after it," he called back as he left.

For a week the days passed quietly. Julian seemed more

than ever involved with his normal work. Bishop Ware awaited a few replies from old friends who might be of some help with his prison idea, and he also went to see Dr. Lindsay, who was interested at once.

"From the little I saw, the poor devils could do with a little Christian ministry. The trick is to get to them. Wardens aren't too anxious to let outsiders in to see conditions. Our whole penal system is based on a wrong premise—that the prisoners are there to be *punished*. They are there *as a* punishment. If I can ever be of any help to you, just let me know. But it's a tough nut to crack."

When the men stood at last Dr. Lindsay smiled at the Bishop.

"I happen to know that a wonderful nurse, named Cissie Lansing, is very devoted to you."

"Better say I am devoted to her."

"I guessed it was mutual. I'm going to tell you something. I'm just past my seventieth birthday. For one reason or another I've been a bachelor all my life. But if I were a young man now, I would move heaven and earth to get Cissie Lansing to marry me. She's a girl in a thousand!" He gave a little dry laugh. "You can raise that figure as high as you wish and I'll still go with it."

As the Bishop went home he was filled with an embarrassment that was almost shame. As he had listened to Dr. Lindsay's startling confidence, he heard Cissie's voice again asking her "unmaidenly" favor of him, which he had laughingly turned aside. He realized now with surprising distinctness that she had been in earnest and her call upon him must have been prompted by more than a casual feeling. He had only answered her by saying, in effect, that any effort of his own would be useless and then forgotten all about it. Until now.

The Setpember afternoon lay brightly beautiful upon the garden, which the Bishop chose as the best place to think about his new problem, Cissie and Julian. What tattered fragments of memory did he have to bear upon it? There was that blinding radiance on her face the night of Mrs. Lansing's dinner party when she had suddenly appealed to Julian and after a glance he had withdrawn his eyes as though they had been burnt. Was there, indeed, some tiny flame that fluttered back and forth between them?

It was all confusing to his orderly mind. After Cissie's wonderful playing that night, he saw her eyes turn first to

Julian as though seeking his response, which in turn had been stereotyped in the extreme. And he had steadily refused to discuss her career plans as they drove back that night together.

And yet—and yet—he had almost shouted his dismay when Cissie, after their own dinner party, had mentioned the possibility of danger from Tom and the police. He had been afraid for her safety. And if his ears had not completely deceived him, their final good night had been verging on the tender. From then on, however, every remark Julian had made about Cissie had been with what he himself called, "studied curtness."

Cissie was right. There was an impasse between these two. And who was he, to attempt to break it?

The western light feathered through the leaves of the big maple, the sweet-sharp tang of the chrysanthemums lay upon the air. Marcano lifted his head to have it stroked, and the Bishop spoke aloud as he caressed the dog.

"You never get anywhere, laddie, by not trying!"

5

The next day Bishop Ware concentrated upon his "mission," as he called it, and slowly set down a few points upon which he just might exert a subtle influence to bring the two younger people together. One was their mental congeniality. But here was the block. They had never had a chance to spend any time alone, so they could test the quality of each other's mental processes. And how could he ever serve in bringing this about? No, he wrote the first idea off.

But as to the second, Cissie's work, with all its incidents of humor, tragedy, and drama generally, surely this would serve as the bridge for her to interest any man she chose in it and in herself. But alas, not Julian. He completely disapproved of it and didn't want to hear anything about it. The Bishop sadly struck this off, also.

On this immediate list, there remained only Julian's own work. As to Cissie he was sure she would always feign an interest if she had it not, but somehow he could not imagine Julian pointing out any mechanistic details of running the Diocese to anybody, least of all to Cissie. He drew a line of negation through his third idea and sat still, dispiritedly thinking as his eyes roved over the page before him.

As it reached the end once more he started and sat straight, his eyes bright.

"Good Lord!" he said aloud. "What a fool I was to forget Julian has a problem now that falls into his work as a Bishop and carries love, hate, jealousy, adultery maybe, all the most complicated human relations. Equal to or more than a hospital, that interest! Well, I've something to work on now."

Bishop Ware was at his best when he faced a challenge. Then he attacked it as Marcano did his bone, slowly but with relish. His first move was to call Fenwick the next day, since one of their regular chats was due. Fenwick had a charming wife. It was possible he might drop a hint . . .

After they met in the familiar study at St. Michael's they discussed the affairs of the Church Militant, the vestry's decision to buy new pew cushions by the following spring, and finally arrived where the Bishop intended to lead the way. Fenwick, however, brought it up himself.

"You know, Bishop, when my wife and I get sort of worn down by church business, home problems, the eternal cry of the city, we slip off for an evening to a little haven we've discovered. It's a small restaurant about three miles out on the South Road. It's quiet, they don't serve drinks, but it's beautiful, the food delicious, and the tables far enough apart that you can talk and not feel someone breathing down your neck."

"It sounds delightful!"

"You can sit there for two hours if you wish, just having cup after cup of coffee, or better still"—he laughed—"big confession! We have a second dessert. We hold ourselves down hard at home, on account of the calories, but when we get there, we just let ourselves go. It's marvelous. Maybe you'd like to join us sometime."

"Thank you, I'd enjoy it, though I may prevail upon an old friend of to my youth to go with me. This is why I do want to get all the details carefully from you."

"One little thing I haven't told you, but it's a part of our trips to The Mill Race. About halfway there, a very large,

77

very fashionable restaurant stands behind great trees. No cars are on the road before it, for a sign a little way back points them up a wide drive toward the parking place at the back. There is only a very dim light on the road and soft echoes of music coming through the trees. We always wait there for a little, coming back, and since I know you are a man of sentiment I will confess we feel young again there and it's good for us."

That night at dinner Bishop Ware was so animated Julian asked what he had been doing all day.

"Oh, a bit of this and that. I had one of my occasional chats with Fenwick. I do like that man! He tells me they are getting new pew cushions for St. Michael's, scheduled first for this fall, but the latest decision is to have them in place by Easter. The best plan, I think."

"Did you take your usual walk with Marcano?"

"Oh yes, and held quite a conversation, one-sided, with him. How wonderful if a dog could talk. We could tell him then all we think of him."

"Don't forget that he could tell then how he feel about us! That might be a shock!"

"Dear me!" said the Bishop. "I'd never thought of that."

For two days, hard work—brain work, paper work, oral work—went on in the study; and then Bishop Ware asked Julian at dinner if he would join him for a talk afterward.

"Of course," Julian said, looking surprised.

When they were alone together Bishop Ware began promptly.

"I've been doing some more considering about your Long Falls problem and I've been struck by a new thought. All the information you have up 'til now received on the matter has been given you by *men*, has it not?"

"Why, yes," Julian said. "But I've never thought much about that."

"I believe you should. I think before you go to this coming meeting you should feel an obligation to talk to a woman about all this and get her point of view. It may help you greatly when you have to reach your own decision!"

"My dear Bishop, you astonish me. When did this idea hit you? In the first place, I would certainly not discuss this matter with just any woman and, in the second place, there would be no suitable woman available whom I could ask to listen. Certainly no one from the parish there, nor one picked at random from the Diocese to hear what is actually kind of secret for the Long Falls people. You can see your plan has to be disregarded. There is no available woman."

"There is one," the Bishop said calmly.

"I should certainly like to hear who!"

"Cissie Lansing."

Julian did not reply. He only stared at Bishop Ware, his lips not quite closed, as though seeing an apparition.

"Now I know," he said at last, "that you are temporarily out of your mind."

"Not a bit. I never was more sane. Now listen a bit about Cissie. She is mature enough, almost thirty, she must have known many more types of men and women than you have. She seems to be gifted in dealing with human relations. Now my feeling is you should call her up at once. Don't delay, for you have that meeting ahead of you. Ask her if she could spare you a few hours some evening to hear a Diocesan problem which worries you and upon which you would like to have her reaction."

"I am more startled than I have ever been in my life, I believe. If I didn't have such regard for you and such faith in your judgment . . ."

"I know, I know. You would toss this all out the window, but trust me, Julian, in this. And when you are talking to her tell her you think you should have your talk in a quiet place, in different surroundings—not her grandmother's drawing room, or ours. By chance, I heard from Fenwick of a charming little restaurant in the country, not too far away. I can give you all details later. It's called The Mill Race. Go ahead, Julian, call her."

"Before I lose my nerve?"

"There's nothing of that involved. You know Cissie perfectly well. You don't have to introduce yourself. Try the hospital first. You can use the phone here if you wish."

Julian rose slowly, as if with difficulty.

"I verily believe you've mesmerized me. At least you took me so by storm I had no chance to think rationally. But since there is one chance you may be right, I'll follow your instructions. I'll make the call in my own room."

"Fine! Only please let me know later how it turned out."

When he had left Bishop Ware sank back in his chair. He realized that his legs were trembling; that, in fact, he felt weak all over as a man might after a physical struggle. "Taken him by storm," Julian had said. Well, he felt as though he had done so, and been rather shattered by it.

Little by little he felt his weakness disappear and an exultation fill him. Against all improbabilities he had actually brought about a meeting between these two! He hoped all his statements, some even surprising to himself, would bear the light of Truth. But he really thought they would. He considered them in a sense inspired—humanly speaking, he added to himself.

When Julian came back an hour later, his expression Bishop Ware noted at once, was not one of distaste.

"I got through to her, finally," he said, "and then she didn't seem surprised at my message. She was just sort of graciously calm, I'd say. She has this Friday evening off and will be glad to spend it with me and hear my problem. She said she was flattered I had asked her. She knows the little restaurant, so we will go there. I'm to pick her up at her grandmother's on Friday evening at six-thirty. So it's all set."

"Very good," answered Bishop Ware, trying to keep his voice casual, and failing. "I think this may be of great help to you."

"It's to be hoped so," said Julian, and went off to bed.

On the afternoon of the appointed evening Bishop Ware noticed several things. Julian had had his car washed, something he usually neglected until reminded. At five he was seen in old slacks and sweater polishing the chrome that showed here and there. At six he came to say good-bye to the Bishop, who drew a little sigh of satisfaction as he looked at him.

He wore a black suit of incredibly fine material and tailoring with a clerical vest and collar, above which his face showed strong, smiling, and handsome.

"Perfect!" the Bishop said. "Perfect! I hope you have a delightful time."

"I'm certainly not just on pleasure bent, as you know, and I'm sure Cissie understands my words about it . . ."

"But I can wish you both peace and quiet, and the hope that your conversation goes well."

"I'll accept that with thanks," Julian said, and was off.

Meanwhile Cissie had been tossing out of her closet frock after frock, trying to decide what to wear. It was September, but the evening was warm. The dress must not be too "fussy," and yet she *did* want to look her best. At times she felt a little tingle of excitement over the thought of going out to dinner and the evening *with Julian*. Could there be the slightest connection between this and the favor she had asked of Bishop Ware, of which she was now heartily ashamed? No, she felt sure this idea was Julian's own, growing out of his deep concentration in his own work. Perhaps his problem was connected with a young woman and she was the only one of that class he could ask easily. At all events, it would be more than nice to have a few hours together.

She chose a voile dress of softest pink, its only trimming being the shirred ruffle around a not-too-low neck. She decided to wear no jewelry, and the smallest amount of makeup. The dress itself would take care of the rest. In the lower hall her grandmother stood with one perfect pink rose in her hand.

"Oh, Grammie dear, girls don't wear flowers in their hair, if that's what you had in mind. Only at big balls, perhaps."

"Any girl can wear a flower in her hair if she wants to. You must let me arrange this. It's just heavenly with that dress."

She fastened it with some small pins she held, in the side of Cissie's thick brown waves and then stood back to survey her work.

"I knew it!" she exclaimed delightedly. "That makes you a perfect picture! Go look in the mirror yourself."

She did, but only for a moment, while the blood rose in her cheek. She knew the mirror did not lie.

"I'm off to do some telephoning," Mrs. Lansing went on, "so I won't be here to greet Bishop Armstrong. Give him my warmest regards, though, and have a lovely evening, both of you."

Cissie, through the open door, saw the car drive into the circle and stop at the walk. She went at once out to the small entrance portico and stood beside one of the pillars, waiting . . .If she had planned it she could not have achieved a more striking effect. When Julian came up to her they looked at each other with approving eyes as they gave their greetings, and as they walked to the car Julian laughed.

"I'm sure no man in a clerical collar ever *whistled* at a young lady, but I confess when I saw you first I had an outrageous desire to do so. Your dress is very pretty."

"Why, Julian, you amaze me but you please me, too. I didn't know you could whistle."

"Oh, yes. Just hymns, of course," he added with a touch of irony. "Perhaps the reason I had such a wild thought was that I'm a little excited or rather nervous at the idea of taking a young lady out to dinner."

"You mustn't be. Just think of the kindness you are doing me. I had *such* a hard day and going out to this lovely spot is like balm to my spirit."

"I had a rather tough day myself, so we'll hope we both enjoy some relaxation. Do you mind if I don't talk until we're out of the city? The traffic gets a bit wicked from here on."

"I'll be quiet," she said.

Once they were safely through the crowded streets, over the bridge, and out on the South Road, he spoke again.

"I've been thinking that since we've both had a rather difficult day, might it not be good just to relax completely over a leisurely dinner and I'll not present my problem until later, over our coffee. I hear we can stay on as long as we please."

"We can. I think you'll love this place, and I agree with your plan."

When they were finally in the restaurant, Julian looked about with evident pleasure, and when the head waiter escorted them to a table in the large bay window, Cissie beamed upon him and then gave a subdued expression of delight when they were seated.

"Julian, did you by any chance *reserve* this table?"

"Yes, I did, but quite in ignorance. It was Fenwick of St. Michael's, you know, who told the Bishop he always engaged this, for he and his wife liked it especially. So I just did the same."

"It's wonderful that you did. The other times I've been here my escorts didn't know about reserving this—none of the other tables are reserved—so this is the first time I've had a chance to enjoy it. Look out the window!"

A group of white birches were lighted with darker trees behind them. Near the window ran a very small stream, the last of the old Mill Race, Cissie explained, wandering gently in the foreground.

"Like the little brook you played about."

"Oh, you remembered."

"Why, this is most charming!" Julian said, "and such a beautifully quiet place altogether. I begin to feel rested already. By the way, as you may know, they don't serve cocktails here but they do have sherry. Would you care for some before dinner?"

"Thank you. I would very much."

"So would I. Parson's drink, you know. I always stick to that only. It saves bother as I go about here and there."

As the meal progressed conversation was easy and light, with a good deal of laughter thrown in. The choosing of food provided most, for Julian explained he would select all the richest items on the menu.

"Mrs. Morgan does hold us down with a Spartan hand," he said, "she's so afraid we might gain an ounce. I'm sure in the main it is good for us, but how I yearn for butterscotch pie and chocolate cake. We do get apple pie once a week but it's never sweet enough and I shock Mrs. Morgan by putting more sugar on it and then adding heavy cream. The Bishop, after a few furtive glances, does likewise. But usually we get gelatine concoctions or plain fruit."

"Two big men afraid to speak their wishes as to their dinners! This seems to me rather ridiculous!"

"Ah, you don't understand our situation! We spend half our time doing exactly what Mrs. Morgan tells us, and the other half praying she won't leave."

There was more laughter, and when dessert time came Julian leaned a trifle toward his companion with a conspiratorial air.

"If I can order two double portions of strawberry shortcake, would you be equal to one of them?"

"After a long week of hospital fare," Cissie said, "I can assure you I will be able to take care of it. Let's pick up our last calories with a flourish."

When only coffee was left on the table Julian looked over at Cissie with a new gravity.

"It's time now for me to tell you the problem that has given me so much thought and upon which I would so appreciate getting your point of view as a young woman. I believe I will first tell it to you as I heard it myself from a Mr. Vail, Senior Warden of the church that is involved."

From then on, very slowly and clearly, he told how the story of Miss Dunbar and the Reverend Howard Bell, the Rector, had grown with the gossip, the surmises, the evidence, and the facts until the parish was disrupted.

Cissie asked a question now and then and once spoke out, "Oh, no!"

"What?" Julian asked.

"Holding hands as they looked at the moonlight view! That seems to me a little too much!"

"I agree. I'm nearly at the end now."

Cissie listened with complete concentration until he had finished. "Now," he said, "I would so like to have your own reaction, as a woman, to this situation. Which of these two seems to you the more guilty?"

Cissie turned her head a little aside. "I hate to answer this and yet I know you want the truth. Remember, though, how wrong I could be. I may have missed many little nuances that might change the outline of the story. But, though it seems like putting a *libel* on my sex, I have to say that it looks to me as though this pretty Miss Dunbar has been trying to seduce the Rector, or, shall we say, trying to tempt him into giving her too much of his attention."

Julian drew a long sigh of relief. "I'm so glad you said that. I've been leaning that way all the time and then choking the thought as I tried to be impartial. I'm most grateful to you, Cissie." His voice was low and very friendly. "Do you work tomorrow?"

"Yes, unfortunately."

"Then perhaps we should be leaving this enchanted spot so you won't be up too late."

They had a last look at the little Mill Race stream, Julian arranged for the bill and then they were again in the car.

"I realize now that I forgot to ask you about one important thing. I may stop the car for a few minutes later so we can talk with a little more ease."

"But I know a perfect place to do that," she said. "I've stopped there before. There is a big hotel behind the trees a mile or so along the road. Its patrons are the 'Jet Set' or something like that, and the cars enter at a sign and go up a winding drive to the hotel, so no cars are ever parked on the road. It's a pleasant spot."

"We'll sample it then and I can ask you my questions without having at the same time to guide the car."

It was easy to recognize the place when they came to it. There was a cleared space of a car's width on the side and Julian stopped here and they both sat looking and listening as the dim light drifted through the trees and the soft echoes of a waltz came mutedly to their ears.

"It's the 'Blue Danube,' " Cissie whispered. "Have you ever danced to it?"

"I'm afraid not," Julian said. "When I was very young, I danced, but that has been crowded out, and now it's too late, I fear."

"But it's never too late," Cissie said earnestly. "It's like swimming. You never forget. It would be good for you now once in a while. And there are lovely, quiet restaurants where you *can* drive and dance a little, too. I just drop this as a delicate bombshell of a hint!"

Julian laughed. "I see the downward path you are leading me into and I must be strong to shun it. However, I could take another evening at The Mill Race some time when either of us has a problem!"

"I'll be waiting for that," she said. "But I keep hearing the music and thinking of the last time I danced that waltz. It was in Vienna at the Opera Ball. Then they build a platform over the backs of all the seats in the Opera House and it becomes an incredible dance floor. To dance on it in that lovely place, to the music of the Viennese orchestra playing Strauss waltzes seemed about as near heaven as one could get. But oh, I'm ashamed to keep talking so much. Please tell me the part of your problem you forgot."

"It *is* important. I mean your reaction is important to me. Try to put yourself in this woman's place. It's the Rector's wife, Mrs. Bell. She taught in high school when she was young and he was in her class. She was not too much older than he. They fell in love. He wanted college but had no money. She went on teaching and put him through. Then they were married, but he wanted the seminary also, so she saw him through that."

"How she must have loved him!" Cissie said.

"Yes, and I think there is love between them yet, in spite of the fact that he may have made a bit of a fool of himself. And now when she hears the gossip and even certain facts about him, she will not listen. She says they are nonsense, he is innocent of any possible misconduct, and if there was any indiscretion it was all due to that serpent, Miss Dunbar.

"Now, my question to you is this: Could *any* wife hear such reports as Mrs. Bell has heard, and not feel at least some question in her mind?"

"Oh," said Cissie, "now I am sure of myself and know I speak truly. If I ever love a man greatly enough to marry him, I will believe anything he would ever tell me."

She raised her head, and the radiance, which Bishop Ware had noticed in her face, became bright as her eyes were fixed on Julian's.

"I would trust him *to the death!*"

And then suddenly, as without volition, Julian's arms were around her and he was pressing her to him, while his lips fell upon hers. He kissed as a thirsty man finds water; she kissed as a hungry soul is satisfied with bread. And the kiss went on as though they were being fused into each other by its power, by a kind of utter sweetness that could know no end.

A moment's breath separated them, and then once more they were together as though now they knew the thirst could be quenched, the hunger assuaged. It was neither he nor she who kissed the other, it was a passionate unity which made them one in flesh and spirit.

All at once, as he had acted before, Julian sprang from his position and almost roughly pushed Cissie away from him. He seemed to press toward his side of the car and his low cries sounded like moans.

"What have I done? Oh, what have I done? Can you ever forgive me? For I can never forgive myself! I'm so terribly ashamed. Please say you forgive me!"

Cissie's voice was calm and very tender. "Oh, Julian, my dear, what do I have to forgive? How can you be ashamed of this beautiful thing that has just happened to us? It is what we have both perhaps wished for but could not . . ."

"Please don't say that. It makes me feel more guilty. I must tell you the background for my feelings now. Then you will understand better."

He sat stiffly, his eyes fixed straight before him, never now at Cissie. "I was planning to tell you sometime, but hesitated for lack of opportunity, I guess, and tonight because I didn't want to spoil the pleasant evening. I was afraid you would not understand. Now I must take the chance." He stopped, swallowing with difficulty.

"When I was ordained as an Episcopal priest, I took a vow. It was a private one but I prayed for God's blessing, and felt I had it."

"What was the vow?" Her voice was very small.

"What, celibacy, of course. But it includes more than just nonmarriage. It means you keep your self-control over all of what St. Paul calls 'the lusts of the flesh.' And I've just now lost this control. In one sense, I've broken my vow. That's why I'm ashamed."

Cissie's voice quivered a little but she brought out the words.

"But, Julian, does this vow mean more to you than—than I do, after what has passed between us?"

He hesitated. "I don't know how to say this honestly and still kindly; but yes, it does. It is like a man's honor. If he loses that, he is devastated. With my vow I felt strong, unassailable, safe. I think I was too sure of myself. But I had

86

never faced any real temptation until I met you. Now I know how easily I can be weak. That is why I should not see you again. Can you understand anything of what I've just said?"

"Not very much. Your vow seems to me—an unreasonable —one," Cissie said brokenly.

"I was afraid you would feel that way, but somehow there seemed no easy words to explain it to you. You see, to me it's a sacred thing, part of my very inmost being. I hope that as you think of me later on you can realize that the amount of my pleasure in what we might call the Forbidden Fruit was the measure of my guilt in falling from the confines of my vow. This is why I asked you forgiveness."

"I do not forgive you, as I said before, for there is nothing for *me* to forgive. And I do not understand the intensity of your feeling about the vow, nor why you should feel iron-bound by it."

"I was afraid of this," he said quietly, "but I'm not able to make it any more plain."

When Cissie said no more he started the car. She shrank then, as though stricken, into her seat. Julian sat a little forward, looking straight ahead with only an occasional glance at his companion. So they went through the darkness until, at last, they came to Mrs. Lansing's home in the city where Cissie was to spend the night.

He helped her out of the car and walked with her to the small, arched portico, where earlier in the evening she had stood against the pillar. It seemed as though they were both hearing again their laughter as they went toward the car after Julian's amazing speech, so gay and lighthearted it had been. Now there was only silence until Julian broke it.

"I'm afraid I told my story awkwardly, and I'm so sorry if my bluntness may have sounded harsh to you. I would be distressed if I have hurt you. Did I?"

He was unprepared for the light irony in her voice.

"Oh, not at all! Especially since we are not to see each other again."

She turned the knob, stepped inside, and closed the door after her.

Julian stood for a few minutes, as though movement was difficult, and then walked very slowly to the car.

6

When Julian reached the Old Rectory he had decided to tell the Bishop the whole story of the evening, including that of the drive home. But even as he neared the open study door he changed his mind. He stopped. "I can't do that," he said softly. "That is Cissie's secret as well as mine. I couldn't speak of it behind her back."

When he went inside the room Bishop Ware was just rousing himself from a little nap over his book.

"Well, Julian. So you're back. How did the evening go?"

"The little restaurant was really delightful and the food excellent as Fenwick had told you."

"But about your problem. You told it in detail?"

"Exactly. She listened very carefully. But when she gave her opinion it did not throw any new light upon the entanglement for her view almost exactly coincided with my own."

"Bless my soul!" said the Bishop. "At least, then, she will add a supportive voice. Did your general conversation go well?"

"Oh, yes. I was surprised to find so many subjects were congenial. Well, having given my news, I believe I'll go to bed. For some reason I'm tired."

"I'll follow your example. I'm glad your evening was so pleasant."

When Bishop Ware was safely in bed, however, he lay there with an active mind. The normal questions had been asked, the right answers had been given, but still there was something wrong. In Julian's voice there had been no least spark of warmth or spontaneity. In addition to this, his face looked drawn, as though its muscles were responding to a tight inner control. The Bishop did not consider himself a real percipient, but he knew he was a rather good judge of people's faces. He was sure now that there had been some sort of trouble between Julian and Cissie on that precious evening upon which he had gloated as the orginator of the error-proof plan, designed to bring them more closely together. When every move had gone so easily into place he had felt that Providence was actually blessing the plan. Now, he was not so sure. But what could possibly have occurred?

Where, indeed, did this leave him, with his tremendous commission and his own eager desire to fulfill it? And yet now, more than ever, who was he to attempt to meddle with the emotional inner currents of two hearts? The sad thing was that in either case he would feel ashamed: if he made a new attempt, or if he did not.

Bishop Armstrong also lay wakeful in his room. He had opened his Bible at random as he often did, and it had showed the first chapter of The Song of Solomon. He groaned. How ironic that this had turned up on this particular night! His quick eyes roved down the page:

> *"Let him kiss me with the kisses of his mouth*
> *for thy love is better than wine . . .*
>
> *"Behold, thou art fair, my love, behold*
> *thou art fair. Thou hast dove's eyes . . ."*

He closed the book with a curt nod as though to the author. "I certainly don't need this," he said aloud, and lapsed, at last, into an uneasy sleep.

The next morning a definite restraint could be felt during breakfast. The Bishops, each for his own reasons, did not want to refer to the previous evening. The routine of this new day lay untried before them. So, they mentioned the morning's headlines, and little else. Bishop Ware did speak as Julian was leaving for his office.

"I don't think you should wear yourself out over this church business. The next meeting comes up in a week and will surely give you a basis for decision. By the way, have you thought any more about Cissie's concert, which comes the night before?"

"Not very much," he said, "but at least I have decided to slip in for the main concerto and leave early. I'll just stay in the back. I won't be sitting with you and Mrs. Lansing."

"Oh? You won't be seeing Cissie afterward, then?"

"I think not. There will be plenty of younger squires

89

waiting to speak to her and eager to see her home. I think this plan is best."

"All right, if you feel so. I'm afraid Cissie will think you are very indifferent to her gift of the ticket."

"Oh, well," Julian mumbled as he went out the door.

In addition to his personal reason for not wanting to see Cissie again, just then he had a strong feeling that his evenings now should be filled with some good hard thinking about the entanglement that must soon be cleared. He must pursue any small avenue that could shed even a ray of light upon the enigma even as a detective catches at every possible clue that would aid in solving a crime. And, he admitted, he was interested to see this particular daughter of Eve to assess for himself what her charms were.

On the evening of the concert Bishop Ware stopped a moment at the door to say good-bye to Julian. The latter looked at him with approving eyes: the finely tailored black suit, the whitest of clericals, the smiling face above.

"You won't like my adjective," Julian said, "but you look positively *jaunty!*"

They laughed together and then Bishop Ware sobered.

"If I asked you a simple question, Julian, would you answer?"

"I don't know. You could try."

"Did anything unhappy happen the evening you took Cissie out?"

Julian, too, looked grave now.

"Perhaps you could say that, but I would not like any more questions about it. Now, have a wonderful evening," he finished in a lighter tone.

Mrs. Lansing was ready at the door when the Bishop called for her. They had planned to arrive early so they could be sure to hear the "tuning up," which for some strange reason they both admitted liking. She was wearing a gown of lavender chiffon that seemed to clothe her with a peculiar grace as it fell softly from shoulder to waist, clasped at the throat with a diamond star.

"You are beautiful, Sally," the Bishop said, "and you should be riding in a coach-and-four instead of my not-so-new car."

"You're sweet, Larry, and I couldn't be more pleased than to be just where I am. It's so wonderful that out of our long ago we have found ourselves again. I'm especially glad to be with you tonight, for I have a big burden on my heart and you're the only person with whom I can share it."

"Please let me try. As it happens, I have a burden, too. Maybe we can exchange them."

She laughed a little but was soon grave. "It has to do with Cissie," she said. "The child is unhappy."

"Not about the concert?"

"Oh, no. She's eager to play and has been practicing every available minute. The trouble is an affair of the heart, and I'm sure it somehow has to do with Bishop Armstrong."

"Ah—," said Bishop Ware, drawing a deep breath. "Now our burdens are touching each other. I have been anxious about him. He has not seemed like himself since the evening he and Cissie were together, and I had hoped that a kind of impasse between them would be broken during that time. As a matter of fact, I pulled a string or two to arrange the evening for them. But it evidently didn't work. I asked Julian pointblank if anything unhappy had occurred and he said I might possibly say that, but he did not wish any more questions. So, that's that. What did Cissie say?"

"I was like you. I hoped so much from their *date*, as Cissie called it. She was so happy. I could hear her singing while she was getting ready. And when she came downstairs she looked so lovely I kept hoping he couldn't resist her—this hardly sounds nice, but I almost *prayed* he would kiss her . . . I'm ashamed now."

"I'm afraid my own thoughts were much like yours. A line of poetry keeps coming back to me: 'Great sin is there in taking Heaven by storm.' Perhaps it's the same with love. We had been trying to exert our own pressures. But do tell me what Cissie said when she came back that night."

"I had waited up, of course, to hear the news, so I tried to ask casually if they had had a pleasant time. Cissie just put her arms around me and said, 'Grammie, we are not to see each other again.' And the tears were running down her cheeks. When I started to ask a question she said, 'Please, I can't talk about it,' and went right up to her room. I didn't sleep well. Once in the night I went softly into the hall and stood outside her door. I'm sure I heard her sobbing. But whether this is due to a broken love or a broken friendship, I wouldn't know."

"Friendship?" the Bishop queried.

"Yes. Cissie takes friendship very seriously. I remember once she said to me, 'What I would like to have is a good man friend.' And I asked why couldn't she have one. She said

91

because the good friends always turned into lovers. That *could* have happened here, don't you think so, Larry?"

"I don't know. I'm puzzled and saddened, of course. I believe whatever it was between them had its beginning at the very time Cissie opened the trapdoor in the study at St. Michael's and shut herself into the *Attic*, so-called. When Julian was giving me a very brief account I remember I asked him if the girl was pretty and he said he hadn't noticed. I knew that was a lie and for as great a stickler for Truth as he is, I knew then he must have been deeply impressed."

"And Cissie," Mrs. Lansing went on, "was at first so mad when she told me of her experience. 'That young Bishop,' she said, was 'without a grain of humor, was stern, overbearing, and very proud of himself' and she couldn't stand him. Later, she gave a giggle and said, of course, if that young Bishop would come down off his pedestal and act like an ordinary man he might really be, she believed, quite attractive. And you know, Larry, sometimes real love does start with a little flutter of dislike."

"I know it. At any rate we've paved the way for more private discussions again and just now, here we are at Lincoln Hall. I'll let you out at the door and if you'll wait in the lobby, I'll join you there as soon as I've parked."

It was pleasant in the lobby when they were together for some friends of Mrs. Lansing came up to speak to her and meet the Bishop. Also the Fenwicks, when they saw him through the gathering crowd, came at once and were very much interested in finding that Mrs. Lansing was the grandmother of the guest artist for the evening. There were a few moments of pleasant chat before the Bishop guided his companion to the great doors that opened into the auditorium. There, while he presented their tickets, a voice some distance behind with a rare carrying quality was saying, "Who was that handsome couple you were talking to, Mary? He looked like some kind of a preacher."

They laughed all the way to their seats and then settled themselves to consider the words they had overheard more carefully.

"So we're a handsome couple, Larry. Isn't that a thrill? I'm terribly set up about it."

"And I'm some sort of preacher," he chuckled, "when I've never been exactly famous for my sermons. You see how fame has caught up with me. It's very funny!"

"That girl—I'm sure the voice belonged to a young girl—

would be surprised if she knew how important you really are. I think every Bishop should have a little mitre to wear when he goes out among people. Wouldn't that be a good idea?"

"I'll get measured for one tomorrow," the Bishop answered, smiling. "But just now I have another idea. We got here in a rather depressed state. Now we've had the most wonderful laughter. Why not take it as a sign we should forget all our anxieties and enjoy the evening to the fullest? What do you say?"

"The idea is perfect. Oh, Larry, let's drop every care!"

"Let's," he answered briefly. They laughed a little at the childish words and settled to hear the first number from the orchestra. Cissie would not appear until the second and longest number, the piano concerto.

When the overture was ended, there was a small rearrangement of the chairs where the first violins sat, the grand piano was wheeled to the center front, and the conductor went backstage to bring out the guest star of the evening. He returned with Cissie, and led her to a spot close to the piano and in full view of the audience.

"Lovely! Lovely!" murmured the Bishop.

For Cissie stood there so slim and fair and appealing, all in a virginal white and looking so incredibly young that a wave of applause swept over the audience. She smiled, gave a little bow, and turned to the piano. She sat down, adjusted the bench slightly, and then waited, her hands in her lap, her eyes on the conductor.

The orchestra played first, beautiful reaches of sound, swelling and then receding. Bishop Ware, though watching closely, could not have told just when Cissie's hands touched the keyboard. He seemed to hear, though, a wind blowing through a field of grain, gradually growing stronger until it became a storm with thunder in its wake. He saw her hands, then, running swiftly the whole length of the piano before settling into a clear and sweet melody rising above the orchestra.

He leaned back comfortably in his seat with complete relaxation. Cissie did not need any supportive thoughts from either him or her grandmother. Cissie was mistress of her art. Her fingers were the perfect servants of her brain. It was from her disciplined memory that the exact moment of obedience to the conductor's baton took place, as did the moment of the crashing chords or the delicate dreaming beauty of the treble keys. He glanced at Mrs. Lansing. She, too, sat relaxed, with a happy serenity on her face. So they listened, enfolded, enraptured, by the continuing music. The great audience also seemed scarcely breathing as the time passed.

At last came the climax, with the orchestra's full volume of sound, the piano rising above it now and then like a thin strain of beauty, before its own tremendous climax joined with the rest.

It was over. The conductor left the podium, kissed Cissie's hand, and led her to the front of the stage. The applause was overwhelming! The conductor took his own bows, shook hands with the first violinist, and signed for the orchestra to rise that they might share in the acclaim. But when he and Cissie went backstage again, the applause was louder than ever. It was clear now what the audience wanted and intended to have.

The next time, Cissie came out alone, and stood smiling at the people before her, and then she finally left, throwing a little kiss as her arm swept the sea of faces. But the applause kept on.

At last they returned together, she and the conductor, and this time he went to the front of the stage and raised his hand. Cissie sat down at the piano to the accompaniment of sweeping murmurs of satisfaction.

"Miss Lansing wishes me to tell you that she is deeply touched by your appreciation of her playing and would like to play for you two short encores. The first is one of Chopin's Etudes, the second is a very old lullaby 'Hush, My Babe.' Please do not applaud between the numbers."

He stepped back and Cissie waited until there was utter silence, then she began to play. No doubt many in the audience were familiar with the Chopin, but none had heard it played as it was now. For with an intimate poignancy they heard the cry of a lover's heart, the rise and fall of its changing moods.

When the bright, impetuous staccato movement began, it seemed to breathe happiness and fulfillment. But at last it died away into the first quiet sadness.

Cissie rested for a few moments and then began the lullaby, "Hush, My Babe."

Hardly discernible at first but growing more distinct was the rocking of the cradle and then the sound as of a woman's singing, for the clear, single notes came like the words of a song.

There was, indeed, a hush in the audience as the music

went on. It was gentle but richly melodious with the sounds of the voice and the cradle filling the short breaks between.

At last it was finished, except for the soft rocking of the cradle. This became more slow, more quiet, until it ceased altogether, and Cissie left the piano.

Then came the real ovation. For the audience rose and stood for a few moments in silence as though still under the spell of the music before the applause broke out. Cissie came forward, bowed, smiling, and then withdrew as the great curtain fell. The concert was over.

When the Bishop and Mrs. Lansing were at last in the car, driving again through the city streets, he spoke.

"I can't trust myself to speak of Cissie and the music, but I do have a surprise for you. As I was getting my car, I saw Julian a little way down, getting into his."

"Oh, then he really did come!"

"Evidently, and what is more, remained until the end. I'm glad he stayed for that lullaby. It was the most tender thing I've ever heard."

"Do you suppose he will talk to you now about the concert?"

"I doubt it. And after what you've told me I don't think I should bring the matter up."

"It's so strange about them, Larry. Here is Cissie with men begging her to marry them since she was in her teens, such fine men, too. She has never been interested, at least not for long. And now she is quite evidently all stirred up emotionally over Julian, Bishop Armstrong, the most unlikely person! And he must feel so about her since he is planning not to see her ... Do you think he's just a confirmed celibate?"

"That could be. We've never discussed it. I could shake him for daring to make Cissie unhappy. Has she any one special admirer now?"

"Yes. A young—not too young—doctor, chief surgeon at the hospital. He's been dating her as furiously as she will permit, and he has everything: good looks, wonderful profession, fine family, and charm. I've met him often now and I've asked Cissie what she intends to do. She always says she isn't sure. I suppose it's the chemistry that's lacking. I believe when two people fall in love, the chemistry of each reaches out to the other and they coalesce. That's it!"

"Ah," said the Bishop, "now we come to Emerson. I still read his poems though I think few people do. Listen to these lines:

95

> *"As garment draws the garment's hem,*
> *Men their fortunes bring with them.*

> *"Nor less, the eternal poles*
> *Of tendency, distribute souls."*

"The eternal poles of tendency," Mrs. Lansing repeated. "I like that as applied to Cissie and Julian, don't you?"

"Yes, but just now I would like to talk about the concert itself."

When the Bishop reached the Old Rectory at last he found the house still, and only the lights in his study and bedroom burning. Julian had evidently retired, and he would be glad to do the same, except that he would have dearly liked first to pour out the vehement comments upon the evening's music which still lay in his mind. Perhaps there might be a chance at breakfast.

It came almost at once, and from Julian himself.

"Well," he began, "I went to the concert as I told you I might . . . I sat in the back and heard it all. It was amazing—marvelous, I would say. I was really dumbfounded. And it only confirmed my opinion which I have often voiced . . . With a talent almost amounting to genius, like hers, it is wicked to give it up and go to carrying bedpans."

"Julian, it's unfair of you to sum up her nursing that way."

"A bit too simplistic?" he said, and smiled. "It was at least symbolic. When I think of the way she can control the mood of a thousand people, by her music, I am shocked that she doesn't continue to make a career of it."

"Did you hear the last number of her encore? 'Hush, My Babe'?"

"Certainly."

"Are you not intuitive enough, then, to know that there is a third career she would choose above the others?"

A slight color rose in Julian's face.

"I think we've discussed the concert enough perhaps. I have a busy day ahead and then the meeting tonight. You haven't forgotten about it?"

"Indeed I have not. My thoughts will be with you. I feel sure something will come out of it to clarify the matter."

"I've prayed it may. I talked to Vail yesterday, and there seems to be no new evidence, only the most un-Christian repetition of the old, among the church members. A decision must be made soon. I'd rather take a flogging than go there tonight."

"You probably would, but hard things come up and have to be met. You will do it bravely and be guided right, I'm sure."

"I wish I could be so confident. I think I should leave by six-fifteen tonight. They set the meeting at eight for my convenience. Do you mind early dinner for once? I'll tell Mrs. Morgan as I go out."

All that day Julian had difficulty controlling his thoughts, a new and distressing experience for him. His will had always been strong. While not considering himself master of his fate exactly, he had always felt himself to be a stern master of his mind. Now, as the day advanced and he wrote important letters, made telephone calls, some of them to far away places, and carried the holy Eucharist to an old friend dying in the hospital, there fluttered unrestrained fragments of last night's experience. Of Cissie, so slim and white and smiling on the platform, and snatches of her last number, which had made him clench his teeth to defy the moisture of his eyes.

At four o'clock he went home, doubly weary, and ate the early dinner mostly in silence. Once he spoke rather anxiously. "Of course, first of all I'm going because it's my duty to do so, but I have a curious desire to see what the two women involved look like. Is that too strange of me?"

"Certainly not. I hope you will look so carefully at them that you can describe them to me. I'm curious, too. I'll be reading until late, by the way, so when you get back, if you're not too tired and care to do so, I would be very much interested in hearing your report."

"Thanks. I imagine I'll be eager then to talk about it. And, meanwhile, I'll be glad of your prayers."

"You never need ask for them."

As Julian drove along the road that would bring him to Long Falls, he found his mind surprisingly clear as he thought of the meeting to come. How, for example, could the vestry dismiss Miss Dunbar? For her, it was an excellent job, and she, on her side, had given the church new and beautiful music. All agreed that she had put new life in the choir, making it a viable and vibrant organization. How could they ever go back to more prosaic fare?

And the Rector? In the face of the gossip and near slander, how could he go on preaching with his usual earnestness and appeal?

Could this meeting tonight possibly decide the future of these two and of the troubled parish itself? "God save us," he kept saying earnestly aloud as a kind of steady prayer.

When he reached the vestry room he found the other men already there, several of them speaking their relief that he was with them. "As though I had more wisdom than they," he thought somewhat bitterly. Mr. Vail, as chairman, said the guests were to be there at eight and he thought he had heard the outside door open. In a few minutes the three entered the room.

After pleasant greetings and the introduction of Miss Dunbar and the Rector's wife to the Bishop, they all sat down, the men facing the guests in the three chairs set for them. As Mr. Vail made a few opening remarks, Julian looked at the women. There was no doubt that Miss Dunbar was *pretty*, and every feature, every smile, every glance from her eyes seemed to enhance this. Whether much lay behind the prettiness was a question. Most men would not bother about this as he enjoyed the sight and felt the immediate charm. The wife of the Rector was different. Only perhaps in the late forties, but with a sort of stable serenity. She had a lovely smile when she was introduced, and Julian felt a husband could watch that face for years without feeling satiety.

"And so," Mr. Vail was saying, "we felt it would be more fair to you and to us if you would tell us in your own words what really happened in those incidents which have been most talked about. Would you, Miss Dunbar, speak of why the Rector sat with you on the organ bench while you practiced?"

"I certainly will," she said, brightly. "I've been studying some very difficult new music. It annoyed me to have to stop to turn the pages. So, since I knew Mr. Bell reads music, I asked him if he would be willing to sit beside me and do this."

"Turn the music?"

"Yes."

"It was noticed by people who came in that his arm seemed to be around your back."

"It was along the organ bench," she said shortly.

"Yes. Thank you, Miss Dunbar. Have you anything to add to this, Mr. Bell?"

"Just a little. Miss Dunbar has given you the facts. I might point out that I was very flattered when she asked me to do this. And I enjoyed doing it—for she plays, as you know, so brilliantly—until I heard some of this malicious gossip. I wish to speak of my position. I am nearsighted. I had to sit as near to the music as possible, but I had to be careful not to let my feet touch the wooden keys. You can picture this was not too steady a position. So I kept one arm on the back of the organ bench. That is all."

"Thank you, Rector. We would like to take up with you now a rather questionable eisode in which I, myself, saw you. It has to do with the night you and Miss Dunbar were driving over a lonely road at almost two o'clock in the morning. Would you be kind enough to tell us everything pertaining to that night?"

"I will be glad to do so. In retrospect, I feel that I should have gone that next morning to you, Mr. Vail, and told you all, but something stopped me. It may have been my pride or a bit of stubbornness, but I thought even though the circumstances looked odd, you might have trusted me. If you had stopped your car and come over to me and said, 'What on earth are you doing here at this hour?' you would have known the whole story then and we could have had a laugh and gone on.

"But now the story from the beginning. Some weeks ago Miss Dunbar received word that she was to receive a citation for her work as organist and choirmaster. She was very thrilled and so was I. The citation was to be given at a dinner on the tenth of October at the music center and they hoped, of course, that she would be there. I said I would see that she was.

"I talked it over with my wife and she said she would love to go to that dinner and why not decide that we would take Miss Dunbar. It was so arranged. We were to leave at five that Friday afternoon, for it was a long drive, as you know, to the city.

"All was well until Friday morning, when my wife was hit by a migraine headache. You probably know how devastating they are. She does not have them often but occasionally when she is excited over some coming event. She did not give up entirely until four o'clock, and then she could no longer stand up, the pain was so great. I called Miss Dunbar at once and told her to invite one of her friends to go with us. If one failed, to keep on asking others. At four-thirty she called to say she had asked three people and not one could go. I then called one woman myself whom you would all know and she would gladly have gone on the short notice but a birthday party was on foot. So I picked up Miss Dunbar and we left."

99

He drew a long breath and continued. "The affair was very pleasant. Two other clergymen had come with their organists and we had a good talk. After the dinner and the citations I thought we could leave, but then the program was announced and went on until eleven-thirty. Even then there was much handshaking and talking, and we left a little after midnight. On the way home I realized that in the upset as we left I had forgotten to fill the car up as I had intended to do. So when we came to a little gas station I was glad. We both got out and we stood there looking at a view of the moon above a field. It was then Miss Dunbar caught my hand. I believe now I have a right to say this. I did not draw it away for I was almost unaware that we were joined in this way. My thoughts were upon something else entirely. You may not believe me, but I was thinking of my wife. I was, indeed, praying that the terrible pain might ease and that she would be better when I got home. It was at this point you passed us, Mr. Vail. This is all I have to say."

The chairman seemed less assured than he had been. He looked embarrassed.

"Miss Dunbar," he said, "there is just one small matter we would like you to clear up for us. You have lately begun to play the piano at early dusk, sitting in the large bay window of your parlor. You always dress in white with a soft light behind you. Is there some significance in this?"

"I can't see why I should answer that. Surely I should be able to play my own piano in my own apartment without criticism. I will tell you this much. I have music pupils and at every lesson they each ask me to play for them. I told them I would be playing at my home and they could come and listen at the window."

"You are doing this just for the children?"

"Anyone who passes is welcome to listen."

Mr. Vail cleared his throat. "I believe then, this will conclude the special matters we all had in mind and . . ."

"Mr. Vail," the Rector broke in, "if there are no further questions may I be allowed to speak of another matter?"

"Certainly."

The Rector stood. "I believe I feel more at home on my feet," he said, "and this is important. Away back, six months ago, I had a letter from the Senior Warden of St. Paul's Church in Buffington. He said one of the vestry had been visiting here and attended church. He had liked the sermon and had been impressed with what he heard of general parish work. Their own Rector, whom they love, is very old and wants to retire as soon as a new one can be found to please the Parish. Would I come to see them if a time was set?

"I replied that I was very happy in my parish work here and at the moment felt I should prefer to stay. In two more months the unpleasant rumors about me had begun here. As they persisted and grew, I heard from the Warden again and this time went to see the church. I was very much pleased, and they were very cordial. I told them all the circumstances here and they were sympathetic, especially the old Rector, who, it seems, had known something of this kind in his early priesthood. They were all delighted with my wife. So now to sum it all up, even if you could decide that there was a clean slate against me, I am afraid I could never again feel the same happy confidence in you and my parishioners. I have been bitterly hurt and my wife has been hurt and humiliated. This will be hard to forget, although I will try. So, I have accepted a call to St. Paul's Church in Buffington and will leave here on January first."

He sat down. There was a momentary hush and then a cry. It came wildly from Miss Dunbar.

"No! No! You can't go! You can't leave! I couldn't *stay* if you were gone! Surely, surely you know how I feel! I would do anything . . . I would go anywhere . . . You must think of . . ."

Julian rose in the stunned silence, almost without volition. His voice broke in, calm but positive.

"I'm sure we have all been stirred emotionally this evening and at this point I think the meeting should close. I know I speak for the vestry, the Wardens, and, certainly, for myself when I thank you, our guests, for coming tonight at our invitation and in cooperating so kindly. Our warmest good wishes will be with you all. Will you rise for a benediction?"

Julian spoke it quietly, tenderly, and after it the three left without a word.

The other men looked at each other as though still stunned, and Mr. Vail come over to Julian and caught his arm.

"I can never begin to thank you for what you just did. After the Rector's news and that girl's hysterical cries I felt numb. I couldn't have taken over then if it had been to save my life. But you did what had to be done at once, and did it so kindly and so well. So, our deepest gratitude to you. Perhaps now we can all sit down and hear your opinion as to what we should do next."

The men settled into their chairs with apparent relief, though their faces were still strained.

"I think now," Julian said, "that your way will be easy. There will be no big decision to make such as we all feared, I'm sure, when we came. The good Lord has taken care of that. You will want to see Mr. Bell as soon as possible to wish him well in his new parish and to commend him warmly for the good work he has done here. And if you should feel there should be a fine party for him and his wife later on, I would guess that nothing would bring the women's two factions together better than planning for that . . . And if you should feel there should be an apology . . ."

"There will be mine," Mr. Vail said, quickly. "When I heard him tell about that night, or morning, on the road, his eyes looking into ours so straight and honest, I was ashamed of my part in it. But," he added with some spirit, "the thing did look pretty bad on the face of it!"

Everyone laughed, which was a blessed relief from the tension that had held them.

Julian went on. "As to Miss Dunbar, the way is easy for you there, also. She, by her own admission, would not want to stay after the Rector has gone. You can, perhaps, tell her how much pleasure she has brought to the church, but if she wishes to leave you will do all you can to assist her. As a matter of fact, during her unseemly confession I actually felt a trace of pity for her. I had never seen her until tonight and she seemed to me much younger than I had expected. She certainly feels in love, and, if this is the first time, it may cut deep. If you can put aside the thought that it was because of her that all the sad trouble came you may be able to treat her kindly as she also prepares to go. And that, gentlemen, is all that I could suggest, except for this comment: I feel that Mr. Bell is doing the right thing to resign. It is exactly what I should do if I were in his place. If I can render any service to you as you seek a new Rector, I will be most happy to do so."

He started for the drive home with a warm feeling in his heart. The men he had just left had been more than kind in their thanks. He knew himself that it was good he had been there this night. But that poor little lovesick, unrestrained Miss Dunbar. She still seemed to him a pitiable object. With her wonderful prettiness she probably felt she could ensnare any man and she had chosen the Rector. Julian drew a long breath and found himself speaking aloud as he went on through the dark. "Love is a sad thing," he said, "and self-control must be my watchword."

It was pleasant to gave Bishop Ware all the news, discussing it as they went along. At the end the Bishop said, "I've made a little discovery about you, Julian."

"What?"

"Well, it has always seemed to me you were pretty harsh in judging those you felt were culprits. You remember your attitude toward Will Babcock when he was living with his true wife before they could be legally married? Well, in regard to this little siren who made all the trouble, you've been rather surprisingly sympathetic."

"Come now, Bishop, are you trying to tell me that for a heart of stone I've been given a heart of flesh, as the Scripture puts it?"

"Not quite that," Bishop Ware said calmly while his eyes twinkled. "But maybe I mean a little of each. I'm trying to pay you a compliment, if you will accept it. I like what seems in you a little kinder, softer attitude toward the erring human race."

"I admire kind-hearted people but preserve me from the soft-hearted. They are likely to be spineless. I'm glad anything about me pleases you though I can't feel any change in myself. Thank you, anyway."

So the big incident of the Long Falls church was closed as far as the Diocese was concerned.

7

It was the next morning that Bishop Ware received a reply to the one of his inquiring letters from which he most hoped for some help. It was from an old friend, another retired Bishop like himself:

Dear Ware,

No letter could be a more pleasant surprise than one from you. It brought back memories of meetings when we were both more active. I'm not able to do anything but sit on the sidelines now. I have arthritis, which brings the habit of having a knee give way at embarrassing times.

But to get to your question about prison ministry. I have not a great deal to offer, but must tell you a story given me when I first came to this Diocese. It seems old Bishop White, the first Bishop of Pennsylvania, was anxious to preach to the prisoners at the old Walnut Street Jail but was refused by the Warden. He went over his head to the Sheriff of Philadelphia, who granted permission. When the Bishop reached the jail on the day appointed he found the prisoners all herded in the Yard, where a pulpit had been constructed. Beside it stood a cannon full of grapeshot, with a guard next to it holding a big torch ready to fire at a moment's notice—hardly a situation conducive to the comfortable preaching of the Gospel. However, the story goes that the Bishop went right on with his sermon.

This general type of tension, I fear, does continue somewhat to the present day. That is, the admission of any Christian ministry to a prison depends on the attitude and the will of the Warden. There are so many different kinds of prisons and, therefore, of wardens that one can't generalize. One of our clergy got permission to speak to the men at a meal time. My main advice is start with the Warden but don't give up too soon. You're good to be thinking about the whole matter.

I have a wonderful story that is happening right now. A man serving a life sentence for murder came under the care of one of our clergy and, finally, became completely changed. He was, at last, made a Deacon of the Episcopal Church. He is what they call a "Trusty," living outside the prison walls in a camp for others like him. He is now studying for the Priesthood, and acting as "resident" chaplain to the other inmates. Isn't that a story? Almost too strange to be believed, but it's all true. An encouragement to all who would like to do prison ministry.

My prayers will certainly be with you, my good old friend, as you think of undertaking this.

As ever,

Bishop Ware read the letter over twice. It gave him real encouragement. That last story, inconceivable, but true, was thrilling! As Cissie had pointed out, there was the large jail, just a mile and a half behind the city. Easy to reach if all else was possible. He suddenly wondered if any of the clergy had visited it. A good thing to find out, he decided, and went to the telephone at once.

It took all day, but by night he had reached the ministers of a Presbyterian, a Methodist, and a Roman Catholic church and found there had been no thought of prison ministry.

The Bishop's lips were set tight when these calls were over. But the next morning he sat down again at the telephone. He began with the Warden, which was a more difficult matter. After having been put off by various aides, assistants, and officers until nearly two o'clock, the man himself answered. His voice was quick.

"Yes . . . (as though reading from a paper), Bishop W-Ware, could you state your business with me briefly?"

"I can," said the Bishop, who had decided just what he would say. "I would like permission to visit the prisoner called Big Tom, in his cell quite soon."

"We consider him a dangerous person. I might give you permission to speak with him behind the glass with an officer near."

"Thank you. If it were possible, I would rather see him in his cell. I'm not in the least afraid. You see, I was with him in the hospital when his wife died. I believe you know Dr. Lindsay. He would speak for me."

The Warden's voice changed somewhat. "Ah, Bishop, this alters the matter. We will give you every consideration possible. Would you come tomorrow at three o'clock? That is the hour the men begin to get restless. Big Tom may like to have a visitor."

"I will be there, Warden, and many thanks."

"Come first to my office. I want to meet you. And then an officer will take you to the cell."

When Bishop Ware told the plan to Julian that evening the latter had a shock of surprise.

"To think of you going right headlong into this thing without saying a word! And being successful, too, in getting past Cerberus by phone at least. It's amazing. After you visit Big Tom, then do you expect to go back? I can't quite understand your plan."

"I haven't talked to you much about that, Julian, for I am

105

still not sure how it will work out. I've been quite interested in what is called 'prison ministry.' If I can get inside regularly after this first time, I will do what I can to bring a bit of light to a few of the men there. That's all my story."

Julian was grave. "I honor you, Bishop, for trying to do this thing. You could so easily sit quietly with your books and do nothing. I have a feeling this idea is going to develop into a real service. Those poor devils in the jail, I'm sure, need as much Christian hope as they can get and you are ideally suited to give it to them. I hope you will give me full reports as you go on. I'm interested."

He stopped, smiling whimsically. "This all comes as a blessing to me, for I believe just now I need a new line of thought."

Bishop Ware wiped his eyes. To have Julian show actual interest in his "dream" was so surprising that he was deeply moved. He had expected only disapproval, backed up by logic. Now if anything really worked out as he hoped, he could talk it all over with Julian, which would be of enormous help.

The next afternoon he set out with a fast beating heart for his first visit to the prison. He was not exactly scared, but he was nervous.

When he reached the prison, he felt a slight shudder. It was an old building, built of red brick, and darkly forbidding. The Bishop had a sudden intense desire to go back the way he had come. Instead, he parked the car and went forward to one of the uniformed men who stood at intervals in front of the prison. He gave his name and asked the way to the Warden's office. "The Superintendent," the officer corrected. "He lives in the Front House. I'll send someone to conduct you."

A grave young man appeared and walked with him for what seemed quite a distance before stopping. "This is the Front House," he said. "I'll let you into the hall and you'll find the Superintendent's door marked."

"He is expecting me," the Bishop said.

"Well, in that case I'll take you to him."

In a short time the young guide was knocking at the Superintendent's door and when a harsh "Come in" came, he announced, "Bishop Ware, sir," and left.

The Bishop stood still in a room like any business office. The Warden, as it still seemed easier to call him, sat quietly for a few moments at his desk, looking keenly at his guest with an air of surprise. Then he rose to his feet and said, "Sit down, Bishop. I must say I was startled to see such a big man.

For some reason I always thought Men of God were of smaller size. Well, now what's all this about Big Tom? I'll be obliged if you will tell me."

"You remember you gave him Compassionate Leave to go to see his sick wife?"

"Yes. How did he behave when he got to the hospital?"

"I wish I could describe it to you," Bishop Ware said, "but I'll tell you as well as I can."

When he had finished the Warden looked at him strangely.

"I can hardly believe that Big Tom has a soft side to him. He's been an ornery enough devil all the time he's been here."

"What was his crime?"

"Oh, vicious assault, attempted murder, something like that. He's been here before for the same thing, and the Judge is getting testy. He says if Big Tom comes up again for the same, he'll call it *murder* and be done with it."

"Does he want to kill somebody?"

"No, that's the point. He just doesn't know his own strength. So when he gets roaring mad at a man he lets fly at him with those great arms and fists and next thing the fellow is in the hospital and they don't know for a day whether he'll live or die. You see the problem? So far the various victims have lived, but it was touch and go with the last one. So you can understand why the Judge is irate. It all shows we know very little about what goes on inside these men; however, that's not our main business."

"But that is mine," the Bishop said quickly. "My business through the years has been what you might call the care of souls. I must not look upon the outside of men, but rather the inside of the heart. Since I've gone this far I think I'll take courage and tell you the plan in my mind, if you have time to listen a little longer."

"All right. Go ahead."

"What I wanted most of all was to see Big Tom. I know his heart is very sad. I hope I can bring him a little comfort. And if I do, if he should ask me to come again, I wonder if you would allow one other man—a friend of his perhaps, to come into his cell so that I would be speaking to two instead of one. Would you?"

The Warden gave a little dry laugh. "I have to have sharp wits in this job, Bishop, so I knew at once what was in your mind. You would like to become a chaplain for this prison. Isn't that right?"

"Yes, but so far it is only a sort of dream. However, I have learned that in many large jails and penitentiaries they do have chaplains."

"I know they do. I've never even considered the matter here, for no clergyman has so far presented the idea to me until now you have done. I certainly would never think of it for I'm not a religious man myself."

Bishop Ware smiled. "I've known so many men who have said the same thing, and I have always found they do have religion, though it may not be the organized kind."

"You mean a man can be religious and never darken a church door?"

"I think that could be quite possible. Religion is a matter between a man and his God."

"Well, that's a new one to me. I'll think about it. But now, this 'dream' of yours. If Big Tom wants you to come back, I'll get an officer to sound Tom out as to what man he likes best, then see if he is a quiet, well-behaved prisoner, and if *this* is *so*, I'll allow him to join Tom the next time you come. But I can't go any further than that."

Bishop Ware rose. "You have been more than kind and I thank you. I've taken up too much of your time, I fear, and I think I should be going to Big Tom."

"I've been interested in the conversation," the Warden said. "I expect to be in the office here all afternoon, if you would care to stop on your way out. I would like to hear how you got on. The officer who will escort you is a good one. His name is Henry and is what the prisoners call a 'white hat.' "

Henry certainly was a big man and was armed, the Bishop could see. The man had a nice face, however, above his gray uniform, and smiled as though it was not an unusual expression.

As the Bishop remembered that journey from the Superintendent's office to Big Tom's cell, it seemed to him to have been made up of great steel doors, or gates, as Henry called them, through which he had to pass and then wait some time on the other side. He remembered waiting while the movement of men's feet passed and died away, as the prisoners came from work, from exercise in the Yard, or even a late mess.

Bits of the journey kept returning to him afterward. He had once glimpsed the library and had asked if it was much used.

"Not too much," Henry had answered. "You see it's only

them on good behavior that gets to go and some officers are pretty free with their demerits. I use 'em, too, of course, but sometimes I give a guy a break."

At long last the Bishop found himself in a wide corridor with cells on either side. stacked one above the other. Each had iron bars across the front so the prisoners could look out if they wished to see what went on in the corridor. He could feel the eyes looking down. They seemed scornful, to him, perhaps because of his collar.

Suddenly there came over the Bishop a feeling of sheer panic, like terror itself. Here he was with five great steel doors locked behind him. He was as much incarcerated as these men in the cells. What if there should be a *riot*? What if there should be a *fire*? But something within him rose to check the fright. He went quietly on, listening to Henry's low voice.

"We're comin' close to Big Tom's cell. You can hear him pacin' back and forth. He does that every day, like the old lions in the zoo."

Then he spoke again. "I want to tell you, Bishop, that I'll be right outside the door. If there's any trouble, I can hear the least sound. I've a key, of course, and I'll be right with you."

"Don't worry about me. You know I've seen Big Tom already. I'm not at all afraid."

"Well, good luck, sir. We're here."

The key turned, the door opened. Henry said. "Hello, Tom, I've brought you a visitor." Then the Bishop stepped in, the door shut and the key turned once more. Tom stared at the Bishop as though he were seeing a dream made flesh. Then he sprang toward his guest and caught his arms in a grip that made the Bishop catch his breath to keep from wincing.

"Ain't you the man what spoke to me when the policemen was walking me out to the elevator *that day?*"

"Yes, I am, Tom, and I'm so very glad to see you again. How have you been?"

Big Tom's arms slipped down until his hands clasped those of his guest.

"Would you give me yoh name?"

"I am Bishop Ware."

"You mean you a big man in yoh Church?"

"I don't feel big, but it is an honor to have that title."

"Not too many folks got it."

"Not *too* many, perhaps."

"Then you gottah be proud, Bishop. Come in! Come in! Set

109

down. I wisht I had a soft chair for you, but this ain't no settin' room, as you can see. Set here an' put yoh books on the table. I'm lucky to have two chairs. Lots just got one. I got a question to ask you, Bishop. Did you send them flowers for Baby an' for me, too?"

"I guess that would be true, but I'll tell you how it came about. There is a lovely young nurse, a friend of mine, who took care of your wife and grew very fond of her while she was in the hospital. *That day* after she had died and you had left, I asked her to order some lovely flowers for you 'Baby.' She told me later on that a great many came. She had made a beautiful big arrangement to go with your wife, and what was left over Dr. Lindsay brought to you. So that's how it was."

"You ain't heard the end though. When the doctor brought the box in I never looked at it. You see I been jest about burnt up with sorrow seemed like. An' there was a heavy stone inside me. I couldn't give out one tear. I kep' thinkin' if I could jest cry I might be kep' from bein' burnt up.

"Then the doctor took off the lid an' the tissy paper an' sort of loosen' up the flowers an' laid the box in my arms. An' all at once I jest clear busted open inside, an' the tears come down like a river runnin'. That fella what brung you here brung me water to put them in an' that night I slep' like a baby. I could smell the pink ones. I used to bring two or three to Baby when I had a little change. I know what flowers cost and I know they cost a lot."

"I'm glad they helped," said the Bishop.

"Then the police stopped a minute for you to speak to me *that day,* you said Baby was safe with the Good Shepherd. I didn't get that jest right. Could you say it again? It sounded nice, some way."

"Do you know anything about the Bible, Tom?"

"Not much. You see, I couldn't buy Pastor when Baby always goin' to church. She was brung up to go, but I was jest fetched up the easy way, I guess. But I thought Pastor was a phony. I went to church once when we first come and I couldn't stand him for nothin'. Look at the way you dress, Bishop. Nice gray suit an' nothin' like a preacher but yoh collar turned 'round. That Pastor come into the pulpit with a red tie on an' a swaller-tail coat an' he pranced roun' on the platform with the tail switchin' as proud as though he was God himself. An' he yelled an' pounded an' told about hellfire. An' then . . ."

Big Tom paused for breath.

"An' now he sez, 'We'll pass the *plates*.' And he watched like a hawk to see if they was any didn't put nothin' in; then he preached at *them*. He was only after the dough. Anyone with half one eye could see that. I wish we could have found another Pastor who preached the Bible. I don't know nothin' much 'bout it. But I did like the sound of the thing about the Good Shepherd."

"I'll recite it for you," the Bishop said:

> *"The Lord is my Shepherd;*
> *I shall not want.*
> *He maketh me to lie down in green pastures,*
> *He leadeth me beside the still waters.*
> *He restoreth my soul."*

Tom sat spellbound until the end.

> *"Yea, though I walk through the*
> *valley of the shadow of Death,*
> *I will fear no evil, for thou art with me.*
> *They rod and thy staff they comfort me.*
> *Thou preparest a table before me*
> *in the presence of mine enemies:*
> *Thou anointest my head with oil;*
> *My cup runneth over.*
> *Surely goodness and mercy shall*
> *follow me all the days of my life:*
> *And I shall dwell in the house of*
> *   the Lord forever."*

Bishop Ware broke the silence. "Is that not beautiful, Tom?" His voice came choked. "If only Baby coulda knowed that!"

"But she did better than just *know* it; she experienced it. Don't you see? She went through the valley of the shadow of death with no fear, but with a smile on her face. And, surely, we know she must now dwell in the House of the Lord."

"That mean the Church?"

"No, no. That means heaven, however we think of it."

"An' you're sure she'd be there?"

"I'm sure she is."

"She was so good, an' she went to hear this damned Pastor just as regular an' she had a little part of a Bible she always readin'."

"The New Testament, probably."

"That was it. I never paid it no mind, the readin' of it. Baby was so kind to me. Times I got in trouble she said nary a word. She knowed I lost my job but I didn't send her word I was in jail. I'll tell you how it was, Bishop. I was workin' good an' happy bein' able to save a little. I liked the place 'ceptin' for one son of a bitch. You'd a-said the same about him. He was mean an' he had a dirty mouth. I kep' out of his way but once he come over an' started on me. Was I married? I said, 'Sure.' An' then he started on women. He said every woman was a you-know-what underneath the paint. An' I shet my teeth tight an' never said nothin'. An' it made him mad as hell. An' he sez, 'Don't look so smart as if your wife was better 'n all the other . . .' He meant women, but he used the dirty word. You know what? He sez, 'Your wife mebbe is as bad. . . .' An' that's when I hauled off an' give him a good one on the kisser an' he went down like a shot, an' the damned fool hit his head on a stone."

"And then what happened?"

"Oh, they all come runnin' an' the police, too. What made it so bad for me, they asked who had saw the fight an' there hadn't been no fight. One policeman was good. He come past me an' he sez, 'I know the dirty bastard.' He sez, 'Good riddance if he never gets awake, but no good for you. Keep your mouth shut,' he sez. 'Don't say nothin'.' "

"Did you go before the Judge?"

"Oh sure, when they knowed the varmint was goin' to live. An' I decided I'd tell the Judge everything, but he didn't give me no chance. 'I don't care what the man said. You all but killed him.' An' then he give me time."

"How long?"

"Six months, an' I never got to see Baby again till *that day*."

"I'm so grieved for you, Tom. I wish I could bring you some comfort."

"But you brung it already, Bishop, with that Shepherd piece. An' jest to see you an' . . . have a chance to talk to you. Can you come back soon, Bishop?"

"If you want me, I'll be glad to come next week. Have you a good friend here?"

"I got one. Lucy Roberts. He's a good guy an' never talks dirty. We chew the fat a little when we got a few minutes mebbe comin' back from mess."

"Do you think he might like to talk with us?"

"I'll bet he would. He gets awful discouraged. He's been here so long an' he's got more time to do yet."

"Do you think he can read?"

"Why sure he can. He went through high school even. He's smart."

"I brought along two little books. Each is filled with some of the songs David made up. I put a mark in the place where the Shepherd piece is that I repeated to you. I'll give you one and I'll let Henry give the other one to Lucy. Then he will know it's all right. Here is yours Tom." He handed him the thin black book.

Tom felt the smooth leather tenderly. "For me?" he said.

"Like a present, Tom, because I like you. Can you read a little?"

"Little bit, mebbe. Baby always tryin' to learn me. I'll *work* awful hard to make it out. An' thank you *very* much, Bishop. I feel good you comin' back."

The Bishop knew it was now coming close to the time he and Henry had agreed upon for him to leave. He opened Tom's little book and pointed to the Twenty-third Psalm, reading the first line aloud.

"This will give you something to work at now. And there is Henry's knock, which means I must go. I've enjoyed my visit with you, Tom, and I'll hope to see you next week."

They were together now at the door as the key turned.

"Good-bye, Bishop. Don't forget next week."

"I won't. Keep well till I see you!" The key turned again.

As they walked back along the corridor Henry spoke again very low. "They're all looking down at you. They knew you were with Big Tom and they've been waiting for the fireworks."

"How did they know?"

"They always know everything. I've been here now eight years and I can't answer that yet. It's a mystery. But information flows from tier to tier, block to block, cell to cell somehow. You see now why they are watching you. They can't understand how any man can go into Big Tom's cell unarmed . . ."

"How would they know I was unarmed? I have big pockets."

Henry laughed softly. "At one glance those men could tell, and they were sure there would be some heavy sounds. Now they're disappointed, and amazed. So, they will have some more news to transmit."

As the Bishop heard door after heavy door close now behind him and realized he was on the way to freedom, a great relaxed feeling came into his chest. When he spoke of the Warden's suggestion that he stop on his way back however, Henry shook his head.

"He's got a man in there with him now on some business and the Super don't like to be interrupted. Suppose I just give him your message and you can see him again next week. I heard you say you were comin' back."

"That's fine," said the Bishop. "Please tell the Superintendent that I had a quiet and most pleasant visit with Big Tom, and he invited me to come back next week. His special friend is Lucy . . ."

"Roberts," prompted the officer.

The Bishop took the slim little book out and gave it to Henry. "Could you ask him if it would be all right for you to give this to Lucy and say I brought one for Big Tom, and one for him? And now, my thanks to you for your help and courtesy. If you'll steer me toward the outside door, I'll get my car and be on my way home."

Henry said his good-bye with feeling. "You see, Bishop, I was a little like the prisoners an' I was surprised. I'd really been a little worried. I doubt if even the Superintendent, himself, would have cared to go unarmed into Big Tom's cell the way we all felt about him before this. So you see, you are a bit of a miracle to us."

As the Bishop drove on toward the city, on the road beside the quiet, flowing river, he pondered on his guide's last remark. If there had been any miracle, it had not been of his making. Its inception had occurred in the tears of the young black wife that had touched the tender heart of the nurse, Cissie, and the stout sympathy of Dr. Lindsay. From then on the impossible had come true. The incredible had happened. Up until this very afternoon, when the rows of men pent in their little cells had kept quiet to listen for Big Tom's outburst of fury, as they had heard it before.

Suddenly he knew he should try to forget the prisoners. His heavy head ached as he thought of them. Perhaps they sometimes trembled with that panic, that terror that had struck him as he heard the five great doors locked behind him. Surely they must.

He would stop thinking about it. He would think only of the lovely September afternoon. He would draw deep breaths of the free air. He would fill his very soul with freedom. Tonight he would talk over all his experience with Julian. That would do him good.

There was only one thing he must not tell him, and that was how woefully tired he was.

8

There followed then a most curious freak of weather. A summer heat fell upon the October days. The month had begun pleasantly warm, but this was different. This made people open their doors and windows, sit in shady places, and caused the cooks to serve aspics and iced tea. Julian came in on Thursday afternoon looking hot and tired.

"Whew!" he said. "What a day! But it's had a nice surprise in it. You remember Mrs. James Loomis?"

"Oh, very well. Delightful woman!"

"Well, she's been very good to me and called today to say she's still in her summer house at the shore and the beach is full of bathers. They say the ocean is perfect. Couldn't I come down for the weekend and have a swim?"

"Wonderful!" said the Bishop.

"I think so, too. I've been feeling a bit seedy of late, and a swim is just what I need to 'fettle me,' as Mrs. Morgan would say. So, if I have your blessing, I think I'll drive down tomorrow evening. That way I can finish a few things in the office tomorrow and still have the whole Saturday there for swimming. I'm excited already. Perfect, isn't it?"

"Absolutely. I'm glad you're going to have this chance to relax."

"And what about you, Bishop? As you know, I was interested in every word you told me about your first prison experience, but I did think you seemed very tired. And no wonder! I would have been myself and I'm a younger man. Do try to rest over this weekend so you will be refreshed before you make your second visit. O.K.?"

"O.K.," agreed the Bishop.

When Julian got in his car Friday evening he felt an almost boyish elation. The weather was still hot with all predictions for a continuance of the same over the weekend.

He had not known until he was on his way how desperately he had craved a swim. He smiled a bit sardonically as he thought of his college awards. He knew he couldn't come up to those records now; even so, he was a pretty good swimmer. He practiced often over at the big university pool, but this was mere exercise. Nothing, *nothing* else like movement in the open sea.

He considered his visit as a whole. He was very fond of Mrs. Loomis, a delightful old lady of eighty who mothered him in gentle ways, giving his heart a certain balm it had long missed. She, in turn, was watched over by black Julia, who must have been only a decade younger than her mistress. She called him "Bishop dear" and patted his shoulder each time she passed him. And what an easy, comfortable household! There were no bells or too-evident clocks. Mrs. Loomis breakfasted at nine in bed. This left her guest free to get up when he wished and go out for the early morning swim which he loved. There was never any hurry, so he always swam and rested, watching the dancing morning light on the waves, then leisurely swam again. And when at last he reached the bathhouse behind the kitchen, he would always find warm towels and a glass of orange juice waiting for him.

But the thing that made his mouth begin to water even while he dressed himself for the day was the thought of breakfast. And *what* a breakfast! Mrs. Morgan would have paled at the very idea. Cereal *with cream*, and then delicate bacon and plenty of it with eggs, hot muffins, and ambrosial coffee. Julia hovered over him as he ate slowly. "Would Bishop dear have a touch more of the scrambled egg?" When she whisked them up there was mostly air in them. "Or a hot muffin, mebbe? They're not so tasty when the heat goes out of them."

The rest of the day always fell into pleasant lines. Conversation was easy, for Mrs. Loomis had a keen mind. Also for diversion she worked a crossword puzzle every day and introduced Julian to them for the first time. He was greatly intrigued for he had never done one before and he was sure Bishop Ware had not.

He thought of all this now as he drove along and it amused him. He was certainly looking forward to purely secular pleasures. And yet, not entirely. He and Mrs. Loomis had often struck a serious note in their conversations. And oh, the power and the glory of the great ocean, as he became a part of it, was a sermon in itself.

For his really long swim, Julian had always chosen the afternoon, about three o'clock or a little after. On this Saturday, he sat with his hostess for a while on the porch overlooking the ocean before he "breasted the wave," as he told her. But, at last, he ran down the beach walk, waving back to her, and was soon beyond the breakers, swimming steadily in the more quiet water, down parallel with the beach itself.

Time always stopped when he was in the sea. He felt released from its boundaries. He was at one only with the limitless ocean and the blue sky above. Having now settled into the stroke he liked best, he moved on almost without effort, so quickly did his muscles adjust to the new demands upon them. He would keep on quite a distance, he thought, then when he felt himself tiring, he would get out at once and walk back over the sand. He was no boy now and it would be foolish to overdo it, but oh, the joy of it as he felt it now.

At last he decided it was time to stop. He turned his face reluctantly toward shore and was soon splashing through the breakers and out upon the sand. Here he shook his head, ran his fingers through his hair and slapped his side to help some of the water run off. He noticed a girl had just stepped out of the waves and was standing quite near but with her back to him. As she bent this way and that shaking her hair in the sun and pressing some of the water from her suit, Julian was thinking, "What a lovely figure!"

Suddenly she turned and he uttered a startled word. "Cissie!" he cried, and in a few steps was close to her, holding out his hands.

She put her own in them. "But, Julian, this is incredible! For us to come up out of the water together. How did you ever get here?"

"It's very simple. A dear old lady asked me down for a couple of days to have a swim. So here I am."

"But I never knew you liked to swim, Julian."

He went right on. "But now, for you. How do you come to be here?"

"Same as you. A dear lady invited me down for a weekend. She is Mrs. Steele. You can see her just up there on the beach. That's her son beside her, Dr. Robert Steele, the chief surgeon at the hospital."

"I see," said Julian in a tone completely lacking in warmth.

"Come on up and see them. Mrs. Steele will be so pleased to meet you. She has often mentioned you. Maybe . . . I mean— it might be better if you didn't keep holding my hands."

He dropped them at once. "I—I beg your pardon. I was so startled I forgot I was—was still holding them."

"Let's go up to them. That's their big green umbrella. We can sit on towels while we drip dry. I think I'm still a little nervous over the shock of our meeting."

"I'm sure I am," he said.

When they had covered the little stretch of sand between them and the big green umbrella Cissie spoke gaily. "Look, Mrs. Steele, what I brought out of the sea for you! A real, live Bishop. Bishop Armstrong, this is my hostess, Mrs. Steele, and her son, Dr. Robert."

Mrs. Steele's warm welcome left no doubt of her pleasure. "You see, Bishop, I've heard you speak more than once, and only hope I may have that chance again. But I'm sure I've spoken of this to Cissie and she has never said a word about being a friend of yours!"

Julian laughed. "Oh, I think she's a little ashamed of it or at least embarrassed. You can see how odd it would sound for her to refer to 'my friend, the Bishop.' Yes, I think she's a little ashamed of the friendship."

Cissie came back quickly. "That's ridiculous! I'm proud of you, Julian, of course, but when I have nothing of any consequence to say about you, I just say nothing."

"There it is," Julian said smiling. "A woman always has the last word."

"Not always," Cissie said softly. But the others caught it.

Dr. Steele began at once to talk about what had gone on in the water. "You're a strong swimmer, Bishop. Does this date back to college days?"

"Yes, it does. I worked like anything to win an award. That seemed to me then like the golden apple itself."

"Did you go out for any other sport?"

"Yes, one, the running broad jump. I don't suppose now I could make it over a ditch. How about you?"

"Oh, I was a runner. But it's hard now with my profession to get any practice. I'm like you, though. I won an award once, a little mock-silver figure, and that was the greatest thrill I've ever had. And yet, it was really such a small matter, as we look back."

"No," Mrs. Steele broke in. "It was no small matter for either of you to win an award for your college. Don't you see that the qualities that made you win then have been part of you all through the years, and always will be. Now you are both at the top of your professions. But oh, don't belittle those sweet young triumphs. They encouraged you both to go on and work for bigger things. Don't you think this is true, Cissie?"

"But I know it is, from my own experience. Away back when I was fifteen the music academy I was attending gave a contest for teen-agers. There was to be a prize but no one knew what. I thought I hadn't a chance, but I signed up anyway. We each had to play one piece and beyond belief—I won. I thought my heart would jump out of my breast and the tears were coming so fast, the dear lady in charge had to mop me up a bit before I could go forward to receive the prize."

"What was it?" Julian asked.

"It was twelve lessons with Mr. Helveg, known then as the finest piano teacher in the country. And that, my friends, was the biggest thrill I have ever had in all my life. I mean the biggest musical one," she added with downcast eyes.

Mrs. Steele began to chat then with Julian, and Robert looked at Cissie with a curious intentness, which, when it rested upon the Bishop, was not an affable one.

Mrs. Steele suddenly included them all in her conversation. "I've just had a lovely thought. Certainly for us at least. Do you think, Bishop, that Mrs. Loomis has planned anything for you both this evening?"

"I'm quite sure she has not. We are usually very quiet after dinner."

"You see," Mrs. Steele continued, "my son and I are expecting a great treat. Cissie has promised to play for us. I wonder if you and Mrs. Loomis could join us? I've met her and would love to see her again."

Cissie was thinking, "Oh, he will never accept. He was fairly caught just now but he won't come this evening."

Then she heard him say with animation, "Thank you, Mrs. Steele. For myself I will accept with the greatest pleasure. And I have a feeling Mrs. Loomis will, too. Of course, if she doesn't feel able, I will not leave her. But I'll hope. Now I must be off. I always walk or jog a little and it takes some time from here."

"You're not swimming back?" the doctor said, with a slight edge to his tone.

"No, I never try that. I don't want to overdo it. Are you going to walk a bit with me, Cissie?"

She rose slowly. "Just to steer you in the right direction," she said with a smile. "No more than that."

"I'm her religious mentor," the Bishop explained, "so I have to inquire into the state of her conscience."

"And I'll go in and call Mrs. Loomis right away," Mrs. Steele said, laughing and waving to them, as they set off. But the doctor still looked grim.

As the two walked slowly along the sand, there was no sound for minutes except that of the rolling breakers. Then Cissie spoke.

"Why did you ask me to come with you now?"

"Do you want me to tell you the truth?"

"I am accustomed to getting it from you." Her tone held a trace of bitterness.

"I'll tell you then. I didn't like the way that doctor looked at you."

"*Looked* at me! What on earth do you mean?"

"He looked at you with lust in his eyes."

"Oh, Julian, what a horrid thing to say about him. If there ever was a perfect gentleman in every way, it is Bob. And he's so kind, so unselfish . . ."

"And he loves you?"

"I'm sure he does. And he has asked me to marry him."

"And what do you intend to do?" His voice was strained.

"I'm trying to decide. He's so much of all I've hoped for in a husband, but still . . ."

"You told me once if you ever loved a man *enough* to marry him . . . Is there not quite *enough* yet?"

"Perhaps that's it."

"Then if you are sure of that, you should put him out of his misery."

"I wonder that you of all people should presume to advise me."

Julian looked at the ocean and did not answer.

"I think I should go back now," Cissie said. She reached out her hand.

He took it in his. "Yes, I think you should. Good-bye."

"Good-bye then," she echoed slowly. And again, "Good-bye."

Julian had been correct in his surmise that his hostess would accept the invitation for the evening. In fact, when he got home she had already done so. She was so pleased over Mrs. Steele's call, for she had met her once or twice and liked her. Then she was truly excited over the prospect of hearing Miss Lansing play. She had been terribly disappointed over missing her concert but a favorite grandson had dropped in from California just for one night, and, of course, wanted to talk all evening about himself as young folks do, and although the sacrifice was well worth it she was glad she would have this pleasure tonight.

Dinner was later than the accustomed hour because of Julian's call on the beach, but all was forgiven by Julia, who later on had the joy of seeing them off with many admonitions.

As the car started Mrs. Loomis began to giggle. "I feel like my granddaughter when she's here and goes out on a date. Julia stands right there until they start and says to Liz, 'Now mind you be good, now,' and to the young man, 'Mind you keep both hands on that there wheel an' don't you go too fast.' And, me? Listen to what she told me, 'Mind you don't sit in no draft now an' catch more of them brown kittens.' That's what she calls bronchitis. 'An' don't talk too much.' She blames me for that and maybe she's right. She's incomparable."

Julian laughed. "Wait till you hear her compliment to me. That's the best one. I was down before you were ready and she surveyed me from all sides. She admired my jacket and slacks to match and pinched the material between her thumb and finger. Then she stood off and eyed me up and down and pronounced, 'Now you look like a real *man*.' I thought it was my collar that impressed her before but now she's raised me up a notch."

They were still delighting in the personality of Julia when they reached the Steele house. It looked much larger from the back than it had from the beach, and inside they were ushered into a very long living room. In spite of its size it was distinctly homelike. A small grand piano stood at one end, opposite the ocean-looking windows, now shuttered. There were many easy chairs and two couches, with tables of various sizes here and there whereon lay books, taken no doubt from the tall shelves on the same wall as the piano, with deep drawers below perhaps for music. All of this, the excellent furniture, the easy casual look that excluded all formality, Julian had a chance to feel and admire before their hostess came in to greet them.

"I wanted to meet you at the door," she said. "I'm so very glad to see you both. I was a little delayed for I waited to help Cissie. I had made her lie down after dinner for she seemed so very tired, Bishop, after her little walk with you. Perhaps she went too far. This is so very kind of you, Mrs. Loomis, to come and share your guest with us."

"It is so good of you to invite us. You and I have met before

121

on our shopping tours, and I've been eager to know you better, but a succession of grandchildren has kept me busy. The Bishop here is no trouble when he comes so I count him one of the family. It will be wonderful to hear Miss Lansing play. I missed her concert. What a remarkable girl! You mentioned your son when you talked with me. Is he still here?"

"Yes, indeed. I think he was resting a little while after dinner, too. He had a hard day. He's a surgeon and had two very difficult operations, so he's been telephoning the hospital for several reports. The last news was good. Perhaps he's just waiting now to escort Cissie down. Oh, here they come."

When they entered the room, Julian saw at once that Cissie was wearing the pink dress she had worn on the fateful night when they had dined together. From its soft ruffle her face rose like a flower.

The introductions to Mrs. Loomis were soon over and Cissie sat down near the piano with Dr. Bob taking the seat beside her. "Good," thought Julian. "In that position he can't watch her face as she plays."

"We hear you have had a difficult day," Mrs. Loomis went on speaking. "Could you tell us what the problem was?"

The doctor hesitated and Cissie spoke. "I would like to tell you about the miracle he performed. The operation was necessary to save the life of a woman but the problem was that she was six months' pregnant. The other surgeon who consulted with Bob said it would be impossible to save the child. But he thought otherwise, and with his marvelous skill he did it. This wonderful thing! The woman and her husband had been waiting and praying a long time for a child. You knew this, Bob, didn't you?"

"Yes, I did, but that didn't sway my opinion in the least about the operation. I knew what ought to be done and went ahead against other opinions."

"You took a chance then?" the Bishop asked.

"In a sense. But it was very small compared to what was at stake. I felt no hesitation."

Mrs. Steele laughed. "Oh, he really thinks well of himself. I'll tell you the best story about him. Two years ago, I had to go to the hospital and before I went I tried to pin Bob down as to who would be my surgeon. 'Is he really good?' I said. 'The very best,' he told me. And when I said, 'Well, who is he then?' he said. 'Me. Did you think I'd allow anyone else?' "

"And did he?" asked the Bishop.

"Absolutely. And I felt so at peace to have him. But they told me the talk in the scrubbing room was quite salty. The other doctors to scare him told about a surgeon who operated on his wife and fainted dead away in the middle of it. The nurses said Bob told them to shut up and get out from under foot, the two now were not needed, that if he fainted they could bring him out piece by piece. At all events I had a beautiful time. And I feel now we should forget Bob's profession and turn to the Bishop's while we have some crème de menthe. Will you bring in the tray, Bob, and we'll set it here in the middle of the group where we can all reach it."

Bob poured the pretty liquid into small glasses and Julian rose to help pass them.

"I should explain that this is the only thing Cissie drinks before playing. Tell us why, Cissie, as you told me."

"It's because a liqueur just warms my throat and chest but never disturbs my fingers. Any sort of cocktail affects me all over by making me want to *dance!* Sort of bewitches me, you know."

"Have you ever told her how you danced at the Opera Ball in Vienna?"

"I'm sure I haven't."

"Oh, do tell us then," Mrs. Steele begged.

"Please do. It sounds so romantic." Mrs. Loomis looked up with eager eyes.

"I was on a brief European tour with my manager and his wife, Mr. and Mrs. La Contes. He had arranged for us to spend two nights in Vienna for the opera, but when we got there we found the second night was the great Opera Ball. During intermission, the night of the opera itself, he managed for me to meet some important people, one of whom was a prince of Bavaria. He was very handsome, tall and dark with a blaze of medals and ribbons down his coat. Almost at once he asked if he might escort me to the Ball and I was so delighted I'm afraid I showed it most shamefully, but he didn't seem to mind . . ."

"I'll wager he didn't," Mrs. Loomis said.

"But he was very correct. He talked to Mr. La Contes and gave him all his credentials and convinced him of his being of royal blood, as it were, so the Ball was arranged for. The La Contes drove me over for it, and the prince met me there. This, too, was correct for a young lady. The La Contes found seats as my chaperones and then the prince and I *danced!*"

Cissie's eyes began to shine. "I could not have imagined

123

such complete physical delight. He said he had been taught by his old dancing master that dancing was a manly art and should be treated seriously. He had learned it well, and there was such grace in every move he made that I felt I was dancing for the first time. At least it had never been like this before. You must try to picture how it was—dancing in that lovely place to the Vienna orchestra playing Strauss waltzes."

"With a prince as a partner," supplied Mrs. Steele.

"Oh, yes, but it wasn't his rank that impressed me: it was his wonderful dancing. At midnight we went to speak to the La Contes and then we found a quiet spot where we could sit down and talk for a bit, but soon we went back to dancing and danced until dawn. Even then I didn't feel tired. So that's the story of Cinderella at the Ball."

Cissie sat back in her chair as though finished with her narrative, but the two older women begged for more details.

"Now Cissie, my dear, you can't expect us, after your description of such an evening, to believe the handsome prince just said 'So long, nice to have met you,' as his good-bye." Mrs. Steele chided the storyteller laughingly.

"You set the stage so beautifully for romance. When the night ended I was expecting the prince to say he would follow you to America!"

The Bishop watching carefully saw Cissie give a little start at the words and then experience a flush which rose in her throat and swept over her face. It had evidently come from extreme embarrassment. He went at once to her relief.

"I'm not so sure," he began. "I believe it is more artistic to allow the prince and his beautiful maiden to end the wonderful night with the coming of dawn. That would be the normal time he would return her to her chaperones who would then take charge of her. But aside from this I am getting eager to hear the music. I'm not allowed to keep Mrs. Loomis out late."

"You are quite right, Bishop. Cissie, I hope, will excuse our last remarks. We saw the picture of the Ball so clearly we felt it was like a storybook, and we wanted to turn the last page. This was very rude of us, but surely a tribute to the storyteller, herself. Let's have a little more crème de menthe and then whenever you feel like it, Cissie, we will be honored to have you play for us." Mrs. Steele's calm voice took away all the tension. Fresh glasses were brought, and the two men saw they were circulated as before.

124

Then, when conversation dwindled to a silence, Cissie went to the piano bench.

"Has anyone a favorite?" she asked the little group.

"I'll ask for my favorite Chopin," Mrs. Steele said. "You know the one."

"I would like to hear the one you played when you and your grandmother took dinner with us. It's very quiet."

"Yes, it's just called 'Pastorale.' Well, that will start me off."

Before beginning Cissie made a little bow toward her hostess. "Julian, you and Mrs. Loomis don't know that Mrs. Steele is herself an accomplished pianist. I feel honored that she asks me to play here in her home." She smiled, turned to the piano, and began.

Julian, now able to watch the side of her face, was thinking that she looked pale. Perhaps it was by contrast from that deep blush of embarrassment she had experienced. But to him, it seemed more as though she were faint.

She finished the Chopin and began on the Pastorale. He watched her fingers going more and more slowly. Suddenly he saw her sway and he was instantly beside her, had caught her as she was about to fall. Bob was only a few seconds behind him. From the position of his chair he had not seen her growing pallor.

"Put her on the couch," he said quickly now to Julian. "My bag is in the hall."

The Bishop gathered her closer. She felt so light, so soft and lifeless. A little wave of fragrance came from her hair. Her face still frightened him. It was so white. He knew that what he wanted most of all was to go on standing there, holding her . . .

He laid her gently down as Dr. Bob came up and began to check her heart. He was skillful and quick, and soon stood up, smiling. "Just a simple faint," he said. "The only thing wrong with her is she's hungry. You know she hardly ate a thing for dinner, Mother. Could you fix her a little cream soup while she's getting awake, and plenty of bread and *butter*. I'll see she eats it if I have to feed her."

It was only a few minutes until Cissie's eyes suddenly opened and she viewed the scene with Bob standing close by, his stethoscope still around his neck, and Julian only a little farther away with such anxious lines on his face as she had never seen there before.

"Good Heavens!" she cried. "What did I do to make you all

125

stand around like that. Did I faint? Oh, Bob, surely you didn't have to *carry* me over here?"

"No, I didn't. The Bishop here got ahead of me. He could see you better where he was sitting, so he took a leap and caught you before you fell."

Cissie's voice was broken in distress. "Oh, Julian, to think I should have brought this on you!"

But he had regained his poise. "Nonsense! I simply fancy myself as the knight going to the rescue of the fair lady. I think I can feel the plumes in my helmet tickling my neck even now."

Bob laughed. "I'm only the poor old herb doctor wandering in the forest and finding Maid Marian almost starved to death. And," he went on, changing his tone, "that is just what is the matter with you, young lady—you are hungry. You must be properly repentant for making all this trouble because you ate only three bites of dinner."

"That's ridiculous, Bob."

"True, just the same. You can sit up now and be ready for a little tray my mother is arranging for you. And when you eat what's on it, *all* of it, mind you, I can guarantee your head won't feel swimming anymore."

"I'm too ashamed to look at any of you. Why"—she said as though the idea had just come—"I was playing—your piece, Julian."

Dr. Steele had just taken the tray from his mother. "You can sit up now and finish your supper and then you can go back and finish your piece."

"Oh, Bob," his mother said, "she should not play again."

"Why not? She'll be fine after she eats what you've brought. Then she will feel better to finish her program."

The doctor was right. Cissie rose at last, refreshed, the color back in her cheeks and her eyes bright.

"I'll start just where I left off," she said. "I think it was at the green field and the nibbling flocks."

"I think that's right," Julian added.

When she had finished the Pastorale she turned to smile at her listeners.

"From now on perhaps you will allow me to choose the numbers. I have tried to vary them."

So the music went on, drawing upon the height and depth of emotion as it proceeded. At last the doctor spoke quietly, "I think we should make the next number the closing one," he said.

126

With a glance at him, she nodded, and then used a brief part of a practice piece allowing her hands to chase each other furiously up and down the keyboard in a brilliance of technique but little melody. She sat quiet for a few moments and then began softly upon the "Lullaby" she had used at her concert.

Mrs. Loomis and the Bishop left as soon as the thanks and good-byes could be said, for the hour had grown late now. She told Cissie with tears what the music had meant to her, and begged her to take plenty of rest.

"I'll put her right to bed now," Mrs. Steele said, "and she can rest all day. Bob is driving her up tomorrow afternoon."

The Bishop held Cissie's hand in both of his. "Thank you," he said, and then stumbled over the rest. "Be sure—I mean, please don't. Be careful of your health," he ended.

The two men shook hands and said the proper things. But underneath there was an air of constraint.

When, later on, he and Mrs. Loomis were back at her house, he helped her up to her bedroom and received her good-night kiss. As he did so, he realized again how tenderly it seemed to fall upon his heart, motherless now these many years. Yes, this would be the significantly best place for him to wrestle with those thoughts and desires that lay upon his soul.

The evening was gently mild, even warm. The wind was still. He decided to go down to the porch, taking out with him his small copy of *The Imitation,* which he always carried if he went for only a night's stay, rather than a larger Prayer Book. With the porch light he could either read or be in darkness, as he chose.

When he settled there at last, he felt more alone than he could recall ever feeling before. There was only the slow, steady rote of the waves to enter the enveloping darkness. There was nothing now between him and his soul, which he must have the courage to consider.

As he thought deeply upon what had happened to him during the last hours of the day he felt crushed, drowned in shame. That very afternoon, as upon a pinnacle of spiritual pride, he had dared to criticize another man for unbridled thoughts while stating his own superiority. Oh, the unspeakable arrogance of that, even if it had been his only sin! His head dropped in his hands as he considered it.

But still darker guilt was to follow. He must acknowledge it honestly. Only a few hours later, when he had held the girl

127

in his arms, close to his heart, every nerve of him had felt hot with desire. And he a Bishop! Trying to live under a holy vow!

He sat on in the darkness, feeling he had tasted the depths of shame.

At last he picked up the small book and turned on the light. There was a marker at a page which had signs of many readings. The words came to Julian as if spoken aloud.

> There is therefore no holiness if
> Thou, Lord, withdraw Thy hand.
> No chastity is secure if Thou leave
> off to protect it.

> Oh how humbly and meanly should I
> think of myself!

What a natural yearning cry of humility. But from many readings of the words of the priest-author, he was struck now again by the general pattern of the chapters. After those in which the spirit seemed to sink in abject contrition, there came the rise, as on Angel's pinions, of the light of a high and holy hope. Could it possibly be so with him?

He sat on, leafing through the pages, reading here and there, stopping once with something like a smile on his lips. The verse marked was the one in which the author reminded God with some slight acerbity, of the weakness of his creation.

> Even stars fell from heaven!
> What then can I presume who am
> but dust?

"A comfortable thought for the fallible race of men," Julian mused. "And certainly for me."

He still sat quietly thinking. This was indeed the time for penitence and humility, which he felt in his very being. And yet, and yet . . . There was that holy hope, which, breaking all bonds, flooded the soul with light, as the author pointed out. While he waited as though for a sign, a feeling of peace took slow possession of him.

He was no longer fighting a battle. Instead, he would walk steadily in his chosen way, doing his best in the place to which it had pleased God to call him.

He closed the book, rose, and put out the light. He stood

then, alone with the ocean and the depths of air. He spoke into the darkness the very words he had found and committed to memory the night years ago when Bishop Ware had given him the little book.

> *"Give all for all; seek nothing,*
> *Ask back nothing; abide purely*
> *And with a firm confidence in Me*
> *And I shall possess thee;*
> *Thou shalt be free in heart,*
> *And darkness shall not tread thee down."*

When Julian reached the Old Rectory late Sunday afternoon, Bishop Ware cried out with pleasure as he saw him.

"Well, well, Julian! I'm surely glad to see you. You must have needed that swim though, for you look like a new man now."

"Oh, a splash or two always sets me up. And I always enjoy being with Mrs. Loomis and her housekeeper, Julia. She says I was named for her! She fusses over me, calls me 'Bishop dear' and pats my shoulder. I'm always afraid she's going to kiss me."

"I must say you look right kissable to me at the moment if any lady so desired. Apropos of ladies in general, Mrs. Lansing told me that Cissie was at the shore this weekend, too. You couldn't have seen her, I suppose?"

"Very much so. We both stepped out of the Atlantic at the same moment. How's that for timing?"

"Incredible. Tell me some more."

"She took me up the beach to meet her hostess and her son. Then this Mrs. Steele invited Mrs. Loomis and me to her home that evening to hear Cissie play. So it was very pleasant all around."

"It must have been. Was the young man a doctor?"

"Chief surgeon, Cissie said."

"That's the one, then. Mrs. Lansing said he was giving her a mad rush and she can't make up her mind. Poor child! Her grandmother is worried about her. Did you like the man?"

"Oh, yes. We only spoke very casually. But he was pleasant."

"How did you think Cissie looked?"

"Tired! I told you that hospital work was too hard for her."

"Her trouble may be an uneasy mind. She's trying to decide whether to marry this man or not. You don't think it's settled then?"

"I can't be sure, naturally, but as of yesterday evening I don't think it was."

"And at all events," the Bishop came back happily, "I'm glad to see you looking so well."

"Oh, I feel like work, just plain diocesan work with no big problems. But where has your mind been traveling these last days?"

"I've been pondering over what to say when I go back to the prison. As I told you, the theme of the Good Shepherd seemed just right with the psalm to illustrate. But next time I will be having a new listener. I don't know whether to repeat what I said the last time or try something new."

"Well, you can't wear out the Twenty-third Psalm by two usings. Why don't you just go over again what you did on your first visit? You said Tom liked that very much and with the new man present he may have a little feeling of pride in being one jump ahead of the story."

"That, of course, would be easiest for me. I could then give them several subjects to choose from for the next meeting."

"Only don't wear yourself out over this, Bishop. You certainly looked tired after your last trip there."

"Nonsense!" said the Bishop stoutly. "This is something of real interest to me. If I get to feel I am doing some good, it will be a real bracer."

"Has Fenwick said anything to you about his Vespers?"

"Not lately. Why?"

"He was doing errands downtown last week and was near my office, so he dropped in. He is definitely going on with the Vespers. I told him it was a beautiful idea if he could get anyone to come to the services. But he has it all thought out."

"I'll wager he has," the Bishop said, smiling.

"He knows the score all too well. How the big part of the morning congregation rolls off afterward to their big homes in the suburbs. But he's planning for a city audience. Perhaps people who don't go to church anywhere. He thinks the music may attract them. It's going to be unusually lovely, he says.

"No sermonettes?"

"Ten-minute talks by 'people who really have something to say,' to quote him. I couldn't refuse him for he is so bound up in the thing. You may be sure he has you down, too. But is there anything in the world harder to do than a ten-minute talk that says something?"

"That's a tough one," the Bishop agreed, and then chuckled. "Do you remember the story about the old clergyman who

130

was asked by a young priest how long it took him to prepare a sermon? The older man said, 'If it's to be a ten-minute one, I would want two weeks; if a twenty-minute sermon I would take one week. And if there is no time limit, I could start right now.' "

Julian laughed. "That's good. I'd never heard it. But I'm really very interested in the Vespers plans. Fenwick may just have got hold of a great idea.

"He says also he is going to angle for the university students. He believes there are hundreds of young people in this city who have no religion at all and who think the church is an outgrown institution. Oh, he will be over soon, I know, and give you more details. I think I'll go now and write a note to Mrs. Loomis. I'm glad to be back home, Bishop. I hope this week will be a quiet one."

But it was not to be so. In the midst of his first morning's work a call had come to Julian. The man who spoke to him was agitated in the extreme. He was from the Mosely Episcopal Church and they needed his help as soon as possible. Could the Bishop see him that afternoon?

Julian pushed away a pile of letters and notations placed by the secretary in his easy reach.

"Of course," he said cordially. "When would you like to arrive here?"

"I could be there at two o'clock, if that would suit you. My name is Jack Hunter."

"Very good, Mr. Hunter. I will see you at two o'clock." Then he added, "You sound as though your voice was trembling. Are you able to drive with safety?"

"Oh, yes. I guess I was just a little nervous when it came right down to talking to you."

"Don't be," Julian said kindly. "I'm an easy man to talk to."

"So there goes my quiet day. I'll talk to this man here in the main office, Miss Lamb. Can you be comfortable in the smaller one?"

"Of course. You can maybe dictate a few answers to those top letters and I can type them while you're busy with your guest."

In the back of his mind Julian wondered about this guest. He pictured him as an older man, for there had come a break in his voice. What could have happened in the church? He hoped it was not another scandal—or bordering upon it. This would be, of course, one of the vestrymen who was coming. He drew a long sigh and began upon the letters.

131

When they were done he went downstairs to the main hall and spoke to the doorman.

"Hello, Mr. Mayer," he said. "I'm expecting a man to see me at two. I have a feeling he is elderly. If he seems a little weak or trembly, better send him up in the elevator. You can tell him the direction to take when he gets off. My name is on the door, as you know."

"I'll treat him nice, Bishop, that I will."

Julian hurried back up the stairs, straightened his desk, put on a clerical vest and fresh collar, and ate the lunch of sandwiches and tea that Miss Lamb always produced for him when she saw his day was becoming too crowded. Then at exactly a quarter to two he heard quick feet on the stairs.

So, the old gentleman spurned the elevator, then, Julian was thinking.

There was a knock on his door and he moved at once to open it, then stood, amazed, on the threshold. The caller who faced him was a big young man, only a year or two out of his teens perhaps, tall and handsome if his countenance had not been marred by bloodshot eyes and lines of deep anxiety.

Julian reached out his hand. "Do forgive me for staring at you, but you see I had expected a very much older man, a vestryman, in fact. I suppose you couldn't be that?"

Then the little laughter wrinkles around the boy's eyes came into full play. It seemed easy to guess the merriment lurking in them. "Vestryman!" he said. "Good heavens, no! I'm just the guy who stirred up all this trouble, and that's why I'm here."

"Come in! Come in!" Julian said eagerly. "At least it's good to meet an honest man. And that last sentence of yours strikes me as the most honest I've heard for some time, considering its frame of reference. Take this chair. I think you'll find it comfortable. I have a good many callers and feel I've an obligation to make their stay as pleasant as possible. I wonder, however, if I've made it *too* comfortable. The last man fell asleep in that chair while I was searching for a book in the other office."

"I wish that could happen to me," the boy said. "I haven't been sleeping too well lately."

At once Julian's face became grave. "Would you like to begin right away with your story?"

"Yes, I would. But if I tell you just as it is, you wouldn't be—be shocked?"

132

"I'm sure I wouldn't be," Julian said. "At this point, Jack, I believe I've heard everything."

The boy drew a long breath and began. "I know you've been in Mosely, for the people of our parish still talk about a speech you made there once in the church. They liked you. It's a small town and not much money in it. Many men work at their trades. Once a year when the members pledge what they will give to the church another year there is only one large donation. That comes from Mr. McPhail, who lives not too far from town on a big, rich farm. He has no children, so the church is his center of interest, especially his Sunday School class of boys. We were about twelve or thirteen when he first got us together. We all liked him. There was always a Christmas gift for us, and, oh, the parties out at the farm. He would invite the girls' class that corresponded to ours in age and then the fun grew; picnics in summer, corn roasts in the fall, and the big winter party at Christmas. Then Mr. McPhail and his hired man would drive into Mosely for us with the huge farm sled filled with hay and blankets, drawn by the two big workhorses with ropes of bells around them. There always seemed to be snow. Then the big tree in the farm sitting room and Mr. McPhail, his face just beaming, calling out, 'Merry Christmas, Girls! Merry Christmas to My Boys!'

"And this, now," Jack said, "could be called the prologue to the story."

9

Julian smiled at the young man. "I've been very much interested in what I've heard so far. You told it excellently. Are you in college?"

"Yes, sir. I've finished my second year."

"Good! And your major is English I would guess?"

"You're right."

"So was mine. It's a good choice no matter what you do

133

later on. Do you feel now like going on with your story at once?"

"Yes. I'll be relieved when it's finished. Well, our boys' class went on all through our teens. We liked Mr. McPhail, we loved the good times, and we enjoyed the old Bible stories. We questioned nothing. Then two years ago something momentous happened. A deep but rich vein of coal was discovered under one of Mr. McPhail's farm fields. We are only about twenty-five miles from the biggest 'works' in our end of the state so, of course, one of the operators there wanted to buy this coal. They thought it would be easy since the owner was an old farmer. But Mr. McPhail was smart. He got the best lawyers and then sat tight. He refused two offers, and then took one. He received two million in negotiables and signed a release to the whole vein of coal forever."

The Bishop gave an involuntary whistle.

"You can imagine what that news did to our little town! As to Mr. McPhail himself, all he thought of was how much good he could do as fast as possible at seventy-six. So," he continued, "that's how I got to Princeton. I was heading for a small college; he said it must be Princeton and he would make up the difference, but he wanted me to take a course in religion each year. I couldn't the first year as I had one course to make up, but I signed for the next one, which all the fellows said was wonderful. I took it and found it so. It was called 'The Miracle of the Earth.' "

The boy paused and said, "I'll try to tell it all quickly for I do want you to understand. The first day, the professor read the description of Creation as it's found in the Bible. He said he wanted us to feel the beauty of the language. Then he spoke of the beginning when the waters covered the earth. So they did, he said, and we yet after all the quintillions of years bear the mark that we all came out of that first great sea. He asked us if we had ever wondered why our tears are *salt*. Then week by week he went on explaining how the dry land appeared with the great upheavals of fire from the earth's center, and, at last, the way it is thought life started. We had two weeks on celestial bodies, and at the last we had the Garden of Eden story. I'm ashamed, Bishop, but I had never thought much about it before. I knew the story, but it didn't do anything to me. But when the professor read it aloud, as beautifully as he could, it became real to me, for I could feel what the writer was trying to explain to simple people who needed sort of a picture to make them understand some of the

134

great truths. When the course was over, every man went up to shake hands with the professor and tell him he had helped our minds to grow. I'm up now to the sad part, Bishop, but I have to tell it."

"I'm sorry it must be sad. All I've heard has been marvelous so far."

"While I was busy at college Mr. McPhail was busy at home. He had decided that the greatest gift he could give the church was a very large and beautiful parish house. You see, we had never had one of any kind, and the loss had always been felt. Now as the new one was described the parish was beside itself with delight, for there would be elegant space for every form of activity. The excitement was felt all through the town, for there was to be a large auditorium on the second floor where all sorts of entertainments could be held that were not possible before for lack of space.

"When I got home I was as excited as anybody. The foundations were all in then and the first uprights were put up. It was really going to be huge. I went to my class the first Sunday as usual and at first we all talked mostly about the new building. Then Mr. McPhail said since I had been taking a course in religion he felt it would be nice for me to tell some of the things I had learned. 'What was the name of the course?' he asked. 'The Miracle of the Earth,' I said. He was pleased at this. 'Ah, yes,' he said. 'The Creation. Just turn to the story in your Bibles, boys, Genesis, Chapter 1. We'll just go over this day-by-day account as the record describes it.'

"I began then to feel a little nervous. I said the professor had first read this chapter over aloud so we would feel the beauty of the language. And then he said that we must all realize that the word *day* as used here did not at all mean our twenty-four-hour day.

" 'What was that?' said Mr. McPhail.

"I said the professor told us we must not think of the 'day' spoken here as a twenty-four-hour one.

" 'And how must we think of it?' he asked sharply.

"I said the time might even have been a million years long.

" 'What you mean is that you were taught not to believe the Bible, that is the inspired word of God. You are denying your faith, that's what you are doing,' he fairly shouted this, and I was so scared and so angry I just shouted back, 'I'm not denying my faith. I'm just using my common sense. Any reasonable person knows this whole world from the tiniest clam at the seashore to the big Sequoia trees of the West with

135

all mankind in between was not created in one *week* of our time!' "

"Good for you!" the Bishop said.

"Thank you. But he went on then to question other boys in the class. One boy said he had wondered about it once when he was with a digging party and had learned the different times different layers of rock had been formed. The other boys said they'd never thought about it.

"Mr. McPhail was so upset," he went on, "he had a vestry meeting called after church that day and the devil of that was that they were about evenly divided between those who said they thought the church should stand by its belief in the inspired word of God as contained in the Scriptures and the others saying that everyone should keep quiet and let this little tempest in a teacup blow away. Let Jack Hunter believe what he wanted to. It wouldn't hurt anybody. Mr. McPhail said it mattered to him whether the beliefs of the church were *sound* or not. It might affect his decisions.

"He took some more samplings. One was from our bachelor Superintendent of Schools. He's very much liked and respected in Mosely. His housekeeper heard the conversation when Mr. McPhail came to talk to Mr. Hanford and she told it. Mr. McPhail asked him how he interpreted the word *day* in the piece of Scripture being discussed. He said he could hardly believe that God just pushed a magic button and all we see had come about in six days' time. He thought it all came very slowly, each stage developing from the one just before it. And Mr. McPhail had said, 'Oh, you're one of those people that think their grandparents were monkeys, are you?' And then Mr. Hanford said just as confidential as you please, 'Do you know that sometimes when I'm *shaving* I think I look just as if my great-grandfather *was* a monkey. Only I believe I parted from that line a long way back. But, as to your college professor, I think he's doing a good job.'

"Poor Mr. McPhail, I do really pity him. He's so thin and haggard now and looks so sad. I will only mention one more person he questioned. A friend of my mother's is the President of the Altar Guild, an important position. She said when he asked her, she told him she had never thought about it at all. She said she believed there was more important work to be done. And when he asked her about her husband, she felt duty-bound to tell him that when the verses about the days were being read once in church, her husband muttered, 'Must have been some long day!'

136

"This was I think about the end of Mr. McPhail's many interviews. They had covered three weeks. He asked the Rector if he might make an announcement the next Sunday and the Rector happily agreed, thinking it would be good news.

"When the time came, Mr. McPhail stood up in front and said he had been dumbfounded, first of all, to find out that one of our own young men had been taught at a large college that certain statements of the Bible could not be true.

" '*Now*,' he said, 'I know what that professor had been reading. It is called the *Higher Criticism*. I think it's pretty *low* myself, but the big professors and the big authors have that name for it.' He said he got such a shock over this college boy for his faith has been broken down. 'He no longer believes that every word of this inspired book is true.' (Here he held up the Bible.)

"He had felt so bad he was sick for several days. Then he knew what he must do. He must find out the way most of the members of the church felt about this. So he had talked to a great many people and to his shock and utter distress found that they felt there were some statements they couldn't believe now in our time, especially about Creation. 'But don't you see,' he kept saying, 'this is not a trivial matter? If you don't believe the miracles described in this chapter of Genesis, you will soon begin to doubt the one about Feeding the Five Thousand. And some might go on from this until they had no religion left at all.'

"I tell you, Bishop, my eyes were wet then, for the tears were on his face.

" 'So I come now to my decision,' he said, choking a little. 'Since so many parishioners do not believe this Holy Book is God's Inspired Word of Truth, I feel I cannot go on with the Parish House.'

"There was a sound, Bishop, as though everyone present had oooh-ed at the same moment.

"Then Mr. McPhail added, 'And please don't speak to me. For one reason, I couldn't bear it, and, for another, my decision will never be broken.'

"So there, Bishop Armstrong, is the story. You can imagine the tumult it has caused back in Mosely. Everyone blames me for not giving way to him at once. Maybe I should have."

"No. You had a right, even an obligation, to speak the truth, as you had learned it. But the problem is a tough one, and no mistake. Do you think Mr. McPhail would come down to see me if I made the invitation *very* special?"

"I've an idea he would feel sort of proud to be asked."

"Well, I'll certainly admit this needs thought and prayer if any problem ever did, but I'll try to give it everything I have in the way of reserves. As to you, however, I can say at once that you did exactly right. If you had agreed with Mr. McPhail, you would have been telling what you know is not true. You can't ever do that. So just have a good sleep tonight and have faith this will all clear up. Do you feel better now?"

"There's just one more thing." Jack again looked anxious.

"Mr. McPhail said if anyone doubted that account of the Creation, they might even begin to doubt a miracle like the Feeding of the Five Thousand. And that just hit me where I live. I've often doubted that. What will I do?"

Julian smiled at the boy's troubled face. "That's a favorite of mine. Let me tell you how it seems to me. The whole scene must have been beautiful. It was in the spring and the slopes of Batiha would be covered with grass. Below, the lake would be blue and dotted with little sail boats. It was sunset. The disciples, who were practical men, realized that it was past supper time and there was no place in this lovely spot to buy food. One of the men said, probably with a smile, 'I notice a lad here who has five little rolls and two small fishes. But they wouldn't go far in this crowd.' The boy could hear what he said and at once went to Jesus and offered his little lunch to him. Jesus evidently took it without surprise, asked the disciples to have the people sit down and then held up the food and blessed it with a supreme confidence. Now, right here I want you to think of something. Does it not seem incredible to you that out of all that great crowd there was only one person, a little boy, who had brought something to eat if they should stay past supper time? Do you think that sounds reasonable?"

"Why no, I don't," the boy said, his eyes fixed intently upon the Bishop.

"If then many people here and there had brought something to eat with them, what do you think happened when Jesus raised the little rolls and fish before them all and blessed them?"

Jack's eyes held a look of wonder. "Why, the ones who had some food might have shared with those who hadn't brought anything."

"That's the way it has always seemed to me. A wonderful lesson in unselfish sharing. And one verse that has helped

138

me in this: the *letter* killeth but the *spirit* giveth *life*. If you read the Bible only by the letter, you will have trouble; if you read it for the spiritual meaning, you'll find life on every page. How does the miracle seem to you now? For, of course, it *was* a miracle, no matter which way you look at it. And I think it was a greater miracle for the teaching and personality of Jesus to change the indifferent hearts of the crowd into unselfish ones than if He had used some supernatural power, which we could not understand, to multiply the little lunch into food enough for the multitude. How do you feel about it, now?"

"Bishop, I can't ever thank you—if I live to be a hundred. You've lifted two burdens from my heart. I'll still try to have faith about the parish house, and I'll always love to think of the miracle."

"Oh, yes. I hope I'll be asked to help dedicate the new building one day."

But as he drove back to the Old Rectory that late afternoon he did not feel so optimistic. This problem of a good but stubborn old man's archaic beliefs seemed, on the face of it, unsolvable. There was to him an almost ridiculous quality in it, as though by treating it seriously they were all being carried back to the early part of the century. But the fact could not be dodged that the problem was disrupting a church and bringing unhappiness to many people. One encouraging thought stood out to him. He would soon be able to pour the story into Bishop Ware's ear and have the benefit of his wisdom and sense of humor.

The weather, though now edging into October, was still mild with the rich fragrance of the last chrysanthemums and the first small fires of leaves. Julian found the Bishop in the midst of the last sunset light on the front porch. He looked up eagerly.

"Well, my son in the Lord, how was your quiet day?"

"Anything else but that," he said, dropping into the second big peacock chair. "It's a new problem and, if I may describe it in slang, I'd say it's a *lulu!*"

"Good heavens!" said the Bishop. "I never heard you use that word before. This *must* be bad.

"Take a comfortable chair, Julian. From the look on your face, this may be a long, hard session."

"I fear so, and I'll begin right now if you are ready."

He started the story with the coming of the boy, Jack Hunter, and continued with his clear eloquence to the end.

139

The Bishop sat, listening intently, once in a while giving an explosive comment but asking no questions.

"So, that's it, Bishop. And what, in heaven's name, do I do now?"

The Bishop sat silent for a few moments and then said, "I am amazed that this problem should have raised its head now. It belongs to fifty years ago. At that time there was a real spiritual battle fought between those who believed in what was called 'verbal inspiration'—that even every *word* of the Scriptures was directly inspired by God. We must have had members of both views though nothing at all like a conflict. But others waged regular battles and even the papers were full of it. My wife was interested. She said that while I was certainly not a Fundamentalist I was still a little bit critical of the Modernists for the way they presented their case. I was young then and about to go to my first General Convention. So she wrote a verse for me to take with me. I remember it. I never can forget a rhyme. I'll say it for you.

> *"Be kind unto the Modernist*
> *And do not pull his hair*
> *Nor bite, nor scratch his principles*
> *Nor trail him to his lair.*
>
> *"Be gentle to the Modernist*
> *And pat him on the head,*
> *For some fine day, far, far away*
> *When all of us are dead,*
>
> *"And all the noisy arguments*
> *Have passed as incidentals*
> *His liberal views so much abused*
> *May then be* Fundamentals."

"That's simply great!" Julian said. "And that's really the way it has all turned out over the fifty years, isn't it?"

"Pretty much. It was bound to do so. But here and there you will still find people who believe as this Mr. McPhail does. And I must get back to your first question. What can you do about this problem? I would first, of course, follow your plan to invite him to your office. If you can use some extra vestments, I would do so. He should be impressed by your position. Then I would tell him that in the Bible there is at least one definite reference to the way God looks upon

140

time. It is found in the Ninetieth Psalm: *'For a thousand years in Thy sight are but as yesterday when it is past or as a watch in the night.'* The watch was only a few hours. Show him how you could read the word *day* in the verses from Genesis as a thousand years, or even more, and you would be still quoting from God's own word. Give him a Bible, let him read it aloud for himself; talk about it. I think this will soften his stony decision."

"I'm ashamed that I didn't think of this verse myself. I was stunned by the situation and scared over what should be my part in it. As a Bishop I feel I've been pretty weak."

"Remember I've had a few more years than you have and met more curious problems. I have used the two verses I am giving you myself, only in different contexts."

"You mean you have still another suggestion?"

"One more. You might use this one to disprove that God inspired every word of the Scriptures. It is the most utterly cruel and bloodthirsty cry which ever came from the bitter heart of a slave. *'Happy shall he be who taketh your little ones and dasheth them against the stones.'* Try that on your Mr. McPhail and see if he can believe a just and loving God inspired *that!* I'll write it down and the place it occurs. This compares in savagery with our terrible modern wars."

The two men sat on talking until midnight of the strange human events in which any Bishop might be called to take part and also of what had happened to Bishop Ware that day—a letter from the Superintendent of the Prison.

"It was certainly a surprise. He said Tom had been quiet ever since my visit, and he was allowing his buddy in the next cell to join Tom at my next visit. This man had been a well-behaved prisoner but had to be watched as he had tried several times to take his own life. The Warden said he had been looking over some old records and found that a room next to the Library had been called the Chapel. Some years ago a minister had come and held meetings there when a few well-behaved prisoners were allowed to attend. After my next visit he would like to talk to me. That's something, isn't it?"

"Very encouraging. Only as I say . . ."

"Don't get too tired. I heard you the first time. What about yourself?"

"I can't wait for tomorrow to begin my own crusade! If I can carry it through sucessfully, I will feel a little more self-respect. But all the same, I'm so grateful to you."

141

Bishop Ware's next visit to the prison came before he had heard anything more about Julian's problem. As he entered, he realized he was not as nervous as before and glad to see Henry, the guard, waiting for him.

"Good morning, Bishop. Well, the men are all waiting to have another look at you. Big Tom has been as quiet as you please, even going to and_ from mess. They don't get it. 'Course he's been better since his wife died, but still he yelled plenty. It's O.K. about bringing young Roberts in with you. The Superintendent explained that to me. I'm to stand close outside the door and ring for help if I need it."

"I don't think you will. We'll be quiet," the Bishop said, smiling.

"O.K. then, if you're ready."

As door after door clanged behind them, the Bishop felt only a great interest in what he would find in Tom's cell and none of the sheer terror he had experienced before. Tom came toward him with a rush when the door was opened, and the Bishop grasped his hand warmly.

"I was scared for fear you wouldn't come," he said.

"But I told you I would."

"I know, but you might ha' been sick or somethin'. The Super is lettin' my buddy, Lucy Roberts, come in. He's a good guy but awful solemn, sort of. Mebbe hearin' you talk will brighten him up. Here he is!"

A tall, slender young man came in. He had light brown hair, deep-set gray eyes, and the saddest face the Bishop had ever seen. There was no return to the smile that had greeted him.

"Come on, now, Lucy, limber up a little! You're goin' to like what the Bishop here says."

Bishop Ware had reached out his hand cordially and the other put a limp one in it.

"May I know your first name?" he inquired.

The young man hesitated a moment. "It's Lucien," he said. "The guys here all call me *Lucy* and I hate it, but nothing matters much to me anymore."

"It's a good name, Lucien. I'll use it," said the Bishop. "I see you have the little book I left for you. Could you read it?"

"Could I read?" Lucien asked. "I graduated from high school with pretty good grades. I was even thinking of college before I got into trouble."

"I'm glad you got that good start on your education. That's fine. Would you read a little piece out of your book for us?

You see Tom didn't get as far in school as you did. I'll find the place for you."

In a few moments the Bishop handed his book back to him opened at the Twenty-third Psalm.

"Read that," he said. "It's meant for a song."

Lucien looked surprised but not exactly displeased. It was a long time since anyone had asked him for a favor. He began to read in a clear voice: "The Lord is my Shepherd." He read on slowly and with meaning until the last line: "And I shall dwell in the house of the Lord forever."

"That's like real poetry," he said. "It's like we had once in class."

"It *is* real poetry," the Bishop answered quickly. "It's a song. Tom, can you tell your friend something about David, the man who wrote it?"

"I sure can. He was some guy, Lucy. He didn't just sit around writin' poetry. His old man kept sheep an' the young fellah took care of them. An' I mean he *took care*. Onc't a bear come sneakin' round an' he killed it jest like *that!* He went to war, too, when it broke out an' come out a general, wouldn't you say, Bishop?"

"Yes, I think that would describe it."

"An' then, after the war he got himself elected king. What do you know about that, Lucy?"

"Some man, I'd say."

"Let's move our chairs now around the table. I see you've got a third one, Tom."

"That's from Henry. He's a good guy."

When they were seated more closely together, the Bishop said, "Now let us try to understand what David was attempting to say in this poem or song. Can either of you explain it?"

"Sure, I can," Tom said. "He means that God takes care of us the way David used to take care of the sheep."

"Very good, Tom. Does that explain it to you, Lucien?"

"Not much, it don't. I'm sure the Lord has never taken care of me. If he had, I wouldn't be here now."

"How do you make that out?"

"Because I was framed."

"Could you tell us about it?"

"I don't mind. It goes through my head all the time anyway, so I guess I might as well speak it right out."

"You may be sure we'll listen with sympathy."

"Well, you see it was like this. My father was dead and as soon as I was big enough I did everything I could to help my

143

mother. I—I loved her. When I was in high school I found jobs for after school. It was a pretty tight schedule, working hard at school all day and at my jobs after that. I began to long for a little fun."

"Damned if I blame you," Tom broke in. "Go ahead, Lucy."

"There were three big fellows who lived on up our street. They always passed, laughing or singing mebbe, as if they had a good time, and one night I asked if I could go with them. They took it very serious. The big one said, 'He may be just what we need tonight,' and another asked me if I could keep my mouth shut and do what I was told and I said I could. So I went along."

Lucien paused for breath. "I can finish this soon. We all went around several streets very quick and then they stopped opposite a little jewelry store. While we were watchin' we saw a man go in and speak to the old fellah who evidently owned the store. Then he bought what looked like a ring and he and the owner both laughed and looked pleased. Then the man came out and walked away. It was nearly nine o'clock, but I thought nothing of this for a good many little stores and shops around those streets kept open until nine. In a few minutes I felt my arms being grasped and the big boy said, 'Here's where we rush it, and don't you even cheep!'

"I thought the boys were going to buy a ring like the man had done so I never suspected anything wrong until we all got into the store very softly and then the big boy began to strip all the jewelry out of the window and slip some of it in my pocket. I know I kept saying, 'Hey! You can't do this! Get this out of my pocket,' and one of the boys pinched my ear until the blood came. He told me to shut up or I'd get worse. The old man looked out once and then went behind the high counter at the back and I was sure I heard him talking very low, like on a telephone. The others were so busy I guess they didn't notice. When he came out again, he walked right up to them and told them to put the jewelry they had taken back in the window. He had called the police and they were already on their way and would be there in a few minutes!

"The big boy caught him and shook him like a rat. His head once hit the sharp edge of the counter and then just wobbled as though his neck was broken. I went to him and caught his head to see if I could help him somehow. I was holding his head up against me and sort of slapping his face to try to bring him to when the police came. You can imagine what happened then."

144

"Don't leave anything out, Lucien, please. I would like to get the whole story."

"Of course the police took over. They said the old man was nearly dead and called the ambulance. When they took him away, I cried. It seemed so terrily sad when I thought how happy he had been just a short time before and his little shop was such a nice one. He must have enjoyed it and now . . . I was thinking more of him than myself until I heard the big boy telling his story. Then I began to shake all over. He was putting everything on me. I was the one who planned the *heist* and they had just gone along to see I didn't get into any big trouble. And look, he said, what I had done. Of course they took me to the station house and while they were questioning me, word came from the hospital that the old man had died. I think now you can tell what our danger was."

"But didn't you have a lawyer?" Bishop Ware asked quickly.

"Yes, my mother got one for me right away, and I'm sure he did his best, but no one could get away from the fact that I was in the store with the others when the murder was committed and there could never be any complete agreement about which story was true."

Lucien looked up over the bare, dreary cell. "I liked the lawyer but once in a while I wondered if he really, in his heart, believed me. Even to me, my story sounds a little fishy."

"Not to me," the Bishop said quietly. "I think it's perfectly credible. How much *time* do you have to serve?"

"I was only seventeen, you see, and the others were twenty-one, so the law gave me a break on that. I got ten years with the chance of parole in five. Only two more to go for that."

"How can you think, then, that you have not been under God's care?"

"Does my story sound like it?"

"We are free agents, you know. God can't prevent our mistakes. I suppose you know you made one."

"Sure I do. I didn't tell my mother what I was doing that night for I had a feeling it was wrong. I just went ahead anyway. And, here I am. But it's not just me, Bishop. It's my mother. She died six months ago, and I think this thing that happened to me just killed her. So, now, I have nothing to live for and I'd rather die if I can manage it."

"Don't say that. It makes you seem like a soldier running away from battle because he's afraid. We're sorry for him but we don't respect him very much. He's got to go ahead. And so

145

must you. You must remember that life is a gift of God, and if you take care of yourself you will probably have a good long one. What subject did you like best in school?"

Lucien started in surprise. It took him a moment to recover. Then he said, "Why—why—why, history. I was pretty good in that."

"Fine," said the Bishop. "I'll find out what history course a freshman in college would likely have, then I'll get you the books for that course and bring them to you next time I come. Would you like that?"

"I sure would. You see I never—I mean nobody ever knew about my liking history until you asked."

"I think now you are just ready to take God for a partner."

"How's that?"

"You can ask Him now to give you courage and a keen mind and a cheerful heart."

"You mean, *pray?*"

"Yes. Nothing's easier. Here are two old lines you can remember:

> " 'None have ever found Him wanting,
> Who have called on Him for aid.'

I wonder what we could think of for you, Tom, to make the time worthwhile?"

"Readin'. That's what I want to learn, Bishop. I'm not much good at it yet."

"You don't mind starting at the bottom?"

"Not a bit. Jest so I can work up."

"I'll do my best to find something for you."

"There's one thing else I want to tell you, Bishop. It's about an idea I had. I always like to sing an' one man once said I had a good voice. Lucy here has a nice one, too, sort of tenor. Now why couldn't we find out a couple more who'd like to sing an' let us try. Late afternoon is the worst time. The men are tired an' bored an' mad an' they jest raise the devil. They yell an' bang things around. Now if a few of us started to sing some old song everybody knows, they might all listen an' then a lot might join in the singin'. It sure couldn't do any harm an' jest might help. Whadda yuh say, Bishop?"

"Why, it sounds fine to me. I am invited to see the Warden before I go home. I could mention this to him."

"That's great. Why don't we give it a try now, Lucy? Do you know 'My Old Kentucky Home'?"

"Sure!"

"Well, start her up then. I'll fill in."

"I'd feel like a fool, singing in this place."

"Not at all," said the Bishop. "Let's see what we can do. I used to sing a lot myself. Start it, Lucien, and I'll try a sort of baritone with you."

Lucien began in a clear tenor voice. The Bishop blended in his second tones. But the real musical ear belonged to Tom. With never a mistake or a hesitation he provided what seemed like deep chords to the song of the other two. By the time they reached the chorus, they were all singing in full voice, sure of themselves.

When they stopped, there was a call across the corridor. "Sing 'er again."

"You see?" Tom said exultedly. "I knew it would work. We'd better just sing the same over an' then we can try a new one next." It was just as the three were feeling for the tone and their first notes together, that a new sound was heard. It came from the upper tier of cells and it was the one by which a rooster ushers in the dawn. In a matter of moments the sound was multiplied seven times.

Tom fell back as though he had been struck, a stream of profanity flowing freely from him. "That tears it. There's nothin' now we can do. Them damned shriekin' roosters will stop us. You'll see. An' the guards can't do a thing. Look how well we was doin'. The guys across even wanted more. Oh, I feel sick about this."

"Can't the Warden do anything?"

"What can he do? All them damned bastards up there has to do is to shut their mouths tight an' look innocent. Then who can tell who give the crows?"

"Couldn't we drown them out if we sang louder?" The Bishop was very upset by the turn things had taken.

"Not a chance," Big Tom replied sadly. "There's too many of them. They done break us up that's what they done."

"Let's try again softly and see what happens," the Bishop urged.

They did. Very softly. And all was quiet except the song along their own corridor.

"You see," said the Bishop. "The roosters couldn't hear us, and they think we've given up. And that's just what we want them to think. Until I can come again. Why don't you men, each in your own cell, practice singing quietly. Have you thought of another song?"

"Bishop, you're all right," Tom said, grinning. "Seems like you mighta said a hymn or somethin'. That wouldn't go down so good with the boys. But this here one they know, all right."

"We'll try to get to the hymn yet, Tom. But now I suggest you and Lucien practice your own singing separately and don't give up on the plan, Tom. Meanwhile I want you to do a little homework for me. Does either of you know what is meant by the Lord's Prayer?"

"I do," Lucien said. "We used to say it in school."

"My Baby used to say it but I never really learnt it."

"I would like you both to be able to say it next time I come. I have a little slip of paper here for each of you. This tells you where in your books you can find it. I'm sure it must be time for Henry's knock. He's giving us a little longer because there are two of you today. I'm glad to see Tom again, and it's been good to have you with us, Lucien. Would you like to join us again next week?"

"I sure would."

Henry's knock came on the door, as he opened it.

"That's good," the Bishop said. "I'll be expecting you again, then, Lucien."

Henry was eager to talk about this second visit when he and the Bishop were alone on their way back.

"This Lucien boy shaped up all right then?" he asked.

"Very well, indeed. He's a nice boy."

Henry lowered his voice. "I sure did like the sound of the singing. I didn't know we could have that much talent in one cell. If it hadn't been for them she-roosters up there—that's what I call them—they're always making trouble some way. I wisht I had the job of knocking their heads together. I'd fix'em!"

"I hope we can think of some way we can go on with the singing. You think the men liked it?"

"Sure they did; all of them on this corridor sat as still as mice as long as the song lasted, an' then they asked for more."

"I am hoping the Warden may want to help when he knows how much the prisoners liked it."

"He's got a ticklish job with those roosters. They didn't commit regular crimes, but a bunch of them were arrested for parading without permission, blocking traffic, and getting rough generally. A few people got hurt so the Judge sent the leaders in here. They're pretty mad and there's always the danger of them starting something. I'll be glad when they're gone."

"I had a message to speak to the Superintendent on my way out."

"Yes, I got it. We have a little way to go yet. So the new kid did all right?"

"He was fine. He wants to join us next week, too."

"That's a good sign. What do you do, Bishop? Preach to them?"

The Bishop laughed. "No, I don't think that would be wise. We talk together about certain verses or about their personal problems."

They walked on quietly, through gate after gate, until Henry stopped at last and the Bishop read the words:

SUPERINTENDENT'S OFFICE
PRIVATE

Then Henry drew back.

When Bishop Ware entered he found the Warden friendly.

"Well, how's your little Sunday School class going?" he asked.

"Surprisingly well," the Bishop returned. "That new member, Lucien Roberts, is a very bright boy and a nice one."

"He's given us plenty of trouble. Three times he's tried to kill himself, and the last time it was close enough so that an extra watch was needed. Do you think he'll be better from now on?"

"Yes, I do. When he told me he was a high school graduate, I asked him what his favorite course had been. He looked at me and said, 'Nobody ever asked me about that before. It was history. I made fine marks in that.'

"I told him I would get some history books a college freshman would be using and bring them to him. He was completely delighted. If these men had something pleasant to think about they could stand the confinement better, don't you agree?"

"I suppose so, but now I want to speak to you about something else. I knew that there was a sort of unwritten law that each Warden when he ended his term of office should leave a brief record of the time of his guardianship. I suddenly felt curious to read some of these, so I got them out from their cupboard. A few had grown yellow but most were easily read, some longer, some very brief. I kept reading here and there until I came on a short record with one item very interesting to me and I think to you. It read:

Religious Service held each Sunday in the Chapel, so called, being the room next to the Library.

Dr. Denby officiating.

Average attendance—20

So you're not the first man who thought of a prison ministry. Now this means that some forty years ago there was a room called 'The Chapel.' That room is just used for storage now, but it could be easily cleared out. How would you like to use it?"

The Bishop drew a long breath. "You must never say again there is no answer to prayer, Warden. This is even *more* than I've been praying for."

He told then about the singing, of Tom's surprising voice, and of his dream of having a quartet. "If two well-behaved men who could sing were allowed to practice with them, they would soon build up a prison quartet. And here now would be the perfect place for them to practice. I would be with them, of course, as a sort of guide. I used to sing myself and could perhaps train them—a little. Warden, would you feel this could be tried?"

The Warden sat, stroking his cheek. "You have pushed a great deal on me at once. I think first, we can make the storage room into a little Chapel and call it by that name.

"As to the quartet, we must work toward that very slowly and carefully, for it will take time and patience. But if it becomes a reality, I don't see how it could do any harm and just possibly might do good. Taking Big Tom as an example of what can be done, and if your young Lucien decides life's worth living there will be two of them. Two men saved from hell, would you say, Bishop?"

"Rather, saved to a Vision of Light, I would call it.

"There is one thing I've omitted from my story. Here it is: We practiced one song, 'My Old Kentucky Home,' with Lucien as a sort of natural boyish tenor, with me a baritone, and Tom with his marvelous bass-like chords. At the end a voice from our corridor called 'Sing 'er again, boys!' We were just getting ready to repeat it when from above us came *crows* apparently from a number of roosters. Big Tom was beside himself with rage. He felt the whole dream would have to be given up. I suggested another singing, but a *very* soft one. And it was not interrupted."

150

The Warden's face was set in severe lines and his voice had sharpened. "There will be no more *crowing*, I can promise you that. For the rest, as I said, we must be willing to wait. I doubt whether it will ever be possible to have the quartet that Tom has been dreaming about, but we will leave it there for the present and concentrate upon the little Chapel, which, Bishop, may be of use to you in some way. A man is coming to see me now so we'll have to leave it there until next week. I'll admit, Bishop, I feel a bit of interest myself."

"Thank you for your kindness," the Bishop answered, and went out quickly.

As he drove home, his heart felt light. Already he felt he had accomplished something. Certainly he had brought a little light to the two men, Tom and Lucien, and as he thought of the Warden, he humbly thanked God and took courage. Somehow he had gotten through to the man. And with his willingness now to arrange for the little Chapel, the Bishop, like Tom, felt a great dream growing in his mind.

That evening the sky was bleak and the west wind sharp, as though no benison of summer had just repeated itself a weekend ago. The two Bishops had to forsake their porch sitting room and repair, somewhat disgruntled, to the one indoors.

"I don't like these sudden changes of weather," Bishop Ware lamented. "To be pitched from summer into something that feels like snow is just not right somehow. And I'll tell you how I think it happens."

"I'm just waiting to hear," Julian said, smiling.

"I think it's the whole Space Program that has done it. When our rockets go off up there in those far stellar regions with those crashing blasts of noise, why wouldn't they affect the air, and disturb it down to the earth's envelope? And then, take the moon," the Bishop went on, warming to his subject. "I've always *loved* the moon. And the idea of men tramping around on its surface and leaving some tawdry things behind just sickens me.

" 'That orbed maiden with white fire laden
Whom mortals call the moon,' "

he quoted.

"They should have left the moon alone. Well, Julian, I believe that is all of my invective for the present."

Julian laughed. "I won't challenge you on anything except

151

the weather. My habit is to take it as it comes and forget it. It's what we have to do, in the long run, so why not at once? 'Accept it and don't worry,' is my motto. I'm afraid from your tone, however, you've had a hard day."

Bishop Ware laughed, too. "No, that's the funny thing. I am actually happy over my 'work' today, as I call it. I can't wait to tell you. But that sharp little wind that blew on my face as I came in rather set me off."

Mrs. Morgan entered with her tray. "It's turned a bit chill," she said.

"Aye, it has and all," Julian said wickedly, in her own vernacular. But she didn't seem to notice.

"So I brought you sherry at room temperature, with a light bit of something to go with it. I might add, sir," she said, turning to the older Bishop, "that I think there may be a mite wrong with the dog—with Marcano, sir."

"Why? What makes you say that? He hasn't come in to me."

"It's just that he lays in front of the dining-room fire, which I made about four, so the room would seem cozy to you both at your dinner, and, as I say, he just lays there and now and again a grue runs over him, what you call a *shiver* . . ."

"Yes, yes. What was he doing this afternoon?"

"The gardener was here and made the beds up just beautiful for the bulbs, and when I let Marcano out he made straight for them and rolled for a good hour before I could get him in."

"And then you washed him?"

Mrs. Morgan all but jumped. "I had to, sir. He was a fair sight, and I wouldn't have let him into the livin' quarters of the house the way he was."

"Have you given him anything to eat?"

Mrs. Morgan hesitated. "Sometimes he's slow gettin' at his food."

"So he wouldn't eat?"

"I'll try him now on a little warm soup. It goes down easy and it's nourishin', too." And she left rather precipitously.

"I'm worried," Bishop Ware said. "Dogs can get what in humans is called pneumonia."

"Oh, I would guess he just likes the fire. Finish your wine and let him lie warm and quiet a little longer."

"You never owned a dog, Julian, so you couldn't understand. But I'll get to him as fast as I can."

He drank his wine quickly and left for the dining room.

Here he heard the faint sound of Marcano's feeble effort to wag his tail. The Bishop knelt down beside him, stroked his head, and uttered gentle words of affection. The dog licked his master's hand while making small sounds of pleasure that seemed more moans than barks. The Bishop felt his legs and body with a practiced hand and then called the Vet and described the case.

"It could really be a chill such as a man would get from overexposure to the cold. If you'll bring him over, I'll watch him through the night."

"I can do that myself and he will be more content if he stays here. Any medication?"

"Get some children's aspirin and give him one now. If he seems restless or feverish through the night, give him another. Keep him warm, and let me know how he is in the morning."

Julian demurred a bit over the Bishop's plan to bring in the chaise from the porch and set it next to the dog, where he expected to lie.

"You can't sleep on that, Bishop. You'll get no real rest at all. I'll stay here if someone needs to. It won't hurt me in the least, and I'll watch him just as you tell me."

"My dear Julian, thank you but it wouldn't be the same to Marcano. He knows my touch. What you can do now is to drive to the nearest drugstore and get a package of children's aspirin. I'm to give him one. I hope you can get there before the stores are all closed."

"Good Lord," Julian said. "We've come a long way since a dog was put out in all weathers to eat cold buckwheat cake or any leftovers thrown out for him. All right. I'm on my modern errand."

Meanwhile the Bishop had told Mrs. Morgan to hold dinner back for a half hour and during that time to bring down bedclothes for the chaise where he intended to sleep and a nice warm comforter for Marcano to lie on. "He's on the cold hard stone now," he said.

"That's more fittin' for a dog than a feather comforter, sir."

"I want the comforter, please." And Mrs. Morgan brought it speedily. The Bishop turned the dog over upon it. He made no movement to get up, only uttered his small moans of satisfaction as he felt the softness beneath him.

"I can't understand it," the Bishop told Julian when he returned with the aspirin. "He's just like a person who is

153

plain tired out. I think after he's slept all night he'll be jumping all over me in the morning."

"Of course, he will. Is dinner on the way, or shall I settle to a book?"

"As soon as I give Marcano the aspirin and have him take a little nourishment, we'll eat. I'm sorry to have held you up."

"Nonsense! I'm not *that* hungry. Take your time over the poor dog. He's not shivering now."

"I know. That's a good sign."

When Bishop Ware had mashed the aspirin to a fine powder he mixed it with sugar and offered it to Marcano on a large enough spoon to keep it from being spilled. The dog licked it greedily.

"Aye, he's got a sweet tooth, that one, I've always said," Mrs. Morgan put in.

"Then why not a sweet custard? He would probably eat that."

When he held the bowl the Bishop waited for the dog to get up, but he still made no move to rise. But he licked the custard daintily from the spoon, settling down again upon his comforter.

When the two Bishops at last began dinner, Bishop Ware's mind was still upon the dog. "I can't imagine what could be wrong with him. He just seems too tired and too weak to get up . . . Of course, I try to pretend that he got a shock from that bath she gave him in the cold basement. The heat there hasn't been turned on yet. And I picture how it will be when he jumps all over me to wake me up . . ."

"Just hold that picture. I'm sure it is a most reasonable one. Eat your dinner now and tell me a little about your day. You said it was a happy one."

It was an effort, but the Bishop told of the new young man, how he had come to be there and would rather die than live; then he told the story of the singing. At this Julian's eyes began to gleam with interest.

"What a day you've had, Bishop. You dare not let anything mar that now. Look at Marcano, warm and comfortable and sound asleep. What more could you ask?"

"That's true. You put it so well, Julian. Thank you. But I've been selfish. What about your own problem?"

"With my old gentleman? I made a beginning, thinking the time element was very important. I phoned Mr. McPhail to invite him to come to see me. I know you'll understand when I tell you he seemed quite bowled over by what he called 'the

154

great honor' I was doing him, and he will come tomorrow. Then I will use all the ammunition with which you have provided me and a bit of my own, too, and try to do gentle battle for the Modernists. So, I hope to give you a good report before long."

When it was bedtime Mrs. Morgan came in to arrange Bishop Ware's improvised bed, and to look carefully at Marcano.

There was no light but the fire. There was a warm, quiet pervasive peace in the room. The Bishop leaned over his dog and softly stroked the silky head, then allowed his fingers to play gently behind the ears, the sensitive spots. At this there was the slightest movement of the dog's head and a feeble sound.

"Oh," the Bishop said softly, "he knows I'm here."

He continued the soft caresses until Marcano lay completely still and apparently sound asleep. Then the Bishop lay down under his blankets and his own comforter, and began, as usual at this hour, on his devotions. When he had finished he lay thinking. He had always believed in prayer, that strange link between the finite and the infinite which no one could explain or understand. But did this nullify its truth? So many activities now in our ordinary days remain mysteries beyond our understanding, and yet we accept them casually. We *use* them. Electricity is one. A man in New York talks by telephone to a man in California as though they were sitting in the same room and think nothing of it. They simply accept it. Could this be so with prayer? Of course, the analogy was not perfect but, at least, it had some significance.

He watched the shadows on the ceiling made by the firelight and went on thinking. The reason the whole question of prayer was now sharply in his mind was because he suddenly wanted desperately to pray for something for which he had never before petitioned, this was the life and health of his dog.

Would such a prayer be but a sort of childish impertinence to the Almighty? Or, considering the attention paid to a sparrow's fall, might it seem a reasonable cry for help to the Great Heart of all?

He thought for a long time but the urge was too strong, the habit of supplication too great. He folded his hands above the bedclothes and began softly: "Dear Lord of All Living, I pray Thee for a blessing upon my dog, Marcano. I pray that he

155

may have health and strength returning by tomorrow and a normal, happy day."

He stopped. "I must be honest," he murmured and then went on with a catch in his throat: "But if this cannot be, may he this night, as he lies beside the fire with his master near, fall upon the long sleep."

The Bishop wiped his eyes and spoke as though answering a critic, "I'm glad I did it. Why shouldn't I? He has the same qualities that make a good man. I feel better."

The Bishop had once found a rare watch in his travels. It delicately chimed each hour as it came. This sound would wake him if he dozed off at any time. So he would check the fire now and perhaps take a little nap. It was not quite five o'clock. He put a fresh log on the fire, as he had done twice before that night, then he stroked Marcano tenderly, trying to pretend there was some response. That effort on the dog's part to get up must surely be a good sign. He got into his bed and was soon asleep.

On the chime of six he wakened, saw the fire was bright, and got up quickly to look at Marcano. He looked down at first and then knelt to listen closely. He waited only a few moments and then rushed to the phone and called the veterinarian. The voice came promptly.

"Dr. Morse, this is Bishop Ware. I'm terrified about my dog. He isn't breathing right. Can you come at once?"

"Yes. Right away."

Before he arrived, Julian came in, hastily tying his bathrobe. "Is he worse, Bishop?" he asked anxiously. "I heard you at the phone."

"I can't tell, but Dr. Morse is coming at once. Julian, I've met all kinds of sorrow in my life, with fortitude I hope, but what I may have to meet here breaks me all up. I'm weak. If I lose Marcano, it will be almost like losing a child. I'm ashamed."

"Don't be. And don't give up hope. There, I imagine that's Dr. Morse. I'll go."

The doctor did not wait to speak. He went right to Marcano, knelt down, and put his hand on the soft hair of the dog's chest. He used the stethoscope, moving it a little, listening carefully, and, at last, knelt very still. When he stood up, he looked at the Bishop and shook his head.

"Oh, no!" the Bishop cried. "You can't mean he is . . . is *gone*! Only an hour ago he tried to get up. He tried so hard and then had to give up and lie back again. I thought it might be a good sign!"

"It was Nature's last effort to bring him to life. But, Bishop, he could not have been more comfortable than here by the fire with you beside him. It was his heart that just got too tired and stopped. How old was the dog?"

"He was twelve years old. Only two when I got him and I've had him for ten years. I can't think of life without him."

"I know. I know. In my work I learn what treasures pets are. I would like to tell you though, first, that if I had seen him last night it would not have made any difference. If you had left him his last night with me you would never have forgiven yourself. This could have happened at any time. I would like to add that if you need anything in the way of practical advice or help you have only to call me. I have a good deal of experience. I'll leave you now but will hope to be in touch." He shook hands with Bishop Ware, his kind face full of sympathy.

When he had gone, Julian made the Bishop go up to his room and get into bed. "You know you hardly had any sleep last night, and you are shaky. Please do as I say and I'll ask Mrs. Morgan to bring up some breakfast for us both. I'll get dressed at once and join you. This will do us both good. Now *please* do as I say."

He dressed quickly and made a telephone call which somehow he felt impelled to do. It was Cissie herself who answered.

"Why, Julian, is anything wrong?"

He told her. "The Bishop is pretty well shot. I felt you should know and perhaps come to see him before too long."

"I'm coming at once," she said. "I think I know something to comfort him. Luckily, this is my day off."

"Have you had breakfast?"

"No, but that's no matter. I'll snatch a cup of coffee over there."

"But we're breakfasting up in the Bishop's bedroom. My idea. If you join us, it will be wonderful for him. And for me," he added in a lower tone.

There could have been no better cure for Mrs. Morgan's attack of remorse over Marcano than the order to serve three hot breakfasts in the Bishop's room. She gloried in it. The Bishop had his own bed tray which he occasionally used, and then, with Julian's help, she placed a table close to the bed with two place settings upon it. As soon as Cissie arrived, Mrs. Morgan started up with her hot plates of food.

Cissie had kissed Bishop Ware at once, and her eyes were still wet. "I *grieve* with you about Marcano, but the reason I rushed over when Julian called was because I think I know something that will be a comfort to you."

The Bishop could eat nothing except a bit of muffin with his coffee, but even this was enough to bring some color to his pale cheeks. He watched the younger people eating with hearty appetites their bacon and eggs, and when the last plate of hot muffins was presented, they each helped themselves to another.

"I think we needed that good breakfast," Cissie said. "I want to tell you . . ."

"It was such a nice intimate breakfast," Julian broke in.

Cissie only smiled and went on with what she had been trying to say. "I brought a little information I think will ease your mind, Bishop. I want to tell you about it. A while ago I had a lovely patient who had a very dear dog. He was often brought to see her but was so delighted it became too much for her because she was very weak. So they had to stop his visits. Her husband did his best, but the little dog simply sickened and died of a broken heart. He was a little cocker spaniel and they are so sensitive. The husband inquired everywhere and finally found what he wanted, a special place where pets could be buried. It is called 'Animals' Rest.' The story is that years ago a very wealthy man lost his dog. He bought this sizable plot of land out of a piece of sparse woodland and had a low stone dyke built around it, and tall iron entrance gates built with the words *Animals' Rest* carved at the top. There were two big oak trees on the plot already, which were trimmed and kept. My patient got well and then insisted I must visit the place with her. So I did. That's why I speak with such feeling. It is a sweet, quiet, lovely spot. There are many little white headstones scattered through it, with many large empty spaces. It is all beautifully kept, for the original owner arranged its care in perpetuity, if that's the right word. We were there on a lovely autumn day, and we saw a man sitting on the low wall, smoking his pipe and looking down at the stone below him. Does this all have any interest for you, Bishop?"

His voice was husky, but the words came pouring out. "Cissie, my dear girl, you have lifted one big hurt from me. Could I go to see this place?"

"Of course."

"Very good. Cissie dear, I can never thank you enough You'll give the directions to Julian, won't you?"

"I'll write them down, so we'll be sure. Is there anything else I can do for you, Bishop? Then perhaps I should be getting along to the office. May I drop you off at your grandmother's, Cissie?"

"If you will I'll be glad. Wouldn't you know on my day off my own car would be laid up for repairs?"

She blew a kiss to the Bishop, and then she and Julian left the room, discussed the directions downstairs, and then, after a few words with Mrs. Morgan, went out to the car and moved very slowly along the way. Cissie spoke first. "Julian, at what point in man's upward ascent do you think he became possessed of a *soul?*"

"How odd for you to ask me that just today, for last night the same thought came to me. I didn't sleep much myself, and once when I was uneasy, I went down through the kitchen into the dining room in the quietest way. I stood there listening and I could hear the Bishop speaking very softly. Cissie, he was praying for his dog. It was a gentleman's prayer, for he gave God an option. He prayed that Marcano might be returning to health by morning. Then he stopped and gave the option with a break in his voice. 'But if this cannot be, then as he lies by the fire here beside me, grant that he may fall upon the long sleep.' I slipped away as fast as I could for I was so moved. When I got to my own room, I broke down completely. I cried as I have never done since I was a boy as I thought of that good man praying for his good dog. I know, of course, that theologians say it is a moral line that separates man from animals. But I wondered if during a few moments of that little prayer the line might have been dissolved. Does this sound absurd to you, Cissie?"

She laid a hand gently on his arm. "Oh, no!" she said. "You can't imagine how much comfort you have given me. I know now what I never did before, that you have a very tender heart."

He got out of the car and walked her up to the entrance. Here their hands clung for a little and then he was gone. He tried as he drove into the city to concentrate upon the points he expected to introduce to Mr. McPhail, but through them all came remembrance of Cissie's eyes as they had looked at him as he was telling his story. How could it be so easy, so comfortable, to tell her what he could not imagine himself telling to any other person? Perhaps it was because of the light on her face when she looked up quickly, with a smile. But hardly so, for the time at which he was most aware of her beauty was at the moment when her face, eyes shaded by her long dark lashes, was fixed in sadness over Marcano. He must put all these thoughts behind him and think only of his coming guest.

When Mr. McPhail was at last welcomed and seated in the office, Julian, looking every inch the Bishop, faced him with a friendly smile. Under cover of the first general amenities, the younger man studied the older. A strong face certainly, with kind eyes but an implacable chin. There was a generally friendly expression and a little touch of—could it be arrogance? Perhaps only pride. There were lines of sadness, too.

"It was good of you to come," the Bishop heard himself saying.

"And very good of you to ask me. I guess you've heard about the trouble we've run into in church?"

"I have, and now I'm eager to hear all about it from you rather than from a vestryman, for instance. Could you start at the beginning now and tell me just what happened?"

"Yes. That's the way to go about it. I suppose you heard then about the coal? That's at the back of it all. I suddenly got all this money and I determined to build a big parish house for the church. You know the story that far?"

"Yes, I do."

"Very good then. I'll just begin at what happened in my Sunday School class on that particular morning. One of my boys had been to college and taken a course in religion called 'The Miracle of the Earth,' and I said it would be fine if he would tell us about that and we would all open our Bibles at the first chapter of Genesis, where it tells what God made each day of the week. But just then the boy said the professor had told them that they must not think the word *day* as it's used there means a day like ours. If he had struck me, I wouldn't have felt worse. I said, 'It's part of the inspired word of God, which we believe. Don't you believe this?' And, Bishop, he said, no, he didn't.

"By this time, Bishop, the foundations of the parish house were all solid and the first beams were up. I was sick at heart and really sick, too. The days I spent in bed I decided what I must do. I must find out more about this defection and how much it has spread amongst our people."

"And did you?" the Bishop asked.

"I did. To my distress, I found many who believed—or

160

disbelieved—as the boy did. And worse still, an even greater number who said they had never thought about it and didn't feel it made much difference either way."

"So what was your conclusion?"

"It was a terrible decision. I felt shattered by it. But I decided to stop building the parish house at once and let it stand until some secular group would like to have it. I couldn't build it to the glory of God and the work of Mosely church when I found the membership was riddled with unsound doctrine. How could I allow my name to stand as the donor?"

"You were planning to have your name carved on the face of the stone?"

Mr. McPhail looked embarrassed. "It was just suggested. I had not given my full consent."

"I was about to say that if this use of your name was planned by the vestry, you could easily change this by saying you could not have your name used in connection with the overall sculpturing, 'To the Glory of God, etc.' You could not have your name used on the building."

Mr. McPhail's face looked stricken and his voice was unsteady.

"You mean go ahead with the whole thing as planned but just leave me out of it?"

"You couldn't be left out of it, as you say, Mr. McPhail. Everyone knows of your wonderful gift and is grateful beyond their power to express it. I only meant you might decide not to have your name engraved on the stone at the entrance."

Mr. McPhail still spoke with difficulty.

"I'll be thinkin' that matter over again," he said.

The Bishop spoke quickly. "There is something else I would like you to consider. I feel you have taken a very narrow meaning of the word *day* as you have discussed it. I believe you should think about the fact that God does not measure time as we perhaps do. For example, take this verse: 'For a thousand years in Thy sight are but as yesterday when it is past, or as a watch in the night.' The watch was only a few hours, you know."

"Where is this from?"

"From the Psalms. The Ninetieth. You must have read it, but maybe only hastily. Think now what it means with reference to that word, *day!* You could read it, 'And a thousand years were the second day,' couldn't you?"

The older man looked confused. "I can't grasp this all at

once," he said. "You see everything about religion was always as sure as rock under my feet. I'm too old to stand anything shakin' it."

"But nothing can shake this verse I read to you. Read that whole Ninetieth Psalm over yourself, and you will feel religion is stronger than ever."

"But I've just thought. Suppose I would get to believe I was wrong about everyone having to believe that word *day,* how could I ever let people know? I even made a speech in church about it one day. I couldn't bear to go around to all those people and say I'd made a mistake. That is, if I decide I did make a mistake."

"If you ever feel you can change your interpretation of the word *day,* I suppose you would go on with the building?"

"I suppose so," he said, but without much warmth.

"Then," the Bishop went on, "you would need only to speak to the Rector and the vestry and everything would take care of itself. Can't you imagine the joy and excitement it would create if the news went around that the parish house was to be finished after all?"

"Yes, it would. I only wish I could feel better about the whole thing."

"Dear Mr. McPhail, my advice to you is 'don't hurry.' Stay quietly at home for a few days until you are entirely sure in your own mind what you believe and what you want to do. Then will be time to tell it and be happy in the doing of it."

When Mr. McPhail left, Julian held his hand warmly in his own.

"I'm sure this story is going to have a wonderful ending, Mr. McPhail. I'm so glad you came, and be sure to let me know if any other problems arise . . . I would like to be in close touch with you."

Mr. McPhail gave his thanks again and drove away. Julian stood a few moments, watching as he left. A great sympathy for the man had been rising in his heart.

"I wonder," he thought, "if he will ever again be as happy as he was over his first dream of the parish house. Too much had been connected with it. And now his own thinking had been stirred by new and startling suggestions. Was this the reason for the sadness of his face?

"And yet," Julian kept thinking, "I could do no less than I did. I might perhaps have led up more slowly to the relevance of the verse, but the meaning would be as clear one time as another." One thing he did regret. The man had come to him,

162

as the Bishop, expecting to receive support for his views and his decision, and thereby go away strengthened and comforted, and perhaps just a little proud. And while there had been no direct question posed, he could not help feeling that this had not happened. Surely Mr. McPhail's mind itself would undergo a change as he pondered. But even if a change occurred, there would be then, as he himself had pointed out, the hard business of retraction, apology, and explanation. Poor McPhail!

Julian climbed the stairs slowly to go again to his office. His face was very sober. There was no one within hearing so he spoke half aloud.

"I'm not satisfied with that interview. I wish I had the chance to do it over. I should have taken more time and gone carefully, step by step, making sure McPhail understood clearly what I was trying to do. It was all wrong to tell him to go home and think it out. I should have done it here with him. I think he went away disappointed and rather puzzled. I'm ashamed I didn't do the whole thing better. After I had invited him to come, too."

When he entered the office, he saw a neat stack of letters to be signed and Miss Lamb smiling.

"When I'm in the little office I never can help hearing the rise and fall of the voices in here and I thought this time you sounded really moved by the Spirit when you talked to that man. He seemed sort of sad looking, I thought, when he first came in. I guess you cheered him up."

"Thank you, Miss Lamb. I need a little compliment to cheer *me,* for I was afraid I hadn't done as well as I should with Mr. McPhail."

"You always help people, so you must never be discouraged."

"That's very kind of you, Miss Lamb. I have to leave early this afternoon. I'll finish these letters first and then be on my way. You go on whenever you are ready."

As he drove back he was thinking of the strange diversity of sorrows that wound the hearts of men. Just now, for example, there was McPhail, whose great dream had been marred, perhaps never to regain all its golden beauty; there was he, himself, suffering bitterly from what he felt was inadequacy; there was Bishop Ware, his grief for his dog still fresh upon him. Did the heart of every man always hold a secret sorrow? Was this the price for the first eating of the tree of good and evil? He must think of this seriously. It might suggest a speech and he had one coming up before long.

He was almost at the Old Rectory where Bishop Ware would join him to go to the quiet spot about which Cissie had told him, thinking it would be a lovely resting place for Marcano.

How good Cissie had been to come right over. Did her heart ever hold a secret sorrow? At the violence of the answer that welled up in his mind, Julian felt a wave of color rising in his face. He got out of the car at once and went to meet Bishop Ware.

10

And the fall slipped gradually into winter. The two Bishops sat now in the study before a blazing wood fire each evening and discussed the affairs of the world and their own spheres of activity. For each man there had come some satisfaction like a little breath of hope that blew the clouds away. In Julian's case there had been a letter sent to the Old Rectory "to prevent any secretary person from reading it," the writer explained. It came from Mr. McPhail and was an effort to adjust the new thought and the old.

"I'm not just settled in my mind, yet, and so I would thank you for your kind thoughts and prayers."

Julian spent hours explaining what he felt he had not done fully enough before. "The good thing is," he kept repeating to the Bishop, "that he is still thinking this all over. I believe it will come clear to him yet."

The Bishop, on the other hand, had several bits of what he felt would be lasting satisfactions. Each Wednesday he met Big Tom and Lucien in the Chapel, which had become a very modest little church. The pulpit, fashioned in the workroom, had a white strip of fabric across the top, and there were eight or ten chairs in the room. The Bishop longed to add a little to the Chapel's decoration but had waited to allow that to come slowly. Big Tom, however, was full of plans. There was another man he wanted desperately to add to the three of them now. This, he said, was Angelo, the "Eyetalian," who sang, he had discovered. He sang bits of opera, but sometimes when he hit a very high note there was likely to be a crack from some fool, "Why didn't you stay up there," and then he would get mad. "He's a good guy too, except when they tease him." Tom said he had spoken to Henry and he said Angelo did not have many demerits.

So Tom had ended by asking if the Bishop wouldn't see what he could do to get Angelo into the Chapel to sing with them.

It had worked out. The Warden was pleased with the quiet way the Chapel so far had been used. The men quite definitely liked the music and listened to it.

"I see no reason why we can't try out this new man, this Angelo. If it is not a success we will stop it. But if he is well behaved and improves the singing, we'll let him continue."

Then he had added a few words that touched the Bishop's heart. "Funny thing," he said, "about the music. I never once thought of trying it. And yet it's a simple, normal activity. It was Big Tom and you who got this started."

When the Bishop described to Julian Angelo's first visit to the Chapel, his own voice grew husky. "He says his father 'sings while he push the cart and much people stop to hear him.' But when he, himself, began we were too startled to go on ourselves. We sang one of our songs to give him an idea of what we were doing and he was delighted. 'You very good,' he said. 'Now I sing along and make it more better.' "

"He must have perfect pitch; he sang at once in a rich countertenor, we might call it, and he went along with Lucien beautifully. Even as I was singing I knew what had happened. Without suspecting it, we had become a really passably good quartet. There wasn't a sound from the cells when we stopped. It was the best kind of applause."

When the next practice came Angelo was enthusiastic. "We do good. Maybe next week I learn you new song. Mr. Bishop you know 'Last Rose of Summer?' Yes?"

"It's one of my favorites."

"I sing it by myself."

Before anyone could say a word, he moved close to the door and began.

"I tell you, Julian, that song as Angelo sang it could have

165

kept a concert audience still. I can't describe it. The voice is pure and rich at the same time, full of Italian sunshine. But to sing that song of all others in a prison. I waited to hear some raucous comment, a few whistles, or some kind of mockery. There was none. Angelo sang it all, bringing out every shade of plaintive sadness. And the men listened."

The first snow fell early, on Thanksgiving Day itself. Mrs. Morgan was in her element. She had the fires laid ready for lighting in the study and the dining room, with the drawing room added belatedly in case someone might come to call.

In the kitchen now, with Cook gone for the day, the turkey was ready for the oven, its stuffing for once light and dry as Mrs. Morgan always felt it should be. When she saw Cook moistening it with *water* she felt sometimes she couldn't endure it, but knowing the delicate wire she had to walk, umbrella and all, to keep the peace with Cook, she decided to let the problem of the turkey stuffing rest. Just today, however, she thought with solemn pride it would be perfect as everything else was.

The matter of the two Bishops' being alone on this family day had been carefully explained to Mrs. Morgan. Mrs. Lansing and Miss Cissie had been invited weeks before to go to Cissie's mother's, staying until Sunday. Mrs. Morgan had gloried in the plan that she alone would be mistress of both house and kitchen and monitor of the two dear gentlemen who really did need looking after sometimes.

They in turn were more than satisfied with the arrangement. Julian had had two invitations to dinner, both of which he had declined. Bishop Ware was again battling in silence with a great feeling of lassitude and would be thankful for a very quiet dinner.

So, as the light snow fell gently outside a great peace settled within the Old Rectory. It was as perfect a dinner as Mrs. Morgan had intended it to be, and the Bishops were both ready to enjoy it. Strangely enough, considering that they had been at home all day, there seemed to be a constant flow of conversation. Bishop Ware often looked off to the portraits above the fireplace but studiously avoided letting his glance fall upon the wide stone hearth now empty.

"I suppose you know that Vespers have already begun at St. Michael's."

"Yes. Of all things, I read an ad in the paper to that effect. How the commercial world does encroach," Julian answered.

"In this case I believe it's justified," Bishop Ware said. "There is no other way to let the general public know about these services. And you know Fenwick is expecting a completely different audience from the regular morning one. He will need advertising to accomplish this. By the way . . ."

"Yes. So do I."

"You are incorrigible, Julian, the way you always know what I'm thinking before I speak. We'll see if you're right this time."

"You were about to say that you thought it would be very nice if you and I attended Vespers this Sunday, now weren't you?"

"Oh yes. Right as usual. Well, can you go?"

"I'm sure I can. Give me some credit. I had thought of this myself."

"You're free, then?"

"Not entirely. I was asked to preach at the eleven o'clock service at Mosely, the home church of my old Fundamentalist. I must tread carefully, which scares me a little."

"Take something from the Sermon on the Mount. You will not encroach upon either faction with that. Maybe you will only bind up wounds. But this makes you a heavy day, doesn't it?"

"Oh, no. I'm used to this. I can be back here before two. I should think this will give me time for a little breather before Vespers. Shall we go over together? Oh, no, that would not be wise. Fenwick will want you to sit among the mighty, somehow, and read a little prayer, perhaps. I want to sit back of center then, and try to judge the audience."

"There is one big bit of news about St. Michael's that I have not told you yet. After a year's search, Fenwick has found his second assistant!"

"You don't mean it! I had decided he just didn't really want another."

"Far from that. Now he's jubilant, and I must say the new man sounds like a paragon!"

"Tell me more!"

"He is young—thirty—but with five years' good experience; he is tall, good-looking, and the possessor of a very fine voice, which has been one of Fenwick's definite requirements, if he could get it. He also, according to Fenwick, has a compassionate heart, and sound business sense with it," the Bishop added.

The big fire in the study burned brightly all evening, and

the great holiday ended for the two Bishops at ten o'clock.

"I'm ashamed of my sleepiness," Bishop Ware said. "I used to feel midnight was too early for a man to think about going to bed. And look at me now!"

When Julian entered St. Michael's Sunday afternoon, he sat just back of the middle distance. He was glad to see that while the church was not full, the pews held what parsons always call "a goodly number." The ads, then, had been worthwhile. It was but a few moments until he was conscious of someone pausing to come in beside him. He rose, quickly, to usher the stranger in. It was Cissie.

"I was feeling so like a lost sheep. Thank you for taking me in."

"It is not *my* house," he whispered, smiling. And she smiled back. Strange, he thought, how seldom he had seen her smile. It was more like an illumination. The late Indian summer sunset shone through the stained glass windows; the shadows of the vacant spaces lent a soft blessing, and the music! Julian could feel Cissie catching her breath as the beauty of it smote her heart, as it did his own.

When the service ended with the final prayer in Bishop Ware's quiet gentle voice, Julian took Cissie's hand and they moved toward the great outer doors before which Dr. Fenwick stood.

Julian waited hesitantly. "Perhaps you should drop my hand," Cissie said softly.

He was manifestly embarrassed.

"Do forgive me," he said. "I didn't realize I was holding it."

Cissie gave a small laugh and Julian was puzzled. "I don't see anything funny about that," he thought.

After warm mutual greetings with Dr. Fenwick they walked out in the early dusk to Cissie's car.

"I don't like to see you driving around alone at night," he said. "The times are becoming too dangerous."

"Oh, thank you, Julian, for your solicitude. I like to think you sort of protect me. But I talked about all this with our nearest policeman and he gave me what he called 'the score.' He said there was always danger of muggings when a woman walks alone with no one near, but for the big crimes, murder and like that, he says there is always a lot behind them that the policemen know but don't tell. 'You get me?' he said. 'Well, I'm sure you are not in any danger, Miss Lansing. And besides,' he went on, 'Tim McShane says you saved his kid's

168

life in your hospital. He'd carry you round the block and back if you needed it. You got *friends* on the force, Miss Lansing.' Isn't that wonderful, Julian?"

"Yes, it is. And it does relieve me. I'm sure Bishop Ware will be glad to know this, too. Thanks for telling me."

"But I have a real favor to ask of you if I may."

"You know you may."

"It's about that last little short prayer that Bishop Ware gave."

" 'Support us all the day long . . .' "

"That's it. I had never heard it before, and I can't wait to have it so I can learn it and use it. Could you possibly . . .?"

"Oh, I would so love to send you a Prayer Book, which has this one at the back among Family Prayers, and also a typewritten copy. I picked up that minor skill in college days. Then you'll be doubly fortified. This prayer is Bishop Ware's favorite and also my own. So if you join us it will make us a trio."

"The Bishop and I," Cissie repeated softly. "I don't deserve that, but I'll be happy thinking about it."

"So will we—I mean, I will."

That night after the two Bishops had talked over the vespers with full hearts, Julian went to his room and typed the prayer and selected one of his Prayer Books to send to Cissie. He put his favorite bookmark at the proper page and added one small note.

> This is often called Bishop Potter's Prayer, made long ago while he was Bishop of New York. I like it best when it stands alone, with no human claim upon it.
>
> *Julian*

As he fastened the small package he had a sudden thought. He had never given Cissie anything before. Not even a flower. This seemed selfish and actually boorish. He knew that flowers were but a kind gesture, meaning nothing in the realm of affection. They were only a friendly courtesy. Why had he omitted this? Because he was a coward, that was why. He was afraid of having his precious decisions tampered with. Well, he would try to repair the rude omission now. This very morning.

He said good-bye to the Bishop, after their early and delicious breakfast, the ending of Mrs. Morgan's sole reign, and taking his little package drove off along the Avenue. At some distance he saw the large florist's shop that he had heard the Bishop himself speak of, as he ordered flowers for Mrs. Lansing. But of course he would know how to do these things!

Once in the shop he found it was easy enough. He decided upon pinkish-rose chrysanthemums, one dozen, in a box to Cissie's address, with the small package upon which his card was fastened to be put with the flowers. His heart felt a peculiar warmth as he paid the bill and went on his way. Presumably the incident would be forgotten. Instead it kept rising as he attended to his routine duties.

Would she have the flowers by now? Only if it was her day off. She may not like the color when she does see them. Perhaps—oh ghastly thought. He should have stuck to yellow and white. How would she answer? By phone or note?

Would he tell the Bishop what he had done?

On the afternoon delivery, a letter came from Mr. McPhail. He was afraid to open it, but after he had scanned it quickly, he looked up at Miss Lamb with a smile.

"From the old gentleman who was so troubled."

"That one was up to no good. I could sense it as he came in."

"Oh, but he is now up to *wonderful* good."

"Well, I'll wager you put him up to it. He was stubborn looking to me!"

"Miss Lamb, do you believe in the Holy Spirit?"

"Do I what?"

"When I have to give a benediction, as I often do, I say, 'May the blessing of God Almighty, the love of Jesus Christ, and the guidance of the Holy Spirit, be with you all.' I think that's a beautiful benediction, but I wonder if we think enough *about* that last phrase, *the guidance of the Holy Spirit.* I expect to concentrate upon it more than I have ever done. Won't you, too?"

"My dear Bishop, it's after three and I'd like to get to my work. Thank you for talking religion to me, but sometimes I don't just understand what you mean."

The Bishop smiled gently. "You have lots of company. Keep on serving God in your own way, and you'll be all right. I want to go over this letter carefully again, and then answer it myself, Miss Lamb."

When she had gone, he smoothed out the sheet of paper and read aloud softly.

Dear Bishop Armstrong—

Your last long letter set me thinking, especially the benediction part about the Guidance of the Holy Spirit. I knew that I had tried to guide myself. I knew I had been selfish about stopping the parish house just to show a kind of power I have with the money. That was all wrong. I'm humbled. I want from now on to seek the Guidance of the Holy Spirit in letting my neighbors decide their own religious beliefs even if they are not mine. So I am starting the Parish House at once. As you say, everyone will be happy. The news spread like fire and already many have come out to see me and shake my hand. The Rector says I have learned a great virtue because of all the trouble. And that is *tolerance*. He explained it to me.

Thank you, dear Bishop, for your wonderful counsel. You must be sure to help us dedicate this new building when it is ready. It will not have my name in the front.

Yours truly,

McPhail

The Bishop leaned back, more relaxed than he had been for some time. He felt the ease of a heavy burden rolling off. He folded the paper and put it carefully into his pocket. He wanted to let Bishop Ware read it. Then he wrote his reply, allowing his hope and his thankfulness to show in each line. He added his blessing and congratulations, stamped the envelope, and left it with Miss Lamb's neat stack to be mailed in the morning.

Miss Lamb appeared at the door. "There's an urgent call for you. I think you had better take it on your private line. I've switched you to it."

He took the phone at once. She had a sixth sense when the call could be put on the Arch Deacon's wire, and when it meant trouble to be handled by himself. He heard the cultivated voice now of a gentleman, first of all, and then of a rector, who was shocked and embarrassed.

"Bishop Armstrong?"

"I'm speaking."

"This is Reverend Harrison Wilde, Rector of St. James Church on the East Side."

"Oh," Julian said heartily. "I'm very glad to hear your voice. I always think of your parish with pleasure."

"And I always have, myself. Our work has gone so smoothly, and so well up until recently."

"What is the problem now?"

"The new Prayer Book! I thought it would be a simple matter for discussion and then a quiet decision. But it is a live, hot issue. On one side are all the older people—and incidentally those with the most money—who want to keep the old book. On the other side are all those who are younger and eager for the change in the new book. The clash between the two is becoming worse."

"I'm very sorry to hear this. I don't know of any other church that has had serious trouble over this issue. Did you feel I could be of any help?"

"Yes, I do. It is a great deal to ask, but I know your ability as a preacher and speaker. Could you possibly come to us on one Sunday very near Christmas and preach a sermon of peace and love and *good will,* which seems most tender in that season, and leave the thought that of all places where these qualities *must* prevail it is in the church. Could you do such a thing? I would be greatly in your debt."

"You speak well, Mr. Wilde. I think you could preach this sermon yourself."

"Oh, no! You forget I've heard you, and I know your wonderful ability. Besides, I'm like the poor. I'm always with them. A new voice would be like a clarion call to them, even without your special magic. Could we count on you?"

"Of course," Julian said. "I'll be more than glad to do what I can. Would you prefer the Sunday just before Christmas?"

"I think so if it suits you. And I cannot tell you how grateful I am. I would have come to your office to speak to you in person, but my wife is having a large missionary do here in the Rectory and I've promised to lend a hand."

"You are married?" Julian said, almost without volition.

"Married?" Mr. Wilde returned. "I should say so. I can't imagine a clergyman starting out to run a parish without a wife to help him. Thank you again, Bishop, so very much."

For the second time that afternoon, Julian considered Cissie and the flowers. Now the thoughts came pouring in. Would she care for that color? Would she call up to give her thanks, or maybe write a little note? He could not decide which would please him most. One delightful thing, he could think of her now without pain. That must mean that his feelings were completely controlled, a condition he had long hoped to attain.

He set down this new engagement along with many others in his book, signed some letters, endured with outward patience a call from the Arch Deacon, thinking as always how wise the man was in all administrative matters and yet how likely he was to take up a good half hour when ten minutes would have sufficed. Ah, well! He was a good man, and gave the balance of age to their discussions, which was needed.

He left the office at five, and drove off thinking of Mr. Wilde's remark about marriage. From that it seemed somehow quite natural to consider the flowers and Cissie's possible reply. It might come that very evening. But he kept hoping it would come by letter. A phone conversation could so easily become confused.

When he reached home, however, he found Mrs. Morgan trying to make a business of waiting in the front hall.

"A letter just came by special messenger a few minutes ago, Bishop Julian, and here it is, sir."

"Oh, thank you, Mrs. Morgan. Just leave it on the table. I do get the strangest kind of mail sometimes." He felt his voice sounded very casual.

He went up to his room and prepared for dinner. Why, he wondered, had he not brought the letter up with him? It was *blue,* and it must be from Cissie. And by special messenger! That somehow warmed his heart.

As soon as he was refreshed, he went hurriedly down the stairs and picked up the letter. Bishop Ware was evidently waiting for him in the study. He opened the letter and read:

Dear Bishop Julian—

It was good of you to remember that I always ate dinner at home on Wednesday, so I saw the flowers at once when I got here. How very beautiful they are. I had never seen that color. They meant so very much to me because I was so sad. A patient died last night. I wanted to stay with her and she wanted me, but hospital rules were against it. When their implacable rules run across a patient's needs, I resent them. So, your flowers meant much to me in taking away that resentment.

Thank you again so very much.

With good wishes always,

Cissie

173

He read it twice and put in in his pocket. It was a nice enough note, but he was somehow greatly disappointed. Her hospital work, which had made him jealous, seemed to form the background of her thanks or her interest in the flowers. McPhail's new letter which he had expected to be the crowning subject of their conversation now seemed to have lost a little of its importance. But this could not be allowed to remain in any secondary place. It was in his own mind that the relation of the two ideas must be made clear.

Mrs. Morgan came in sight.

"Dinner is served, Bishop Julian. I am a bit worried over the Bishop himself. He would take no walk today and it's not good for him, sir, to miss his walk. Of course, it's because he doesn't have Marcano now to go along with him. Ten years they always went off, so happy. Now it's different. Oh, if I could only be like Cook and tell the priest all my remorse and get shet of it, once for all. I still gotta carry mine about. Givin' him that cold bath . . ."

"Mrs. Morgan, you must not think about that. The doctor said he would have gone this same way *any* time. The bath may have made him weak just at once, but he would have been gone in a day or a week, anytime."

"Well, I'll try not thinkin' about it. But it's hard when I'm used to havin' him 'round me every day. An' then, the poor Bishop. My heart just aches for him. Would he want another dog, think you?"

"I doubt it," Julian said.

When he reached the dining room, he found the Bishop already seated at the table.

"Do forgive me, Julian, for my rather indifferent welcome. I'll have to confess that I got completely lost in a book—a novel at that. I haven't been able to do that for a long time. Did you have an interesting day?"

"Oh, very. I'll tell you all about it later. I even heard again from my old Fundamentalist."

"No!"

"Yes, good news. What about your day?"

"Not much, of course. I've been muddling over the question of whether to try using the short prayer just after the solo, and also looking through some old songbooks to see what we might add to our quartet. We definitely need new pieces."

"I'll discuss these all later with my colleague."

They laughed together then and went on with their excellent dinner.

When they were in the study again Julian produced McPhail's letter and handed it to Bishop Ware, who read it slowly, a smile growing upon his face.

"I suppose you know, Julian, that you have been an ambassador of good will, and also a wise peacemaker?"

"I didn't think of that. I felt the tribute belonged to the One who gave the guidance."

"Ah, yes. I read your benediction. Very beautiful I thought.

"The Blessing of God Almighty, the love of Jesus our Lord, and the guidance of the Holy Spirit, be with you forevermore."

"I expect to ask more of that guidance; I think I've neglected it a little."

"That is a good shock for me, Julian. I've repeated the words without much feeling myself. I thank you for that shock."

There followed then one of those rare and precious evenings when each man bared his soul to discuss the mystery of the Trinity, their minds slipping into cosmic questions and drawing back again, afraid of the answers.

They discussed their views of the Creation. Here they somehow felt they could be on firmer ground. Julian's view was that the Creation came about because of a vast cataclysmic burst of fire. The Bishop held to a gentler beginning. He believed that the waters covered the earth and darkness lay upon them. From this, small fires erupted to send the mountains into place and the dry land, until one all encompassing sea became several, and all life, vegetable, animal, and human, came out of the sea.

Julian always challenged this general belief.

"Don't you see, Bishop, in your view, you'll have to *posit* God to get your first complete sea!"

"And what about you?" the Bishop would come back. "Who's going to set off that first enormous blast of fire? Won't you have to posit *God* for that?"

"I guess so," Julian agreed. "Unless we have a mechanistic universe and I just can't settle for that! How would we explain the various colors of the flowers—just one thing—if there was no mind at work!"

They went on, probing deeper and deeper into the mystery until their minds, dizzy from cosmic questions, returned at last to the comfort and peace of their usual evening prayer.

Julian went early to bed, claiming weariness, and once in his room he read Cissie's letter over again. It did not sound as cold as he at first had thought. She had been sad, and she explained why. The flowers had cheered her. What more could he want, in heaven's name?

She ended with good wishes. Well, so had he. After all that had passed between them, how else could a young woman of pride sign herself? He saw now that he had been a selfish and ungrateful soul. He should be thankful that he still had her friendship!

When the day came for the next prison visit, Bishop Ware was, as always, eager and a trifle nervous. In a sense it had seemed almost too easy to achieve their singing and the use of the Chapel. But it was not enough, if he was to have Christian Ministry. There must be some words from him and certainly a prayer. He would like to have more men inside the Chapel. So he set forth, both pleased and anxious.

When he reached the jail, however, Henry met him with a message from the Superintendent. He would like to have the Bishop stop in when he came. When he was again in the office, the Warden seemed eager to talk, but his first words chilled the Bishop's heart.

"I think," he began, "that we will have to make some changes. I had a rather light week, so I've tried to get the real opinion of men in the various tiers. It seems their only complaint is that they can't hear the music well enough. They like it. I found out that a good many would like a little service in the Chapel that they could come to. On the whole, you see, the report is good."

"Thank God," said the Bishop.

"Now the question is what can we do next. We're not overcrowded here, so I think we can enlarge the present room to make a bigger chapel. One of the men draws well, and he made a picture of how it could be done. Then, several men said they'd like it to *look* more like a church, with an altar at the front. You could help us with that."

"I can't tell you how thrilled I am."

"I thought you would be. But here is the hardest to achieve. How can you sing the music so more men can hear?"

"It's the men in the tiers above?"

"Yes. They barely get an echo."

"Couldn't we singers go up there?"

"Of course, though I think it would be very irregular. However, I feel the three men have proved themselves. I believe we will do it. I want you to meet the guards who will be on duty when you go up, just after you finish in the

176

Chapel. I will have Henry arrange for that. Well, Bishop, I believe your work is having success. One other thing. Since we have a Chapel in which to meet I think it is best not to have more than one man in a cell at any time."

"Very good. And thank you again, for your great help."

When the quartet was once more in the Chapel, they were elated over all the news and promised perfect behavior. As to a new song, Big Tom suggested "When the Saints Come Marchin' In!"

He and Lucy knew it, but Angelo caught on quickly and Big Tom's rolling bass had never sounded better. With a few tries they were perfect.

The Bishop explained that he was going to make a little talk just before Angelo's solo, which was still requested, and the others could sit down then.

The singing went better than ever before, each week bringing some improvement. Then the Bishop stood close to the door with its open bars and read the story of the Prodigal Son. Then very simply he told it in modern words and spoke of its beautiful meaning. The men seemed to be listening. When he had finished, Angelo stood beside him and sang his plaintive solo. As his voice fell on the last note, the Bishop began, "Lord, support us all the day long until the shadows lengthen, the busy world is hushed, the fever of life is ended, and our work is done. Then in thy mercy grant us a safe lodging and a holy rest and peace at the last. Amen."

There was no sound until after the singers spoke naturally as they prepared to leave the Chapel and move toward the stairs at the far end of the corridor, where the new guards would speak to them and conduct them toward the tiers above.

As the Bishop passed along close to the familiar cells, several hands reached down through the bars and the Bishop grasped them as he heard, "Thanks! That was a nice prayer. Thank you, Bishop."

His heart felt warmed and filled with a new blessing. When he came to the high iron stairs, however, he wondered whether his heart would feel as blessed when he got to the top as it did now.

One guard went up smartly, then the other singers who had politely waited for him until he waved them off. "I'm scared," he said to them and they all felt it was very funny. But as he started on his own way up, he knew it was, indeed, the truth. For one thing it was possible to look straight down to all that lay below, if your eyes dropped between the step and the riser, and then the steps were so high! He felt he was straining from one to the next. Halfway up, he knew he had to stop. He felt a trifle lightheaded, and very definitely short of breath. This was ridiculous. He was used to exercise. Surely walking would have trained him somewhat for this. He drew deep draughts of air and started on again. He could hear the other guard starting also to mount behind him with the easy lightness of a mountain goat. "What a thing is youth," he kept saying to himself.

The Bishop fixed his eyes upon the top of the stairs, set his teeth, and moved slowly on. When he had arrived at the end the other three were waiting, it was Big Tom who took his arm in a firm grasp. "That's a hell of a lot of stairs ain't it, Bishop? Just stand quiet a little bit till you get your wind."

Lucien, too, was watching him closely. "It was looking down that caught me!" he said. "I was feeling plenty dizzy till I kept looking straight up."

The guard now abreast of them, paused. "Pretty stiff climb for you when you ain't used to it. Are you all right, sir?"

"Yes, perfectly, thank you. I've got my breath again now. If you'll just show us where to stand . . ."

He indicated a small break between tiers and the four singers took their places. A low mixture of a hum and low voices came from the back of one tier. The guard went there quickly and all was quiet. The Bishop smiled upon them all, and said they would start with an old barbershop song. If any of the men listening would like to join them as they went along, that would be fine.

> *"I been workin' on the railroad,*
> *All the livelong day:*
> *I been workin' on the railroad*
> *Jes' to pass the time away.*
> *Can't you hear the whistle blowin'—"*

And many voices joined in. This was something new. There was nothing raucous, nothing disturbing; the sound came from the throats of men who evidently *wanted* a chance to sing. So they sang it all over again. When the Bishop announced "My Old Kentucky Home," he said their quartet would sing it through first and then he hoped those who wished would join in the chorus. The Bishop realized that the harmony of their own singing seemed perfect. At the chorus many voices joined them, and it swelled into a rich body of sound. Some of the men there certainly knew how to sing.

"That was so good," said the Bishop, "let's take the chorus again."

"Weep no more my lady,
Oh weep no more today . . ."

The infinite pathos came through.

It was time then to announce "When the Saints Come Marchin' In."

As he spoke the words the Bishop could feel a subtle movement of satisfaction spread over the men. They evidently knew this song.

When it was time for the men to join the quartet on this one, it seemed to the Bishop that many more men were singing, some not always on key, but Big Tom's remarkable bass kept up a deep undercurrent, like the waves of the sea, drawing it all together.

When it was over, a voice begged for one more rendering. So once again, "The saints came marchin' in."

The Bishop introduced Angelo next. He told how Angelo had learned this song he would sing from his father, who had a vegetable cart in New York, and often sang to draw people to buy from him. Angelo stepped forward, raised his head, as he always did, and began. The words came distinctly and plaintively as he went on.

" 'Twas the last rose of summer . . ."

When he had finished there was a great silence for a few moments, then the clapping began. The Bishop was startled, but saw the guards were making no move to stop it, for it was not noisy but the expression of sincere pleasure.

By the time the singers had reached the top of the stairs the tribute stopped, but a voice, evidently that of a leader, spoke out to the guard.

"Could you ask him if they're comin' back next week?"

"Are you?" the guard relayed.

"We expect to."

"That's good. We sure enjoyed it. Tell the kid we liked his rose song too."

"Thank you," said the Bishop. "You were a very good audience."

179

The guard had a word of caution about the stairs.

"Hold on well to the railing. The stairs seem a bit steep sometimes. I'll walk slowly first, ahead of you, sir."

"I appreciate that. Thank you," answered the Bishop.

Once again on the first floor Henry met him, with the message that the Superintendent would like him to stop in if he would.

The Warden was very curious to hear how it had gone in the upper tiers. When the Bishop told how quite a good many men had joined in the singing, the Warden looked at him in amazement.

"Well, I'll be damned!" he said. "You mean to say the men, themselves, liked to sing?"

"Oh, not all of them, of course, but certainly quite a good number. They would ask to sing a chorus over again."

"Well, I suppose you'll say next that if we could get them all to sing we'd never have a riot, eh?"

"Oh, I'm not making any rash statements, but this one thing I do know to be true. When you get a man to sing with all his heart, he will have lost his tensions."

"Bishop, I don't think I've given many compliments along the way, but I would like to give one to you. You came here alone; first minister, priest, or whatever, who had come during my stay. You came quietly, spoke your wishes like a gentleman, made no comment on what I said, but thanked me and went out. Now you have brought something to this jail that was not here before. I won't try to name it, but you can feel it yourself. And it's my turn to thank you."

"This will bring comfort to my heart many times over, and I do thank you."

"And," the Warden went on, "I have talked to the man who is in charge of the woodworking shop. We have some quite decent carpenters there. They are all ready to build an altar, and they want to run a wide board up from either end and let them meet at a point at the top. As if sort of a background for the altar or making a little holy place for it. They plan to paint all the woodwork white except the inside of this enclosure, which one man is set on making a light blue—I don't know why."

"It's the Virgin's own color," the Bishop told him. "This man may be a Catholic. The altar will be lovely when it's all done. And I want to contribute the altar cloth and a pair of candlesticks. We'll have a church yet!"

"I think I should say that of course there would be funds to make this a professional job, but the men will be so proud if they do the work themselves."

"I'm sure of it," the Bishop answered. "Do please let them go ahead."

He had much to tell Julian that night and almost forgot the stairs until he suddenly laughed. "We had to climb the most inordinate flight of iron stairs. I actually had to stop halfway up to get a blow."

Julian was at once grave.

"Now listen, Bishop," he began. "You must not take those stairs again until you've seen Dr. Lindsay and had a thorough checkup. It's been a good while since the last one. Now, I'm very serious."

"You're kind, Julian, and I'll go and see my friend to satisfy you. But I'm certainly not giving up those stairs just when I'm so delighted over what has happened."

"Well, let the doctor decide that. And make an appointment right now so you won't forget. Dr. Lindsay always has a nurse there in the evenings. Go ahead, under my eye. I don't trust you."

"A fine thing to say to me! All right, to prevent future nagging, I'll do it!"

He was back after a few minutes. "He will see me Tuesday afternoon at two. Now I hope you're satisfied."

"I'll be more so when I hear his opinion. Oh, I forgot to tell you yesterday that I have had an invitation to preach at St. James the Sunday before Christmas on peace and good will in general."

"Why, that's nice. Everything stable there as usual?"

"Oh, no actual disruption, of course, but a little undercurrent of dissatisfaction that troubles Wilde."

"Good man!" said the Bishop.

"I like him very much. But this trouble as he sees it is that a great part of their parish is made up of older, very wealthy contributors who are inimical to change in any form. They like the status quo. On the other side there is the larger body of middle-aged and younger members who like change, who want to move with the times, and a fig for the status quo. You know, Bishop, I've been thinking. Are rich people always conservative?"

The Bishop smiled. "Maybe that's the way they got to be rich!"

"I wonder. This just struck me. And my sermon has to

spread an aura of good will. How will I do that? It's a big responsibility."

"Julian, stick to the very beginning of the Christmas story, then you can't go wrong. It always melts the heart."

When Tuesday came Bishop Ware was in Dr. Lindsay's office on the stroke of two. He kept saying over and over to himself, "A fool idea! To take up a doctor's time when there is nothing wrong with me. A fool idea!" But when the doctor came in, there was a very warm handclasp between them.

"I've been wanting to see you to tell you the latest about Big Tom . . ."

"And I've been wanting to tell you my sympathy over the loss of your dog. What was his name?"

"Marcano. I named him from the pictures of dogs on my dining-room wall. He was a noble dog."

"And have you ever thought, Bishop, that such a sorrow could affect your health?"

"I suppose it could. I had never thought of it."

"Well, it can. It does. Now suppose while I listen to what your insides are up to, you tell me the latest news about Big Tom."

The doctor went quietly on with his listening; to the heart, the chest, the blood pressure, and then slowly over it all again. They talked for a little while then about the prison episodes, and then once more the doctor listened. "You might cough a little for me," he said, and the Bishop obliged.

"Lungs sound nice and clear," said the doctor.

Then, at last, he laid down his equipment and looked straight at the Bishop. "It's generally a very good report. Lungs, blood pressure, circulation, fine, and the heart doing its work well except that you must not let it get overtired. Now, about those damned stairs, how high are they? Two stories up?"

"That at least."

"Umm hmm. It would upset you to give up climbing them?"

"Oh, I couldn't do that just now, Doctor."

"Well, here is my rule then and see that you *keep* it!" The doctor's voice was stern. "When you feel you must use them to keep you happy, stop *twice* on the way up. And each time rest and relax for about eight minutes by your watch. Will you promise?"

"Of course."

"Good. And one week from today I want to see you again."

"Now, Doctor, surely . . ."

"And if you don't promise me that and come, I'll take the stairs completely away from you! How is our friend Cissie Lansing? I don't see her often now."

"I have some very pleasant times with her grandmother. And she is anxious about Cissie. She says the girl is not happy, and she thinks she may regret refusing to marry the doctor."

"Yes, a fine man, brilliant in his profession, charming, and even rich too. I felt he would be perfect for her. But Bishop, if there is one thing true about love, it is that you can't force it. It has to come unbidden. You can't start it and you can't stop it, as I guess you know."

"I do, indeed," the Bishop said, smiling.

"Now what I think is the matter with Cissie is that she has fallen in love the deep way with a man not free to marry her. She's the kind who wouldn't take anything else."

"I'm sure of that."

"I'd like to wring the man's neck for making her unhappy. Have you any idea who he might be?"

"Not really," the Bishop said slowly. "Once or twice I thought I might be getting hot, and then it was all off again."

"Let me know next Tuesday, if you suspect anyone."

As the Bishop checked his calendar that night he took new stock of his assets. He had found a comprehensive history for Lucien and the boy was eating it up, from his reports. The "Easy Reader" for Big Tom was in constant use also, but he knew their main interest just now was the weekly songs and their reception. Tom often remarked, "We never get nothin' now like them she-roosters did that first time. I wonder what the Super done to them."

The Bishop had often wondered too but had never asked. Now with his calendar before him he made his plans. There were just three weeks until Christmas, which meant not quite that much for learning the new songs he had set his heart upon. For it had come to him with the force of a dart that they must have a purely Christmas program for the men on what must be a hard day for them.

He thought deeply and then decided on "Joy to the World" and "Silent Night" for the quartet to sing. For Angelo's solo there could be "Away in a Manger." He could hear the boy's clear lyric voice singing that. And for a lighter touch "Jingle Bells" and "White Christmas." Certainly many could join in there. A public stenographer often came to the house, and he would try to get him tomorrow to copy the words that needed to be memorized. Julian was away for the evening, so he roamed down to the drawing room, selected two books that would contain the selection he wanted, and then ran over them one by one, for his own pleasure. Yes, he decided, his choices had been good.

On Thursday afternoon he set forth again for the prison with four envelopes in his pocket. He was sure he knew all the words but he would feel safer with a copy for himself as well. The three others were there already, eager to tell him what reports of last week's singing had filtered down to them. The comments had all been good. When the Bishop gave them the envelopes and explained his Christmas plan, they read the songs and looked as though they had struck a tender note in their hearts.

"We ain't never had nothin' for Christmas but a good dinner. I tell you, Bishop, I'll work like hell to learn all these words. Damned if I don't!" said Tom.

Lucien smiled. "Me too," he said. "I may remember some from high school."

"An' what about me?" Angelo added. "I got the most to learn with my solo piece on top of the rest. But I'll betcha I'll know it all first. I learn awful quick."

"I would like to keep these songs a secret until the day itself, so we could spring a little surprise. Let's run over them now to get an idea of the tunes. We'll take the easy ones first."

"Jingle Bells" needed little practice and oddly enough "White Christmas." The words and melody of that had gone to the roots of society. There was recognition as the Bishop started on "Silent Night." This would improve easily with practice. When he began on "Joy to the World" Lucien was the only one who found it familiar. But the others liked the unusual tune. Angelo sang, reading from his paper, with the Bishop as he went over the solo.

"That was all wonderful. How well you caught all the tunes and dropped into the harmony almost at once. Would you like to go over it again before we take up our regular program?"

They chorused approval and once more, this time with surprising success, they tried the Christmas songs.

When it came time to climb the stairs, the Bishop kept his watch in his hand. "It would be easier," he thought to himself, "if I hadn't been so stubborn about keeping this dear old turnip, instead of getting a wrist watch as Julian wanted me to do." He kept his promise about the rest periods, though it did embarrass him to have others waiting for fifteen minutes until he reached the top. But once there he felt a general settling of men in their chairs near the bars, as if they now felt something like anticipation. And the rest of the time confirmed this.

At the end, once again there was the restrained clapping, beginning apparently in one cell and then spreading until it became a soft but fairly general sound.

When it was over, the Bishop repeated quietly but with great distinctness, the short prayer, then turned with the others toward the stairs. The voice of what must be the self-appointed leader spoke to the guard.

"Tell him I guess we can buy that last thing he said."

That night the Bishop felt very tired indeed. It was not so much the stairs, he decided, as a certain tension that he always felt when he was going through their prison program. It should now be a thing of the past, but strangely, it was not. There was no relaxation until he was in the car starting home. But when it did come, it came too much. He felt weak and, once at least, he actually *wobbled* a bit as he got out of the car and started for the house. If Julian should ever see that, what a scene. As to using his cane, that was worse, for it was all bound up with memories of Marcano. Oh, well, the doctor was a good soul, but put all kinds of thoughts into his head. All he needed was to concentrate on his happiness over the way his ministry work was going. Even the little prayer had been accepted.

And that night Julian came home tired also. He explained his day after dinner when the Bishop questioned him.

"Oh, I wrote twenty-five letters today. In each case I had to think out my answer clearly before I dictated it. It was stiff work for that many. Then I had a call from a church in trouble."

"Not more scandal, I hope?"

"No, and not Fundamentalist trouble, either. This is financial."

"Oh, dear. That's a sticky one."

"Isn't it though? When you touch someone's pocketbook, you've hit a raw nerve."

"How bad is this?"

"Bad enough. About a third of the membership either pledges nothing for the year or so small an amount it seems sort of insulting."

"Strange, no big givers."

"Apparently not. Just normally pleasant, comfortable people, all 'seated in the mean,' as Shakespeare puts it, so what pledges there are, are also in the very middle range. It was the Church Warden who called me. He had talked with the Treasurer, and they beg my help."

"Do you know the Rector?"

"Slightly. A very fine fellow and worthy of a larger parish, it looks to me."

"Is he satisfied with his salary?"

"I don't believe he can be. But he likes the people. He has children and he feels it's a good place for them to grow up, so he stays and pinches the pennies! At least that's my opinion."

"You have a good talking point there. But I'll tell you what we did once long ago when I was faced with this question. I suggested the Treasurer would read aloud, the stated expenses that had to be met, and then the amount of each pledge (of course with no name), and finally the totals showing how close they were to the edge. It worked there, and the crisis was past."

"I had thought of something a little like that. Have the Treasurer, or the Warden, read what he called the Honor Roll of those who were carrying almost the whole weight of the church's expenses on their shoulders and then read both pledge and names. Your way would take longer but might be more effective. I'll think it over."

And he lapsed into silence. The Bishop, too, remained quiet until he suddenly rose, merely tossing a remark over his shoulder.

"I'm going to call Cissie!"

"Always a nice idea," Julian said, his face relaxing.

He listened then with intent to the Bishop's side of the conversation.

"It's about the altar for the Prison Chapel, which the men are making. The altar will be painted white except for a light blue inside the little peaked alcove above the altar proper. . .

"Yes. I think so too. But I would like to find some soft material to be gathered gracefully at the front of the altar. I don't like hard painted boards there somehow. Would you possibly know what . . ."

There was a long period broken only by excited exclamations from the Bishop.

"Oh, Cissie! My dear, you don't mean it! But that's *perfect!* Oh, my *dear* child!"

There was much more of this until the Bishop said, "Cissie, must end by asking you one question. Listen carefully. Do ou take off your wings before you get into bed?" Then apturous laughter at both ends of the wire.

Julian pounced at once.

"Now just how did you happen to ask *that?*"

"Oh," the Bishop explained, "she told me once a young loctor had asked her that after they had saved a tiny baby's ife. I've often chuckled over it. But listen to the wonderful hings she now will do. I told her what I wished for at the 'ront of the altar, and she said at once she had a big strip of white velvet laid away, left from a dress long ago. I gave her he measurements of the altar, which of course I knew, and she said she and Mrs. Lansing would hem the velvet to the ength desired some evening soon when she is free, and she was sure that John, her grandmother's man of all work, would be proud to shop for the small brass rod and the rings hat, fastened to the top of the velvet curtain, would make it hang easily." In a burst of elation the Bishop cried, "Cissie is he most wonderful girl I've ever known."

There was a muffled "That's right!" from Julian. Then as he straightened, he added more distinctly, "You might say hat."

The Bishop did not sit down. He paced back and forth in the study, as he remarked at intervals: "I feel *lifted,* as the Scottish say. I certainly feel lifted, tonight. Never better! A fig for the fuss-budget doctor and his stairs!"

"His *what?*" Julian was wide enough awake now. "Why, it's just hit me I didn't get a full report of your visit to Dr. Lindsay. I want to know everything. What about the stairs?"

"Now Julian, you're such a one to get excited. There was practically nothing to tell. Chest clear, blood pressure fine, heart doing good work only 'don't get overtired,' you see?"

"Not quite. Now about the stairs. Does he want you to stay on one floor? We've plenty of room here, so we could easily make . . ."

"Now Julian, listen. He never mentioned my staying on one floor. I told him in fun that as I was climbing the long iron stairs at the prison I stopped once for a good blow, and of course then he had something to talk about. He wants me now to stop twice, which, as our Cockney friends would say, is a bloody nuisance."

"When do you see him again?"

"Next Tuesday."

"Good. And I'll certainly check on you carefully after this

"I believe I actually *like* being worried *over!* Just see ho
precious a creature I at once became. But don't ever g
excited over me, Julian. Just a nice soft little worry like th
purr of a kitten, nothing more."

Julian laughed. "Fine!" he said. "I'll purr but never sho
my claws. And I think I'll be going on up now. I have to wo
hard on that Christmas sermon at St. James. That's why
didn't go to vespers last Sunday. Did you?"

"Yes. A lovely service. But I saw Fenwick this morning.
went over to ask him about a song. He said his wife an
children are down in Florida with her parents, and he an
Morton are getting on alone. Morton is married, you knov
but his wife is coming on a little later. What I meant to as
you is, wouldn't it be nice to ask the two of them over to a
all-male dinner? Perhaps after next Sunday's vespers?"

"I think that would be a very nice, neighborly thing to do
I'm sure Mrs. Morgan and Cook would outdo themselves a
the thought of four clergymen at once. They would feel the
were breathing sanctified air. Do invite them. I would like i
immensely."

And that little half-breathless time came when Christma
waited, as it were, in the wings, while busy shoppers fille
the stores and battled through a light curtain of snowflake
so that no child would be disappointed on the great day. I
was also the time when the clergy strained every nerve to
make sure that this Christmas would mean more to thou
sands of men and women than it had meant last year. A bel
rang out at every street corner, with a kettle to catch the
coins. For this was the time when from faraway hilltops and
mountain slopes great noble fir trees were brought to be
placed in the city's squares, to lift the hearts of men as they
saw the million twinkling little lights and the glory of the
crowning stars. And countless little men, hard pressed by the
cares of the days, went here and there into slushy storage
yards or perhaps even into a bit of city strange to them, to
spend a few precious dollars for just this late cheap buying of
the tree, which would be decked this very Eve. And over all,
from great houses and small, from churches and stores and
street singers and walkers through the snow, came sudden
bursts of the old familiar carols.

Bishop Ware woke on Christmas morning in a state of
dazed happiness. It took him some moments to adjust to the
new day; then as he raised himself on his pillows and put on

his glasses, he knew exactly what had taken place the day before and why a feeling close to delight had burst into his mind like a Roman candle. It was the Christmas visit to the prison.

It had been decided that the singers would arrive a little later than usual, so that their program could indeed be given on Christmas Eve. The guards related this word. The Bishop had been very nervous about the performance. He had borrowed four songbooks from Fenwick, paperbacks, which the children's choir used. The carols were at the front, so each singer could follow the words. Even so, the Bishop was afraid for the music itself. With all their practice the tunes were not truly familiar.

As to the altar, it seemed incredibly lovely. The workmen had wrought a miracle with their eager hands. The altar stood now, opposite the open door, in its delicate blue enclosure, with the lace cloth and candlesticks as its only ornaments and the soft white velvet curtains below. Even the Warden had been impressed. "We must manage some way for each man to see this" was his first comment. So, as each contingent came from mess they were to be allowed to stop for a moment to look.

But if the perfection of the altar had made the Bishop thankful beyond words, it somehow made him more anxious about their program.

He had confided this to Julian when the time came to leave early yesterday evening for the prison. Julian had insisted upon driving him over and remaining to bring him home. "You'll be too tired to see through this first dusk," he had said. "Besides I can hardly wait to hear your quartet."

"That's what scares me," the Bishop said.

"Well, without calling you a proper fool I'll just say your last remark was very foolish."

When they reached the usual parking space there was a car in the space next to theirs, with its door open and a young woman looking out ruefully at the snow below her. They both recognized her and spoke her name at once. "It's Cissie!"

"Heavens! This is the last straw!" The Bishop chuckled now as he remembered his remark.

Julian was beside her at once. "See what the snowstorm brought in," he had said cheerfully. Then he explained how he would carry her over to the wide brick walk by the walls, which was cleared.

There had been quite a bit of badinage as he picked her up

and insisted she put an arm around his neck to steady her

"Whatever made you come out on such a night?"

"I did want to see the altar with the lights on. Then I'm just dying to hear the men's quartet sing the carols!"

"So am I, but the Bishop doesn't seem keen to have us in the audience. He said he was scared having me come, and when he knew you were here he said it was the last straw. So you see how you rate."

They laughed, the two of them, and it had sounded like young laughter.

"What a naughty thing to say about me! But, I could forgive him anything! Anything at all!"

"I wish I were as lucky."

"But you are, Julian. Truly."

"That will be my best Christmas gift, then."

"I'll give you another if it doesn't upset you."

And then after a very short space had come Julian's "Thank you, dear."

What had it all meant?

What was happening or *had* happened between those two? Were the "eternal poles of tendency" still slowly, quietly operating upon them? He loved them both so much it seemed as though the very strength of his affection should bring them closer, and that all his yearning petitions should be answered.

At least they had all been together on Christmas Eve and his short fears had been put to flight by the way the program had gone.

When they reached the door of Front House and were admitted by both the outside and inside guards they had gone at once to the Chapel and stood a few minutes at the open door, looking at the lighted altar. Something was there that had not been there the day before. It was a heavy brass cross around which had been twined, by a florist's hand, bright red carnations and holly, without obscuring the outline of the symbol upon which the flowers and greens rested. This had been a beautiful mystery even to Bishop Ware, but the effect was that of giving the altar something it had lacked before.

"This is a gift from me," Julian had said in a low voice. "If the men like it, I'll be happy. If there are any objections it can be quietly removed."

The other three singers were there, waiting. After the introduction they all spoke their feeling about the altar. "It looks like a church now all right," came from Lucy. And

190

Bishop Ware caught Big Tom's low murmur, "If only Baby coulda seen this."

Henry had set two chairs from the Chapel outside for the two guests, and Bishop Ware, the tightness still in his breast, explained that the singers were to stand in front of the door for the program and they all took their places.

First came the Bishop's tender reading of the Christmas story itself, the most beautiful story in the world. There was a minute of breathless silence, and then a great burst of elation in song, "Joy to the World!"

Before the verses were ended Bishop Ware knew he need have no further fears about the music. One by one, carol after carol, they sang, secure in the words from their books and the melodies that seemed to have become a part of them, as it was hoped they could always be.

When it was time for Angelo's solo he took a step further forward and in his angelic young voice sang:

> "Away in a manger,
> No crib for a bed,
> The little Lord Jesus
> Laid down his sweet head—"

When the last note had died away Bishop Ware spoke. "I feel it is a great honor that we have with us this evening two guests, one is Miss Lansing, who gave us the velvet curtain for the altar." At once there was the sound of applause. Cissie rose and bowed. "You've no idea how much I've enjoyed spending this Christmas Eve here, and I want to thank you for having me as your guest."

After this graceful little speech, Bishop Ware had gone on. "Our other guest is a very distinguished one. As many of you know I'm a retired Bishop, meaning my regular work in the Episcopal Diocese is ended, and we have a new active Bishop. He is here and I am going to ask him now if he will give the little prayer many of you have liked. Bishop Armstrong?"

Julian looked a bit surprised but went forward at once to stand beside his old friend. But even Bishop Ware had never heard Julian's voice so rich in meaning. On the last lines it seemed to grow more tender . . . "In thy mercy grant us all a safe lodging, and a holy rest and peace at the last."

A deep quiet lasted until Bishop Ware spoke. "That ends the religious part of our Christmas Eve program; now we're planning a little fun. How many of you know, 'I'm Dreamin of a White Christmas'? Speak out!"

Before the quartet was more than half through, one by or and then it seemed dozen by dozen, the voices came from th cells. As they repeated it for the last time, the body of soun almost shook the walls.

The men were loath to stop. But at last, Bishop Ware tol them the singers must have a little time to catch their breat before going up to the tiers for the second program.

When they all reached the foot of the stairs, Bishop War saw Julian scanning the rise sharply and then the Bishop own face.

"I will take your arm, but even so do you really feel able t climb these?"

The Bishop remembered his light remarks before.

"Why certainly, what did you think?"

"I don't know exactly," Julian had said, "but lean hard or me."

It had been a great help and the two rest periods also, bu when he had reached the top he had felt strangely weak "Nonsense!" he had said aloud. "*Nonsense*," though no on appeared to notice. They had gone through the whole pro gram again, and he knew now as he thought of it all, that it had been even better than the first one down below. What a relief! What a tremendous satisfaction. The men had liked it. They had really been cheered by it for Christmas. His heart was very happy over that. But even so that organ did not need to pump so fast and hard. He turned comfortably on his pillow and fell asleep again.

He was still asleep when Mrs. Morgan came up with the breakfast tray that Julian had ordered for him. At two o'clock he was still sound asleep.

Mrs. Morgan and Julian conferred. The former said, "It ain't natural for him to sleep this much."

"But," Julian still argued, "he was under such a strain about this prison business, and you should hear what he's accomplished! I was there yesterday and I know. No wonder he's tired to death."

"I think a doctor should be called."

"I would feel like a fool to ask a doctor to stop in on Christmas afternoon because the Bishop got overtired and is still asleep."

"I know it sounds funny, but it ain't natural."

"I suppose I could at least talk to him, and in any case I'll have him come over tomorrow morning. We are to go to Mrs. Lansing's for seven o'clock dinner."

"He's in no shape to go. His color ain't good."

Julian was slightly irritated.

"Mrs. Morgan, you certainly are determined to have a real patient here. I still hope you are wrong, but I'll have a talk with the doctor, if I can."

When he returned from this, he looked anxious. "He's coming over at once. You may have been right, Mrs. Morgan. He says he must check at once on his heart."

"Aye, it's a good job he's coming."

Julian let him in and listened carefully to his brief words.

"When he came to the office, he seemed quite sound except for the heart. I was a little concerned, but after talking with him I felt it would do him more harm to shut down the prison business entirely than to let him keep on until Christmas, which I gathered was a sort of goal. Now I'll see how he got through that."

The Bishop was still asleep. He did not waken until the doctor touched his shoulder gently. Then he roused, opened his eyes, and looked irritated. "Doctor," he said, "why on earth are you here?"

"That's a pretty way to speak to a friend who was passing and stopped in to say 'Merry Christmas.'"

"Heavens! Did you really come for that? And I'm sound asleep. Do excuse me. Sit down do. I'll be up in a minute!"

"Now, just stay still. Since I'm here I might as well have a look at you and hear what you've been up to since I last saw you!"

"I smell collusion here! Hand me my dressing gown, Julian, please!"

The doctor did not alter his movements, except to wave the dressing gown away. "I hear you had a big time at the prison yesterday afternoon."

Bishop Ware relaxed at once and began describing their program.

"And Doctor, at the end when we got to 'Silent Night,' my own eyes were wet. It was feeling all that emotion in the men, for they seemed to be listening *out loud,* if you can say such a thing. Did Julian tell you about our guests?"

"He and Miss Lansing," Dr. Lindsay said.

"I was very nervous when I knew they were coming. But so glad they heard it when it went so well."

"And you did it all twice over, I gather, and climbed the stairs in between."

"Well, yes. Julian helped me up the stairs, and we even took two rests, so you can't go on about that. Why are you looking at me like that?"

"Because you are not going to like what I have to say."

"Now, Doctor, please don't get any foolish ideas . . ."

"I assure you, I'm not being foolish, but when I warned you against getting overtired, you didn't pay much attention. You have strained the muscles of that good old ticker of yours and now you'll have to pay up. I order you to stay in bed and sleep all you want. Eat a very light supper and take the medication I'm ordering for you. I leave it with you, Julian, to see that he stays right here even if you have to use brute force to keep him."

Bishop Ware laughed. "I doubt if it comes to that. Julian has the gift of persuasion. He's all right but just a little too bossy at times. Like today," he added.

"And a good thing he is!"

Julian spoke hesitantly. "The Bishop and I are expected at Mrs. Lansing's for dinner at seven."

"Bishop Ware isn't going anywhere. You can go, only don't stay away too long, if there's no one in the house."

"Mrs. Morgan will be here, but I won't be staying long in any case."

"That's too bad about Mrs. Lansing's dinner. Of course I intended to be there, but since I'm settled in bed with an order to stay here I will confess that it would be a big effort to go out."

Julian went with the doctor as he left and watched him anxiously at the outside door.

"Please tell me everything," he begged.

"First, I'm glad you are here, and I don't like the condition of the heart. It is, as I told him, an overstrain of the muscle, but I can't tell now to what extent. I'll have a heart man come in tomorrow and make a cardiogram. But meanwhile I found something else. He has a little fever and a very red throat. It may be that he has one of these damned viruses starting up. I'll have instructions put on both medicines I'm ordering, and we'll hope all is better by tomorrow. I'll come in then and check. Where is your bedroom?"

"It's on the third floor. But there is a good couch bed in the study, a most comfortable one where I think I will sleep tonight."

"Very good. I see no sudden failure of the heart, but you might slip in once to look at him, and of course you can be in immediate touch with me. I always sleep with one ear open and my bag packed."

"You're an unspeakable comfort to me."

When the doctor had gone, he went to the office phone and called Mrs. Lansing's number. It was Cissie who answered.

"I'm afraid I have some bad news," he began.

And she broke in. "But so have I and was just about to call you. Grammie suddenly became lightheaded and against all her protestations, I just put her to bed. She seems a bit feverish to me and her throat is sore. How is the Bishop?"

"That's *my* bad news. He didn't get up this morning. I called the doctor, who has just left. He says the Bishop has a greatly overtired heart and he will bring their best heart man over tomorrow, and he must *not* get out of bed tonight. He is distressed to disappoint Mrs. Lansing as well as himself. What shall we do about the dinner?"

A small laugh came over the wire. "I'll just rearrange the table a little. Oh, I'm so distressed about the Bishop and Grammie too. She's been planning this for weeks. Do you think you could enjoy a Christmas dinner with only me?"

Julian did not answer for a few seconds, and when he spoke his voice was low and, in spite of himself, very tender.

"With *only you!* I should call that perfect!"

11

The heart specialist arrived in good time the next morning. Bishop Ware had been irritated at the very idea of the visit, but when the doctor came in, he was most disarming. He wore a bright plaid necktie and had a small gray moustache, and his hair was curly.

"Well, now let's have a look at you. For it's the first time in my life I've ever seen a Bishop. You see I'm an old Scotch

Presbyteerian myself and I'll tell you something if you won't quote me. I do believe a Presbyteerian finds it hard to kneel even before God Almighty Himself. They're a little stuck-up, religiously speaking. But if you get a good one, you can trust him to hell and back—that's quite a distance."

The Bishop chuckled. He decided he liked this man.

The doctor sat down on the chair left for him, one hand lightly feeling the Bishop's wrist.

"Now, about this jail business. Dr. Lindsay says pretty soon you'll have all the prisoners out 'on free,' as the kids say at their game."

"I was pretty happy day before yesterday, maybe too much so for my own good."

"No, no. Happiness never killed anyone. Just sketch me in a bit about it."

The Bishop told briefly of the Christmas Eve program, and the doctor was quiet and serious.

"That's a wonderful story, but it was natural for you to be tired from it. You will plan now, of course, to take a little rest from your efforts."

"Rest?" The Bishop was at once excited. "I couldn't possibly think of not going as usual next week. The men sort of—I mean they look forward, for some reason, to seeing me! I feel so humbled about it, but you see I have to go."

"I'd like to hear you pronounce my name. It's MacCloud. Can you say it after me? You have a fine voice. It's not MacClood, nor MacLowd. It's quicker than that. Now try it. MacCloud. See? *au*, it's short. Now, again!

"Fine. You caught it exactly. Now, I'm going to introduce you to a small pet of mine. When Mrs. Morgan let me in, she stopped me at the stairs and took hold of what I was carrying. I made some struggle but I couldn't budge her. She had heard the trill on my tongue and that settled it. She was so overjoyed to hear her own speech I thought for a moment she was going to carry me up, too. I talked her out of that, but you may have noticed this tenacious quality in her."

The Bishop laughed. "Yes, I just may have," he said with delicate irony.

"Right in here with my pet," the doctor said. "Right on this chair, Mrs. Morgan. This creature has soft little paws which touch your breast, Bishop. And when the cord is plugged into the outlet—that's just fine, Mrs. Morgan—you can hear it purr. It goes tickety, tick, tick, tickety, tick, tick, tick, and this makes marks on a strip of paper which I can read. Isn't

196

that clever of me? Oh, by the way, have you ever had a cardiogram before?"

"Never."

"That's all right then. If you had, I wouldn't have needed the explanations. Now just lie back and be perfectly comfortable. This is a painless proc*ee*dure."

The doctor did not talk as the sounds came as predicted. When they stopped, he pulled out the strips of paper, glanced a moment at them, and put them in his bag.

"That was easy, wasn't it?" he asked the Bishop.

"How did the purring come out?" the Bishop inquired.

"Oh, I'll study this at the office," he said. "The marks are nice and black." Then he stopped suddenly. "You can tell I'm specially interested in the heart." His tone was contrite. "I forget people have other troubles. Dr. Lindsay asked me to check your temperature and throat when I was here, so now here goes to save my reputation." He advanced with a thermometer. When he withdrew it from the Bishop's mouth, he looked at it, then took it under the light and looked again.

"I do feel a trifle hot," the Bishop mentioned.

"I shouldn't be too much surprised if you were. Is your throat sore?"

"Just a little."

"Uh, huh. Dr. Lindsay was right. He thought even last night that you had picked up a little virus. Now, I feel sure of it. Plenty of liquids and a very light lunch. Do you know how to make panada, Mrs. Morgan?"

"Mebbe it'll not be by that name, sir."

"Well, here's how you make it anyway. Take a slice of white bread, toast it lightly on both sides, lay it in the bottom of a soup dish, and sprinkle it well with sugar and cinnamon and a wee touch of nutmeg. Then pour boiling water over it and serve."

"Ooh-eye, that's what we call 'boily bread.' "

"I thought you'd know it, Mrs. Morgan. And if you like to make it a bit richer put a teaspoon of cream in the center of the bread. That would be safe for the Bishop's lunch."

The men parted with a real feeling of interest on both sides.

"If I were not a medicine man, I'd like to talk to you longer," Dr. MacCloud said earnestly.

"And I would so greatly enjoy that. And I should like you to meet the real Bishop."

"You mean you're not *real?*"

197

"I'm retired, but the active Bishop is not quite out of his thirties and is a real son-in-the-Lord to me. I'll tell you what," he went on, sitting up in the bed, "when I'm over this thing, maybe you could join us at dinner one night . . . and your wife?"

"I lost her a good many years ago," the doctor answered as he gently pushed the Bishop back upon his pillows.

"Ah, we have a bond then. Don't forget about the dinner. I'll soon be planning for it."

"How could I forget!" came from the doctor.

When he was again alone, Bishop Ware felt upset with his whole situation. Worst of all, he now felt really sick. His head ached, his throat hurt, he felt miserably hot and thirsty. He must, indeed, have caught one of those wretched little virus devils.

Mrs. Morgan entered now with a pitcher of cold pineapple juice and a fresh glass.

"Aye, he's the grand doctor, you one. He says pineapple's good for the throat, so here's plenty for you. And he says to make you lie still except when you're swallerin' something. And here's the pill you're to take steadily till Dr. Lindsay sees you again. You can have a glass of juice now and I'll support your back a wee bit."

"No, Mrs. Morgan, please. I'm quite able to . . ."

His speech trailed off as he fell back suddenly once more against his pillows.

"You see? Pride goes before a fall. You must just get used to a bit nursing when you're sick. Now, we'll try again." With a strong arm she raised him and held him straight until he had swallowed the pill and drained the glass.

"And I may tell you," she went on, "that Bishop Armstrong called to see about you and he's coming home early and right glad I am of it. He'll be here about two, and I'm to tell you not to worry for he'll arrange everything."

"Good," said the Bishop weakly. He turned to find a cool spot on his pillow and was almost immediately asleep. His last thought was of two lines of what he had always said was a wicked old hymn that had come down from the Puritans:

> *We should expect some danger nigh*
> *When most we feel delight.*

What ghastly theology, as though God actually brought

disaster upon the happy! This was true in his present case but certainly not by the Will of Providence.

He did not rouse until Mrs. Morgan appeared again at nearly one.

"An' here's your boily bread," she stated.

"I like the doctor's name for it better. 'Panada,' [long a] he called it."

"It will taste just the same anyway, sir."

"No, I don't think so, no matter what Shakespeare says. A rose by any other name would *not* smell as sweet to me. I'll call this 'panada.' "

"Yes, yes, sir. Just what you like. And don't feel bad if your mind wanders a bit on Shakespeare, an' that. It's just because you've a bit of temperature."

It was nearly three when Julian entered with a few snowflakes still on his hair.

"I'm absolutely full of good business," he began. "I caught Dr. MacCloud by the merest chance, and after his report that you would *not* be able to go out for another week, I dropped by to see Fenwick's new assistant. You know me, thought it strange he didn't appear at vespers. Well, he was like you. He had a virus. He's well now, and listen to this! He will be happy to take your place at the prison! Now, I await praise."

Bishop Ware managed a good smile at least, with his words.

"You're wonderful, Julian, and you knew just what was worrying me most. What is the young assistant like? Name? And qualifications?"

"I'm prepared for that. He is David Morton. He is tall, blond, very good looking, and warmly friendly. But best of all he has a fine baritone voice. It seems Fenwick kept hunting until he found this special quality. He was thinking, of course, of a reading and intoning voice, but for your work the singing voice will be perfect. I gave him a brief sketch of what you have been doing and how the men keep calling for Angelo's 'Rose' song. He smiled and said, 'I think Bishop Ware has got those men. I'll certainly try to keep them.' "

"This is a blessed relief, Julian. I believe I *can* relax now."

"I'm sure you can. I like this Dr. MacCloud unqualifiedly. I'm sure he'll be back."

"What would he come back for? He had this creature, as he called it, making marks on a paper. He's done all that."

"The cardiogram? The doctors often make two close togeth-

199

er. I had them years ago when in college. I had done some fool jumping and swimming tricks. But now, how do you feel in general?"

"For the first time I can remember I feel absolutely *sick*. My head aches, my bones ache, my throat is sore, and I feel completely limp. That's my state. And don't come near me, Julian. You might catch this thing."

"Oh, no. I move too fast. I'm very distressed about you. Dr. Lindsay will be in soon and give you some stronger medicine, I'm sure. Here is Mrs. Morgan with another cold drink. That will be pleasant. Do you feel hot?"

"Very. I'm slowly burning up it seems. I wish you would go out of the room, Julian. And, Mrs. Morgan, don't hang over me. I know this thing I have is probably very contagious. I'm ashamed of having it."

"Ooh-ee, I don't ketch things easy," she said.

"Nor I," Julian echoed.

When Dr. Lindsay came he did not pause for many words but went quickly about his various tests as the Bishop dutifully answered his questions, and obliged politely to his requests. And the doctor finally stood still looking down at his patient.

"I'm going to tell you something I'm afraid will make you mad. I'm going to send a trained nurse here to stay with you tonight."

"Now listen, Doctor . . . I . . ."

"Now *you* listen. I'm the boss now. I'm sure Mrs. Morgan would like to watch over you or even Bishop Julian here, but that's not the same. A good experienced nurse knows a dozen ways to make you comfortable. Also she will *do exactly as* I tell her, and that's important."

The Bishop was still trying to mutter his objections, but the doctor paid no attention.

"Now we have this matter of semantics, Bishop. You know people have had the same symptoms you have time out of mind. But then it was called the *grippe!* Nearly everybody some time or other in the winter got the grippe. But then later on they wanted a new, more scientific name for it. And so no one gets the grippe anymore. They have a *virus*. Funny, isn't it? Well, you certainly have a bad one, but we'll catch it by the tail yet. When the nurse comes she will make you more comfortable and for your dinner—could you drink an eggnog with a dash of nutmeg?"

The Bishop merely nodded. "That's it then, and *cold*. Now don't worry about anything. Sleep all you wish."

And he was gone.

At the front door Julian spoke anxiously. "Dr. Lindsay, will you please tell me his exact condition? I really must know."

"All right, here it is. Dr. MacCloud was not satisfied with what the cardiogram showed. The heart is definitely irregular right now and shows the signs of strain. Moreover, he found, as I surmised, that he suffers from complete exhaustion. He has been doing more than he was able for many weeks, and this condition alone would require bed rest. But he has the weakened heart and now this devilish virus to contend with. I will do my best with the medication, but I want a nurse here until he shows some signs of improvement. Now I've told you everything. I hope you'll back me up."

"You can count on me for anything. He is very dear to me. Can you get a nurse at once?"

"I'm going to try. I know the one I'd like to have, but it may be better for him to have a complete stranger. I had been thinking of Cissie Lansing, but he knows her too well. He would be self-conscious and probably want to talk. No, it must be a stranger, in her forties perhaps, if I can get her. So, now I'm off to try. As I've said before, I'm glad you are here. That door in the Bishop's bedroom, does it open into the study, as you called it?"

"Yes, it does."

"And there is a good couch bed in there?"

"Yes, excellent!"

"Well, tonight with the nurse on watch you can go to your own room, but tomorrow I might make a plan for her to stay on for a few days and nights, and then she would need to rest. For tonight, I don't want her to sleep. You will be here to greet her, won't you?"

"Most definitely, I will."

He was not too much surprised then to have her arrive at eight o'clock. She was a pleasant-looking woman in her forties, with a young smile and voice. Julian felt at once she would be right for the Bishop, calm, quiet, but friendly and with a nice glint of humor in her eyes. He took her upstairs at once, showed her where in the study closet she could hang her coat and bag, and then took her into the Bishop's bedroom to meet him.

He was awake, so she spoke first. Her voice was pleasant, Julian thought.

"I'm Mrs. Leslie, Bishop, and Dr. Lindsay and I are old friends. I was pleased I was free when he called me. Thank you, Bishop Armstrong, for showing me the rooms." He waved to the Bishop and then to her, and went out.

It was nearly ten when he went through the bedroom door again, and then he felt at once a change in the atmosphere. It could not be exactly defined except that everything seemed fresh and clean and the air itself lighter, perhaps because of the open door. The light was very low, but as he advanced he could see the bedclothes had been changed and the Bishop lay in a sound sleep.

Mrs. Leslie got up at once and indicated they could talk in the hall.

"I do not want him wakened now, for I believe it's the first real sleep he has had. The others were just what we call 'fever naps.' I gave him a little tepid sponge bath and he seemed quite better afterward, and, of course, he's had his medicine and a cool pad on his head. Altogether, his temperature is considerably lowered. I'm sure you need not worry about him tonight."

"And his heart?"

"One medication is for that. His heartbeat now is not too strong but much steadier. A good sleep will help him all over."

She was right. In the morning the temperature had dropped to a mere indication, his head was rested, and he actually felt a bit hungry.

Mrs. Leslie was smilingly alert. "Such a good patient. You helped yourself get better, Bishop."

"And what about you? I'll make my terrible confession and get it over. I didn't want you. I mean any nurse. I was very nasty about it. And look what you've done for me. Now, I don't want you to leave."

"I don't have to. I'll have a good nap this morning and then be ready to look after you this afternoon and perhaps tonight also, if Dr. Lindsay wants me. Now, what shall it be for breakfast?"

"Anything I want?"

"Since you've behaved so well, yes!"

"I would love one piece of toast and a scrambled egg. Orange juice as usual. What about coffee?"

"Let's make it tea, good and strong."

"I was afraid you were going to say that. But anyway I like tea, so that will be fine. Will you eat with me?"

"I would be honored, Bishop, at another time, but just now I think you should be very quiet. You are so much better and I want you to keep on the upward trend.

"A little marmalade with your toast?" she added.

Dr. Lindsay decided that Mrs. Leslie should stay on as a home nurse. She was to use the big couch bed in the study and be near the Bishop these first days and nights when he must be kept quiet and content. He relaxed at the news and marveled at how easily Mrs. Leslie had fitted into the household. "Like an old shoe," he said, "and be sure to know that's a compliment."

"It's because I like it here," she said, smiling.

"I'm interested in the young Bishop," she said once. "I wonder if he realizes how attractive he is. He is entirely free from self-consciousness. I should think some young woman would want him for her own. He's not interested in girls, then?"

"Not too much, I should say. But I agree with you that he is quite fascinating when he puts his mind to it."

Mrs. Leslie laughed at the description but asked no more questions and returned to the book she was reading aloud.

When Dr. MacCloud came after a few days with his box he was in high spirits. "Look at this man, Mrs. Leslie. That's the way you always breathe the breath of life into your patients. How do you feel, Bishop?"

"Champion!" he said.

Dr. MacCloud laughed. "Now, that's what they say in the old country. I like the sound of it. If I'm invited I'll sit down a few minutes while we talk about Mrs. Leslie. What do you think of her, Bishop?"

"She's magic!"

"Aye. You're right. This room smells as fresh as a dewy morning, and you, Bishop, look rested and ready for the new day. I brought my little creature in the box over again to have it purr for you. I'll just make the connection if you lie still."

When all was ready he snapped the switch, and there was no further conversation until Mrs. Leslie had carefully wiped the Bishop's breast and the doctor came to stand before him.

"So now," the Bishop said clearly, "I don't wish to hear any more about a creature purring. I want, as man to man, for you to tell me exactly what you learned from this cardiogram."

"Very good. Here it is. Your heart is more regular in its beat than the last time, but it is still weak. It is still a tired muscle, and it will need a long rest to bring it back to something like normal."

"How long?" the Bishop said weakly.

"I would say—let me see. We'll have two more whole weeks in January and four in February—that would just do it, I'm sure. But it must be bed rest, Bishop, with a good nurse to take care of you."

The Bishop's face looked stricken. "You're not *joking?*"

"I was never more serious in my life," the doctor said. "And please don't look so terribly sad, Bishop. You have another trouble beside your heart. You have complete exhaustion. If you follow instructions, you will first begin to relax completely. You haven't yet, but you will. And then for quite a long time you won't even *want* to get out of bed."

"That's nonsense, Doctor."

Dr. MacCloud went right on. "I know what's worryin' you. You think you're irreplaceable. We all get that idea. But here's a little story. I knew a clergyman who was told he must rest or else. He plunged right on, for he said no one could do his work. And do you know what happened?"

"Yes, yes. I get your point."

"I have to tell it all. He went ahead and died of it, but here's the point. His assistant took over and, bless my buttons, he did better than the original man. So you lie there and think about that."

When Julian got home and heard the report from the doctor and also the prescription, he felt, first of all, a sense of shock that the condition was so serious. But quickly then, by the time he saw Bishop Ware he had adjusted to the fact that there was a cure and so he was smiling broadly when he entered the bedroom.

"I don't see much reason for jubilation," the Bishop said as he greeted Julian plaintively. "I suppose you've talked to Mrs. Leslie downstairs. She's the brightest spot on my horizon at the moment."

"Mine, too," Julian said. "I've just had a talk with her, and she's going to stay on. She likes it here, is free, and so can make her own plans. She will sleep in the study at night and take a nap by day when you are taking yours. Are you pleased?"

Bishop Ware drew a long, satisfied sigh. "More than you know."

From that time on, through a long succession of quiet days in the Old Rectory, the Bishop at last reached that perfect point of relaxation that the doctors had prayed for. It was so complete that the Bishop spoke his mind to Dr. MacCloud.

"Look at what you've done to me," he said. "I'm worse than I was when you first saw me! I'm so weak I can hardly lift my fork; and as to lifting my napkin to my face, it's just about beyond me. And you sit there smiling. It's disgraceful."

"Think shame of yourself, Bishop. Here I've been working my fingers to the bone for you, and not a word of thanks do I get! Do you know that fine old English word, hunkers? Did you ever sit on your hunkers?"

Bishop Ware laughed. "I suppose I did when I was a boy."

"Yes. Well now as to your position, you are, at last, completely relaxed and sitting on your hunkers. Our job now, as doctors, is to bring you slowly back to the upright position of a *man*, you might say."

The Bishop still chuckled. "That old expression. I'm sure I haven't heard it for nearly seventy years! When I played marbles as a youngster, I always 'sat on my hunkers' to do it, I remember. Do you suppose kids say it now?"

"They do in the Old Country but I wouldn't know about it here. America moves so fast I can't keep up. If *you* remember it, that's enough."

The days slipped into their steady pattern. Mrs. Leslie with all her nursing skills had proved herself a capable barber, so the shaving and hair trimming were done by gentle but skillful hands. In the mornings a few letters were taken care of, several phone calls made, and after lunch, the real nap, which was followed by the reading aloud until Julian returned at five. Then there was sherry together, and a quick summary of the day, before dinner, with the real visit afterward. At this time Bishop Ware listened eagerly to all the matters, routine and special, which had made up Julian's day. For he was hearing events that had made up his own active life's work.

But as the slow weeks of February moved on, it became clear to the Bishop that there was still something pressing upon Julian's mind. He was not his usual cheerful self during their evening visits. He brought little diverting news in from the outside and often lapsed into silence. One night the Bishop decided to break this stalemate.

On this particular night they made a few comments upon the weather, then Bishop Ware said, "A blind man could see, Julian, that you have a heavy problem resting upon your mind. Considering that I am so much older than you and so very fond of you, don't you think I might be accepted as your confidant?"

The change in Julian was electric. He sat up quickly in his chair, his eyes fixed intently upon the Bishop. "If you only knew how glad I am to hear you say what you just did. I've been trembling on the brink, you might say, about telling you my problem, and I always grew embarrassed and gave it up. But now I'll tell you. I'll make it general.

"If, as a very young man, a clergyman takes a private vow of celibacy, intending to give his whole life to the Church, and then, much later, fears he is falling in love with a girl, what should he do about his vow? So far he has tried to throttle the feeling he has for the girl. He can't tell what his duty is. Could you help him?"

A light spread over Bishop Ware's face. "I'm sure I can. Let's take the vow first. It was a private and personal one, so the young man is free at any time to dismiss it and forget it. It will have served its purpose long enough.

"And then, if this young man you speak of has felt love coming to him, he must let nothing, *nothing* interfere. He must open wide the portals of his heart and let this beautiful passion fill it entirely."

"But his *work*"—Julian's voice trembled—"would it not suffer?"

"I'll tell you how it was with me. When I found myself truly in love, and then later on, *married,* something wonderful happened to me. Not just to my personal happiness, which was complete, but to my work."

"Yes?" Julian prompted eagerly.

"All at once I began to feel what you might call well-springs of satisfaction coming up where before there had often been bad deserts of depression. And even more than that, you know only too well what our profession entails: all those stretches of doubt of our own adequacy, as to whether we could ever rise above these dark, ineffectual hours? After my marriage there kept coming to me more and more a sense of strong incomparable accomplishment, enough to compensate for all the doubts. It was as though love had made me, soul and body, a stronger man. That is my message to your young friend."

"And I'll act on it. Thank you more than I can say." Then he added hastily, "I'll tell the young man."

"Do that!" the Bishop said, with a twinkle in his eye.

12

Bishop Ware lay in bed, smiling. Something had happened during the night. For weeks it seemed to him he had heard no outside sound except the stillicide of the melting snow as it fell in steady drops from the eaves on the porch roof. Now, there was another sound. It was the one that betokened the entrance of March. Of spring!

The Bishop raised himself on the pillows to hear better. The sound at first had been soft and lamblike, but it increased as it moved around the chimneys of the Old Rectory, and ended whistling a bit over the steeple of St. Michael and All Angels. In a gentle elation the Bishop repeated the childish rhyme he always quoted in March:

> O wind a-blowing all day long;
> O wind that sings so loud a song.

It was early yet. Too early for Mrs. Morgan and for Julian, who both would play their parts in the morning of this special new day. For, in addition to the coming of spring, the doctor had said that he could sit up in his chair for two whole hours. He had been practicing the matter of getting out of bed and walking across the room, until now his head felt quite clear when off the pillow. It had all been a long illness for one who had no memory of any other.

He lay now, thinking over one part of it that had strangely brought joy to his heart. This was in connection with Julian. While the Bishop in his love for the younger man had thought of him as his son-in-the-Lord, yet he had been aware of a delicate wall of dignity, a thinly woven web of restraint, and a faint recoil from what Bishop Ware considered normal expressions of affection, in his attitude. But he was remembering now the night when the doctor had admitted, under questioning, that the heart was very weak and the end might not be too far away, when Julian had sat on beside him, as though he could not leave. The few words they exchanged then came back now to the Bishop, and he smiled. For Julian had risen and stood looking down and his eyes were wet.

"Not tears?" the Bishop had said gently.

Julian had used his handkerchief. "I've got a cold." His voice was husky.

"Liar," came softly from the Bishop.

Julian had leaned over and pressed his lips to the Bishop's forehead. "Touché," he had whispered, and gone quickly out, as the nurse came forward.

As Bishop Ware now thought this over he realized that the words used would not be considered the normal ones given by a priest of the Church to a soul on the eve of its departure, but they were the right ones for him. His whole being had been warmed and made happy by them. Almost at once, he had fallen into a sleep that had lasted all the night. As to prayers? The Bishop knew they had not been lacking. He was sure that Julian on his lovely Prie Dieu had agonized most of the night for his old friend.

When he arrived early the next morning to check the patient, the doctor showed surprise at his improvement. "I felt last night we might see a change one way or the other, but I never expected so definite a turn for the better."

"Oh, I had a new kind of medication," the Bishop had said. "I feel able now to get up and preach a sermon!"

"Well, you can hold your sermons yet a while, but you can lie still and enjoy the thought that, by all signs, you're going to live!"

So now, on this first day of March, the Bishop was doing just that. The first bird chirping had begun, and then a clear sweet morning note; the wind had settled into a soft, steady blow, with every now and then a trailing whistle.

The Bishop felt unreasonably happy this morning. He indulged himself in remembrance of things past. There were the doctors, now dear friends, both of them. Dr. MacCloud tried unsuccessfully to teach Mrs. Leslie to say his name properly. "She says it with her mouth wide open. Makes all the difference. Now you say it with your mouth closed really; without trying you bring your under jaw just a thought over the upper one. Good! Excellent!

"I must tell you something for I won't be seeing you so often now. You're the laziest man I've ever really liked. You see, you took to doing nothing like a duck to water! You've been a gra-a-and patient. Keep it up now. I'll see you in a month and then if I find you've been mistreatin' that heart I'll *skelp* you!"

"Is that another Scotch word?"

"It's likely. We've got a good many. How's your young Bishop?"

"I hope all right. I gave him some good advice lately. On the side of the Angels, of course. But I can't say he looks much the happier for it. What made you think of him now?"

"I ran into him this afternoon, and he looked to me as if a few little devils were trying to bite him. What's the trouble? A love affair?"

"I hope so. But I've done only what I was asked to do, up to this point, so I can't go further. But I'm anxious!"

"I would guess it is one of two things that would make a man look as he does today. Either he has asked her and she has refused him, or he has decided he is not worthy of her and cannot bring himself to speak at all. That's a hellish little state of mind. I went through that myself and have never been so absolutely low in my life. I could only think of the many reasons why my girl couldn't possibly love me. I'll tell you, Bishop, it was a ghastly experience!"

"But that changed, didn't it?"

"Aye, did it. And the sweetness of it never left me all the years we had together. I'll wish the same for your young Bishop."

The good doctor spoke more wisely than he knew. For after the elation that filled Julian's heart as he pondered the strong, unequivocal advice that Bishop Ware had given, there had come first a sudden glory to the earth. It was everywhere, giving radiance to the usual dull thoroughfares, brightening the bushes and trees with the first breath of budding pink, and lifting his heart with a burst of joy, like a song. "I'm free! I'm free! I have no bond now. I can give myself up to love like any man. I'm free! And I *love!*"

The plans formed quickly in his mind. He would invite

Cissie to have dinner with him again. They would drive to that same charming spot and coming back where the incredible kiss had taken place, he would tell her there!

But like a chill wind came the remembrance of his own hardness, his actual cruelty there. He had turned from her, he had said he could not see her again, he had told her that the vow meant more to him than she did, when she asked her pitiful question. Oh, how could he believe now that she would forgive what he had said and done to hurt her tender heart?

There was also the memory of their walk by the sea when he had asked her to help him forget her! What kind of an insane fool had he been? All he could see now was Cissie's side, and against her hurts his hard, implacable determination about the *vow*. Now, according to Bishop Ware, it could be resolved, done away with. It had done its duty and could now be dismissed. But all his recent elation was now clouded over by the thought of his own callous attitude when she had twice, shyly, tried to offer her own love, and both times he had refused. Had this not been once too often? Could he ever dare to speak of his own love when he had spurned her timid advances? As he felt now, he could not tell her the joy and the burden on his heart. Not yet! Not yet!

So the spring moved gently on. Bishop Ware was now practically well. The young assistant at St. Michael's, David Morton, was doing so beautifully with the prison work that the Bishop could continue to rest from that. He could have short walks now, and, of course, his usual evening visits from Julian. He was somewhat puzzled, however, by the younger man's lack of enthusiasm. He had expected wonders after his urgent advice.

Julian himself felt it would be too long a story to tell the Bishop all that led up to his present heavy heart. So he kept it to himself. He did decide upon one change, however. He had heard Cissie telling the Bishop once when she came to visit that she always took a little walk, just back and forth in front of the hospital, before dinner. She had been given special permission to do this because on two separate occasions she had fainted just before dinner.

Julian was enraged that her work should take such a toll, but he did see a bright possibility. He would park his car a block from the hospital, and then he would walk over to where he could watch Cissie in her little stroll. The first evening she didn't appear, and Julian was very anxious. But as the nights went on, she came out in full view of her watcher, who moved back and forth. There were many pedestrians so he did not fear detection. Cissie did not look around, but only gazed straight ahead. As Julian watched the slight form in the white coat, however, he realized that his love was so great he needed hard control to keep from rushing across the street, catching her in her arms, and taking her home at once for something must be said that could not wait. All sorts of phrases came and went through his mind. Bold ones to break through all barriers; tender ones to beg forgiveness from Cissie herself.

When she went back into the hospital, he quietly returned to his car, and no one glancing at him could have guessed that the tumult of a hungry love lay behind that quiet face.

Julian found, however, that while his daily watches stirred his love into a vehement flame, they also seemed to diminish his own sense of unworthiness and somehow washed away the bitterness.

Day by day he continued his vigil across from the hospital, watching for Cissie.

One day after he got out of his car, he stood for some minutes looking up. The sky was very threatening. Even now at five-thirty, it was much darker than usual at that time. Great black thunderclouds covered all the west to the horizon.

"Looks bad," Julian said half aloud. "I hope Cissie has the sense to stay inside tonight."

Even as he thought it, he saw a white umbrella emerge from the great doors of the hospital. In a moment, he could see Cissie so plainly that he waved wildly. At once the white umbrella moved a little up and down. She must have seen him and be answering his signal. She began walking as fast as she could toward the end of the sidewalk. She had made it!

Then it came! Suddenly, blindingly, a great jagged bolt of lightning filled the sky with fire, sounding as though it struck nearby, then the crashing roar of thunder, seemingly drawn from the heart of the earth's center. Then, the heavens opened and impenetrable sheets of rain fell, with darkness following.

Julian saw the white umbrella when he had recovered from the shock of what had just passed; Cissie was standing a few steps out in the street, looking over as though to see him. She must *not* cross now. But how to tell her? The traffic lights at the intersection were out.

As he looked over all the parked cars he saw what chilled him with terror. On the other side of the intersection, among the cars waiting for a light, was one driven senselessly, recklessly, coming fast, weaving in and out amongst the other cars, bringing down shouts and imprecations. It was heading right toward Cissie. She had to be moved!

Without another thought he elbowed his way to the wall that ran behind the sidewalk. Not much space, he knew, but it would have to serve. He ran the little distance and vaulted over the hood of the first car in his way; he edged between others; he crawled over tops; he leaped once more when he got a start for he could see the crazy car coming closer. The drivers of the waiting cars, even those far back, were shouting to him, "Stop! You'll be killed if I start this motor!" "Stop, you fool! Get into my car! But stop!"

He could see Cissie now, watching him with terror on her face. He could not call through the mingled noise of small thunders, raucous voices, and shouts of workmen, which rose above the now quiet rain. Julian only pressed on, gambled on one last leap, made it, and clutched Cissie to him, pressing her close out of reach by only inches, as the car streaked past them, the driver singing!

When the two stood safely upon the sidewalk, Julian drawing deep breaths after his most unusual exercise, it was evident to Cissie that he felt he had to speak. The words came slowly, with pauses between:

"My love . . . my love . . . my precious . . . love, . . . will . . . you . . . marry . . . me?"

And strangely, Cissie had stopped trembling. There in the rain, clutching each other as though life would leave them if they ever let go, Cissie whispered, "Yes, yes, oh *yes*, my darling. But what about your vow?"

"It's gone," Julian answered almost explosively. "Gone! Now all I want . . . is to make . . . a bigger one . . . for life . . ."

And then, unaware of the curious glances of the passersby, their lips met once more as the cool rain fell upon their faces.

O sweet vocables of love! They murmured all of them as they walked along the now quiet streets, then Julian realized he had forgotten all about his car. Cissie spoke gently, "What a *lovely* thing for you to do to me, Julian dearest, just these first hours!"

"How, lovely? I feel like such an utter fool. Please don't tease me about it."

"But I'm not teasing, darling. I'm trying to tell you why that made me so happy. Don't you see? A man's car is so much a part of him. As the old mediums used to call it, almost his 'astral envelope,' and for him to forget it shows his mind was completely full of . . ."

"Something else?" Julian prompted eagerly.

"Exactly!"

"You," he said. "Oh, now I see what a blessed thing you were trying to tell me. So now I'm terribly glad I did forget."

"Every time I think of it, I'll be thrilled all over again. Julian darling, whom shall we tell first?"

"I've just been wondering. You choose which. It should probably be your grandmother. More in line with the conventions, perhaps."

"When she hears she will at once have the wedding and the reception and everything to think of and be excited and happy about, but I would rather go first to the Bishop! You are his son-in-the-Lord, as he says, and it's so wonderful he's going to be well just in time for us. Is it all right if we go to him first?"

"Nothing would make me happier! The only thing now is . . ."

"O what? Is anything the matter?"

"It's just that we've been so absolutely lost in each other that I fear we have turned a couple of wrong corners. Can you walk a little bit farther?"

"I could walk forever if you kept your arm around me."

"Precious! We'll watch the signs now."

It was nearly six when they reached the Old Rectory, and the Bishop was sitting in his favorite chair in the study. Julian called from the hall.

"You should see whom I've brought along to give you a kiss."

"Is it Cissie?"

"How did he guess that? Do you go around kissing gentlemen promiscuously?"

"Just older ones. Let's go in together when we get to the door!"

They walked toward him, widely smiling, hands clasped. Cissie then dropped to her knees beside him on one side and Julian did the same on the other, holding his hands out to join hers.

"Now look closely at us, dear Bishop, and tell us whether you can guess our secret?"

"My dear children! It's written all over your faces! I want to hear every word of it, where it happened, how you told her,

Julian, what she said, *everything* you can tell me, I want so badly to hear. Who will start?"

"You begin, Julian darling. It's so beautifully dramatic, Bishop. Just wait till you hear."

"Of course," Julian said, "after that pretty definite advice you gave me, you should have expected some results. I was standing on the street opposite the hospital when I saw Cissie going along opposite me toward the corner under a white umbrella . . ." He stopped. "Oh, my Precious, *where* is the white umbrella?"

She looked back at him blankly. "I've no idea. When you took me in your arms, I never even thought of it again."

"I was planning always to keep it for a memento!"

"Never mind that," the Bishop said. "You can buy her another one. Please go on with the story."

"Well, suddenly a bolt of lightning tore through the sky and seemed to strike something near. I guess it was the traffic lights at the intersection, for all the cars on both sides came to a halt from away back. Then the thunder, as though it was from the bowels of the earth, and then the rain in a torrent."

Julian caught his breath as though he were living it all over, and went on.

"It was hard to see but I could make out the white umbrella, and it seemed as though Cissie had taken a couple of steps into the street, as if trying to come to me. Of course, this could not be, but worst of all I suddenly saw beyond the intersection a car driven apparently by a lunatic coming on at a terrific speed right in line with Cissie, where she stood. I couldn't shout above the noise but I *had* to get to her. I had been a jumper in college so it didn't seem too ridiculous then. I got a small start and leaped over the hood of the first car in my way. Then I edged between others and crawled over many, with an eye on the mad driver who was still bearing down upon Cissie. When only one car was in my way I took a last gamble and made it! I caught Cissie in my arms and pushed her to the sidewalk, with the car missing us by inches."

"Oh, darling, let me tell it here. It's so very sweet. You see, Bishop, he was holding me so close in his arms, breathless after all he had done, but he seemed determined to speak. And then he did, even though he had to stop between the words. He said, 'My . . . love . . . will . . . you . . . marry . . . me?'"

Julian broke in, "And she put her arms around my neck and said, 'Yes, yes, yes, my darling. What about the vow?'"

"And I told her it was gone and I wanted only to make a new one to last all my life. So that's the story, Bishop!"

"Except that right there on the sidewalk, with people passing by, his lips met mine. O Bishop, such a kiss!"

"My dear, have you told your grandmother?"

"We're going right over. Somehow we both felt like telling you first."

"I'll never forget that. Wait a minute for my blessing and then hurry over to Mrs. Lansing."

He put his hands upon their clasped ones and said the beautiful words of grace.

When they rose to leave the Bishop suddenly began to laugh. They paused to hear.

"It's really so funny," he began, "the way I have tried for nearly a year to bring you two together without success and then in a matter of minutes God and a thunderstorm did it!"

Cissie had been correct in her judgment of her grandmother's reaction to the news. After the first rapture, she was at once into wedding plans. If they wished they could set the date four weeks from that day. Julian looked aghast. "Oh," he begged, "not so *long!*"

She beamed upon him. "That is just what a lover should say. But, my dears, the invitations should be out three weeks before the wedding, and that leaves only one to get the cards, make lists, and write them."

Julian was still plaintive. "But I had thought the Bishop and I could just drive over here, and Cissie would be waiting with you and her mother and we would just be married and go on our way. Why can't we do that, if Cissie would like that, too."

Cissie's face was a study. "Oh, darling. I love you for feeling that way, but I'm afraid I'm just a girl and I've dreamed of a big wedding in St. Michael's."

"Besides," Mrs. Lansing broke in, "you are a personage, Julian, and your position demands a very proper and dignified wedding. And Cissie has made a name for herself, so she deserves the most beautiful wedding there can be. I'll get on to the stationer at once and, Cissie dear, you'd better go to the hospital and tell them you have to be free from today on . . ."

"Oh, Grammie, I've some patients who need me!"

"Isn't it about time, Julian, she thought a little about *herself?*"

"And about *me!* I find I'm growing more selfish by the minute!"

"And every word you say makes me love you more. Suppose you both join me here tonight and we'll start the lists."

"I have a date with Cissie tonight, which I can't and won't break."

"Dear me! Listen to him, Cissie. Well, come over after your date, then. We can still do a lot tonight. You must realize there is no time to waste."

Julian stepped closer to Cissie. "Could you wear the same dress you wore that other night when we went there?"

"Of course. I'm glad you thought of it yourself. I was planning to wear it. I love you so *very* much, darling."

"My dearest what about me? How can I leave you now without a kiss?"

"We'll make up for it tonight."

"Would you want me to go with you to the hospital and lend weight to your words?"

"I can't wait to show you off, but I think this once I had better face the lions alone."

If the lovers had needed anything more to draw them closer together they found it that evening as they relived their first real date at the country restaurant and the shock of their kiss on the way back, their first and only until this very day. When they returned to Mrs. Lansing at nine o'clock, even Julian was cheerfully ready to begin upon the lists of guests.

As the weeks moved on, Julian was conscious of the fact that the horrible tension he had experienced had been completely eased. Problems were solved; incredibly, preparations, went on apace; Mrs. Lansing had her capable hand upon florist, caterer, and extra help; and not only was achieving order from chaos, but enjoyed doing so.

One or two matters rose about which she had to ask help. Whom did Julian choose for his best man?

"Good heavens! I don't know. I never got married before." As he saw Mrs. Lansing's face anxious, he said at once, "For a young man, I like best David Morton, one of Dr. Fenwick's assistants. I'll ask him."

The matter of who was to walk Cissie up the aisle and "give her away" was discussed earnestly by Cissie and Julian.

"Of course," he said, "it really doesn't matter who he is

since I'm the one to whom you are to be given. But still there must be somebody. Don't you have a great-uncle or a cousin?"

"Not a single male relative to my name. It's disgraceful. I guess Grammie will have to do it. Mother wouldn't be able. Oh, darling, I just had a wonderful thought! Why not my agent, Philippe La Contes! I've been under his concert care for five years, and I'm so fond of him and his wife, Marie. Why, this would be perfect! I'll ask him to give me away and ask Marie to be my matron of honor and that would solve everything!"

So this was the way it was, to everyone's pleasure.

Cissie came over for a stolen little visit with Bishop Ware. "I just *have* to talk about how wonderful Julian is as a lover. If I try to tell Grammie she just says, 'Yes, yes, dear. That's delightful!' and I know she hasn't heard a word. But I'm sure you'll listen. You see, it's this way. I had loved him for so long without any real hope, that now when he is all at once so completely in love with me, I can hardly believe it. I thought even when he asked me to marry him, he might still have his dignified side, but not to me, Bishop, not to me! He's the most incredible lover! Every word, every little act, is so beautiful. I want to sing all the time, *or* play the piano. Bishop dear, did you ever guess that Julian was capable of such a great love?"

"Once, I did."

"Oh, please tell me if you can."

"I was very dangerously weak one night and Julian had tears in his eyes, and then kissed my forehead."

"I'm glad. Then you will understand about the way he loves me. That was what I came to talk about, but also I have something to show you." And she stretched out her left hand. There it shone. A magnificent solitaire diamond.

"My dear!" said the Bishop. "That's a beauty!"

"I adore it, but I am afraid it cost him too much. Do you think he could afford this, Bishop?"

"Cissie dear, don't worry about that. I'm sure Julian would never have thought to mention it, but he has some inherited money. I'm sure he was able to get you this ring and enjoyed doing it as much as you liked receiving it."

"I'm so relieved for I simply *love* the ring, as well as the giver. The wedding plans are all going so beautifully. Bishop dear, will you wear your wonderful cope to marry us?"

"Would you like that? It's pretty elegant."

"Oh, I'd love to see you in that, and so would Julian. And you should see my dress. It's the most beautiful thing I've ever seen. And the veil. Did I tell you I'm to have a little crown made of sweetheart roses? The florist is to bring it over the last thing. Mother is giving the rehearsal dinner at the hotel, for Grammie's house by the night before the wedding will be all cleared out for the reception."

"That sounds wise. Do I go?"

"I should say so. I told Mother it was good having it at the hotel for then she could give an early sign to stop and go home. Everyone should get some sleep. Julian says he doesn't expect to close an eye because he is so excited. I'll have a little time alone with him when we get back from the hotel. I'll try to calm him down. But, Bishop dear, it's so sweet and lovely to me that he *is* so excited!"

In the morning of The Day itself Julian and Bishop Ware stood in the garden admiring the weather.

"I prayed for fair weather," Julian said, "though I do feel that is hardly sensible."

"Oh, I don't know," said the Bishop. "I did myself, and I feel sure Cissie did. It could do no harm, and *look* at the day we got!"

It was perfect. Warm but not hot, with fluffy white clouds drifting about in the sky like playing lambs. It was June. The time of brides and roses!

Julian went on, his eyes shining. "And we are to have a choral ceremony. I have never heard one, nor has Cissie, and now we are having one ourselves. It's Fenwick's doing. He suggested having the harpist and perhaps four of his best voices from the vesper music sing 'O Perfect Love' when we first kneel and then the Sevenfold Amen at the end."

"What a lovely thing, Julian. I'm glad I'm taking part in it."

"You are the largest part. Tell me, what does a prospective bridegroom do with himself all day ... until time ...? Cissie says I mustn't see her until she comes up the aisle in church."

The Bishop laughed. "That old tradition has upset many a bridegroom, but I think it's much better to stay with it. You can slip over to the church later and watch the florist at work, or do some quiet reading at home. Though you may not believe me at this moment, the blissful hour will actually arrive. Are you allowed to speak to her on the phone?"

"I guess so. I'll do it anyway. It will be a help. Cissie and I discussed what I should wear. She knows about the beautiful cope you gave me, but she said she was not marrying a Bishop, she was marrying a *man*, and she thought I should look as I have always looked to her."

"And she was absolutely right. You are not involved in any duties as a Bishop. You are just a man, like any other man who gets married."

"At least I have a whole new set of clericals."

At Mrs. Lansing's big house, Cissie did not find the time dragging. Indeed, she watched the clock anxiously as the hours passed all too fast for what she had to do. She still had to pack her "going away" bag and the small overnight case. Dresses and lovely lingerie lay tossed about.

"The thing is, I don't want to be hurried when it comes to my wedding gown," she told her mother, "and I simply couldn't get these bags packed before. There were so many interruptions."

The phone rang beside her. "Yes?" she said quickly.

"My dearest, I'm desperate just waiting around. What can you find to do?"

"Darling, I'm rushed to death. I'm just packing my bags now. I have a thousand little things yet to take care of and I must have one whole hour to dress. Do forgive me, darling, if I can't talk long now. I'm *so* busy!"

But as Providence kindly ordains at weddings in general, all those making up the nuptial group were ready and waiting in their appointed places, while the harp and organ made soft music.

The four ushers Cissie had chosen from among her many doctor friends were young enough to be able to take the time. They had now been guiding into the flower-decked pews a surprisingly large number of guests. For Dr. Fenwick had done a gracious thing. He had announced on Sunday morning that the wedding ceremony would take place at four o'clock on Saturday and all who cared to come were invited. The reception would be by written invitation only, but all friends would be welcome at the ceremony.

When all were seated, including the two Mrs. Lansings, a breathless quiet filled the great church. The harp and organ began upon the familiar strains that Cissie had chosen, the audience rose, and Bishop Ware in his very resplendent cope emerged and took his place in the front chancel with Dr. Fenwick beside him, both facing the congregation.

Julian entered with his best man and all heads turned then toward the aisle for the sight for which they waited. Mrs. La

Contes came first, in rose satin and pink flowers, and then Cissie herself, looking as though all the loveliness of the years had been stored up for this moment. Her low-necked satin dress fell into the folds of a train and her veil flowed to its whole length, caught on her head by a little tiara of sweetheart roses. Her bouquet gave off a delicate perfume as she passed. For when Julian had asked her what she wished she had said, "Well, of course, white, darling, but something with a fragrance." So, with care he had selected lilacs, gardenias, and carnations. She moved forward on Mr. La Conte's arm, slowly and with grace.

When she neared the front her eyes suddenly met Julian's eager ones and the look they exchanged was so intensely beautiful that those who saw it were stirred themselves.

Julian extended both hands to meet her and draw her to him, then together they stood before Dr. Fenwick for the opening sentences. After this, as the Bishop walked toward the altar, they did also and knelt there as prearranged for the choral hymn.

It came, clearly and distinctly with the harp its only accompaniment.

> O perfect love, all other loves transcending,
> Lowly we kneel in prayer before Thy Throne
> That theirs may be the love that knows no ending
> Whom Thou for evermore dost join in one.

At the end of the hymn, Julian and Cissie rose and took their vows, given in Bishop Ware's tender voice, then they knelt again for the closing benediction and the choral Amen. And then the kiss! Considering what she had already known this seemed to her rather short. Once in the luxurious car that Mrs. Lansing had arranged for to bear the couple from the church to the reception, Julian was quiet and Cissie waited. At last he spoke.

"I'm scared," he said.

"Oh, darling, why on earth?"

"Because you are so beautiful, so like a dream."

"I would let you know, sir, that I am real." She gave his arm a little pinch.

"Ouch! I'm glad you did that. It relieves my mind. My Precious, can you believe we are really married?"

"It's unbelievable but I'm sure it is true. Wasn't the hymn lovely?"

"So much so we were all in tears."

"I did think my kiss at the altar was a little bit short."

Julian laughed. "If I had done it as I wished they might have asked me to leave. If you aren't afraid of spoiling your veil, I can do better now!"

"I'll take the chance," she said.

The reception was all that any bridal couple could have wished for. When they arrived, the orchestra was playing softly, and a few young early guests were dancing. The bridal table was elegantly set and Mrs. Lansing already there to show them where they should stand to welcome the guests. And then came the steady stream of men and women bringing their good wishes. Julian whispered over to Cissie, "When any of my own clerical friends come, I say, 'I want you to meet *my wife,*' and I nearly throw a fit each time. It sounds so incredibly wonderful."

"You can't go back on that," Cissie told him with a little giggle. "There were too many witnesses."

And the gaiety went on as the whole bridal group sat at the table making and drinking the toasts. Julian had kept an eye on his best man, who was, indeed, in high feather and quite capable, he felt, of making any kind of embarrassing toast. But all was well. David Morton spoke with sincerity but within conventional limits.

There was no haste, time and to spare for the pleasure of the guests between toasts and the final "loving-cup" of the bride and groom. Mrs. Lansing had found it, quaint and wide brimmed. Julian held it to Cissie's lips while she sipped and then she held it for him. After this they left the table and with the bride's train and veil held up by the wide ring that slipped over Cissie's arm, she put her hand in Julian's and they circled the room in the first dance, a Viennese waltz. Then they slipped quietly away to dress, in Cissie's case in "going away" clothes.

Now, Cissie held strong opinions about their leave-taking. "I hate the way some couples do, going to all lengths to confuse the guests and get away secretly. I would like to come downstairs when I am ready and have Julian at the foot, waiting for me, and then go out together and allow the guests to follow us out if they wish and throw all their rose leaves and rice or whatever, and shout out their good-byes to us while we wait a few minutes in the car before we drive off. Couldn't we do that?"

It was Cissie's wish, and therefore to Julian, sacred. The

bags were put early in the new car—a gift from Bishop Ware to his "children," as he called them. Julian waited at the foot of the stairs wondering what Cissie would wear now. When she appeared he gave a little start of pleasure. She was wearing the ruffled rose dress with its memories, his favorite of all the gowns he had seen her wear.

He caught her to him before she reached the final step, and they went quickly out the door with the guests thronging after them, delighted with the unusual arrangement.

Julian helped Cissie into the new car, which had been brought up near the house, got in beside her, and they waited as the good-byes still came from the group on the lawn, and good wishes even in rhyme. David Morton's came clearly:

> Here's to the bridegroom
> We wish him all joy,
> And in another year
> A girl or—a boy!

Loud laughter and applause followed this effort. Julian leaned as far as he could to the window:

> Here's to the Best Man,
> Who steadily grows worse;
> Hope his wife soon joins him
> To take off the curse!

"What curse?" Cissie asked curiously.

"Nothing. It just made a rhyme. But that Morton. He's a dog to shout out that rhyme of his. I hope it didn't embarrass you too much."

"Heavens no. I thought it was funny, but *lovely*."

Julian laughed and started the car. "What a precious little hussy I have," he said. "I think we'd better go on now . . . but listen!"

Some words drifted to them from the nearest guests, " . . . an old Parting Song . . . she's going to sing . . . she sang at the ceremony."

The medley of noises stopped. One clear voice rose above them.

> Hie away, may angels defend you!
> Hie away, may Fortune befriend you!

222

Hie away, our blessings we lend you,
 And with happiness send you
Far away! Far away! Hie away!

The car gathered speed, left the drive, and turned west into the early sunset.

NEW FROM FAWCETT CREST